AFTER HE KILLED ME

ALSO BY NATALIE BARELLI

The Emma Fern Series

Until I Met Her

AFTER HE KILLED ME

NATALIE BARELLI

THOMAS & MERCER

Published by Thomas & Mercer, Seattle

www.apub.com

Amazon, the Amazon logo, and Thomas & Mercer are trademarks of Amazon.com, Inc., or its affiliates.

ISBN-13: 9781542046992
ISBN-10: 1542046998

Cover design by Mark Swan

Printed in the United States of America

AFTER
HE
KILLED
ME

1

They've come to gawk at me; the very people whose admiration I once longed for, the ones who read my novel and stopped me in the street to tell me—a complete stranger—that they loved me. Just like that. Well! They don't love me now.

And then there are the others. They're here too, of course; the ones who are most entertained by the misfortune of people like me, people whose lives until now have been blessed. The higher and more painful the fall, the better, and mine is vertiginous. I'm surprised they didn't bring popcorn.

To think that only a few weeks ago, these were the same people whose adoration I was craving. I was depressed. There were new books to be read, none of them mine, and new writers to be admired. I was being forgotten; the crowds had started to move on. If only that were still true.

I watch them as they watch me. I'm not afraid of them. They make me sick, craning their necks; anything to get a better view of me, and my shame.

I had never seen the inside of a courtroom before all this started, which is incredible when you think about it. They are part of our society: the laws we live by are decided here; as is our fate, should we be unlucky enough to have broken those laws. A courtroom is more important than a museum, and yet most people will have seen the inside of a museum at least once. But a courtroom? Not so many.

If I ever get out of here a free woman, I will lobby for visits to courtrooms to become part of the school curriculum, I decide. All schoolchildren should become familiar with how they operate so they will be prepared, instead of feeling like they've wandered through the wrong door and into a foreign country where people have different customs, and where the language spoken is related to English but not the same, so you don't really understand what's being said, and even when you think you do, you've got it wrong.

"So this 'novel' . . ." The prosecutor sneers a little on the word *novel*. "Sorry, what is it called again?"

"*The Lie*," I murmur.

"Can you speak up, please?"

"*The Lie*." Louder this time.

"Right, thank you. *The Lie*."

I'm on display, on the witness stand. I had an image this morning of myself in the dock, handcuffed, my head bowed in shame, waiting for my punishment, but my lawyer said no, it's not like that. She said I'd be seated at the defense table facing the judge until I was called to testify, and on the opposite side of the aisle would be the prosecutor and his assistants. I'm only up here because I'm being questioned.

"Now, if I understand correctly, you're suggesting you didn't write this novel?"

"Yes. No. I mean, no."

"I'm sorry?"

There are beads of sweat pearling on my lip. I wipe them with one finger; it buys me time. I don't want to answer that question. I don't know how.

"Not completely," is all I can come up with.

"I see. Which parts did you not completely write, Mrs. Fern?"

"Objection, argumentative."

That's my lawyer, and I have no idea if she's any good, but she's all I've got.

"Overruled."

I don't even remember my lawyer's name It's a blank. Is it Katherine? Or maybe she just looks like a woman I knew once called Katherine. But she is arguing on my behalf, even if I can barely follow the proceedings. The very idea that I could go to jail is simply impossible to contemplate. If I think about it, I can't breathe, and so I don't . . . think about it.

"Someone rewrote it."

I hear myself as if I were speaking from a long distance away, and it makes the statement sound even more preposterous. But truth is like that sometimes.

"I see. You wrote it, and someone rewrote it. Tell me, the part where you meticulously plan and then commit murder, and then get rid of the evidence—did you write that, Mrs. Fern? Or did someone"—and here he lifts two fingers in air quotes—"rewrite it? As you put it?"

I lower my gaze. "I didn't write that."

"And yet you submitted it to your publisher as your own words, correct?"

"Yes, but—"

"The entire manuscript delivered by yourself, to your publisher, Mr."—he consults his notes, pushing his thin-rimmed glasses farther up his nose—"Badosa, is that correct?"

"But—"

"But what, Mrs. Fern?"

Katherine, I'll call her Katherine for now until I remember her name, is on her feet again, she spreads her arms wide in frustration.

"Your Honor, my client is trying to answer the question. Now if only Mr. Ackerman here—"

"Yes, I agree. Mr. Ackerman, let the defendant answer the question."

"My apologies. Please, Mrs. Fern, go ahead."

I take a deep breath. "Yes, I personally delivered the manuscript to my publisher."

"Thank you. Would you agree that the last chapter amounts to a confession? Of murder? Committed by yourself?"

Katherine jumps up again. "Your Honor!"

It's hot in here. I look around the room to see if there are any air vents, and my gaze lands upon the sea of faces beyond in the gallery. They've already judged me. As far as they're concerned, I'm guilty as sin. I stare back, give them a good eyeful. There. That should give them something to feed on. And then I spot her and my heart stops. Beatrice is sitting in the gallery and she's staring straight at me.

Without a hint of a smile, she arches an eyebrow, the way she used to sometimes, as if to say, *Fancy seeing you here!* Someone is playing a trick on me. Beatrice can't be here. It's not possible. She's dead. I should know, since I killed her myself. I shut my eyes tightly. I count to ten, taking a breath on each beat.

"Mrs. Fern has unlimited funds available, Your Honor. She has access to resources that could make it very easy for her to disappear."

My eyes fly open. How does he think I could disappear? There are photographers outside, already jostling each other to get to the front. Does he seriously believe I can escape this baying pack of paparazzi? I put a hand up to say something. I want to tell the judge—but Katherine says that I have no money. Great! Now the whole world knows just how bad things have become. I can already see the headlines: *From Riches to Rags.*

"Bail is set at two hundred thousand dollars."

The bang of the gavel resonates loudly and makes me jump. There's too much noise. My head is spinning. I look to where Beatrice was sitting, but it's a different woman there now. I quickly get up from the witness stand and someone in uniform takes my arm.

"Wait, please wait!"

I plead and point to Katherine, who is gathering her things from the table; putting legal notepads away in her elegant attaché case. She's not even looking at me. She behaves as if her work is done here and there's nothing more to be said. I go to her, the uniformed woman by my side, holding my elbow, and with my other hand I grasp Katherine's arm, desperation engulfing me.

"I don't have that kind of money," I say urgently.

She looks at me, almost surprised to see me.

"Then you'll have to go to jail."

"Killer!"

I turn to see who shouted. I'm almost at the door of the courtroom, trying to stop Katherine from leaving me, and when the doors open, I am in full view of journalists and photographers shoving each other out of the way; the others too, people shouting. Someone spits on me.

They hate me. I let them down. They loved me so, and now they think I've committed this heinous crime. If only they knew. Yes, I am a killer. I am a murderer. I am all the things they think I am and worse, but I am not guilty of the crime they have accused me of.

I did not kill my husband.

I tell them, "I did not kill my husband," but they're not listening, so I shout, louder still, over the chants of "Killer!"

"I did not kill my husband!"

Someone is pulling me back.

"Kil-ler!" they chant.

"Kil-ler!"

"Kill her!"

2

"Happy anniversary, my love."

My wonderful, devoted husband gently places a small blue gift box on the table between us. I clap my hands, enchanted.

"What's this?"

Jim raises his glass of champagne in a gesture that invites me to do the same. I follow his lead and we clink them together. I can't stop grinning.

"Happy anniversary to you, my darling," I reply. I feel a little shy suddenly. Sitting across the table from this handsome, powerful man who adores me, makes me weak at the knees.

"Open it."

"But you shouldn't have, really," I admonish gently, looking down at the unmistakable Tiffany box. "It looks expensive."

Jim smiles. He opens his mouth to say something, when I hear a voice behind me.

"Emma Fern?"

I don't know who she is, the elegant woman who is staring at me, eyes wide, bending down slightly to get a better view of me. I hide the tinge of annoyance I feel at the interruption and smile.

"Yes?"

"I thought it was you! Oh, my dear, it's wonderful to meet you!" she says as she takes my hand in hers and shakes it up and down and up and down until I remove it gently.

"Thank you so much. It's wonderful to meet you too."

It's surprisingly awkward when people do this to me, because I feel I should ask something like, "And you are?" but that would make me sound like a snob. *Do I know you? Have we met?*

I know of course why this happens. I am a famous, beloved novelist. I am a Poulton Prize winner—frankly I have no idea who won after me, because who cares?—and I am last year's bestselling author by a long shot.

"Charlotte Harper," she says, reading my mind, "and this is Cornelius." She turns to—I assume—her husband, who even from this distance looks too young to be a Cornelius.

I know who the Harpers are. I've never met them before, but I've seen them in the social pages, many times. They're always photographed at this ball or that charity event.

"I'm delighted to meet you, Charlotte, thank you." I try not to stare at her beautiful dress.

"I knew it was you," she says now. "I wanted to tell you how much I loved *Long Grass Running*. A truly beautiful novel."

"Thank you. It's kind of you." I raise my hand toward Jim. "This is my husband, Jim Fern."

"Yes, of course, the economist. It's nice to meet you. You must be very proud," Charlotte Harper says, and for a moment I think she's referring to the work he's doing at the Millennium Forum, but then she smiles at me and says, ". . . to be married to such a wonderful woman."

I smile my thanks back and Jim winks at me, tells her that he most certainly is, and I try not to grin, because I can tell he is proud of me, and I love that feeling more than anything. Then Charlotte Harper asks, "Do you have another novel coming out soon?"

She asks this very genuinely, but frankly I hate that question. Why do people assume I even *want* to publish another novel? Do they have any idea what I went through with *Long Grass Running*? No. Obviously not. I'd be in jail otherwise.

"Yes, yes," I lie, easily. "It's coming out this fall."

"Oh wonderful! I'll be looking out for it."

She reaches for my hand, and for a moment I think she's going to kiss it, but no, thank God, because that really would be a little too much, instead she takes it in both her hands and squeezes it.

"Thank you," she says, with feeling. "Thank you."

She turns and leaves, just as I reply, "No, thank *you*."

Jim, who sat silent, completely ignored in this exchange, mutters, "Here we go again," although not unkindly.

I laugh. "Well, yes, what can I do?"

Except that it hasn't happened in a while—someone stopping me like this, asking for my autograph, acknowledging me. I've been vaguely aware of a new, creeping anonymity, and it has worried me a little, so it's nice after all to be recognized today of all days, on my wedding anniversary.

"Now, where were we?" I smile.

I take the pretty box in my hand, carefully untie the ribbon, unwrap the pale blue paper and open the box. He strokes my arm as I lift the velvety top and discover the thin diamond and white gold band inside. I gently lift the ring from its cushioned container, and lift it up to admire it. It takes my breath away.

"Do you like it?"

I hold it gently between my fingers and watch the diamonds sparkle in the light.

"It's beautiful." I slip the ring onto my finger. I look up at him, my face flushed with joy.

"You're staring," he says, smiling.

"I know." I love observing him. He's looking better than he ever has, his wavy hair thick and dark, and longer than he used to wear it. I wasn't sure about it at first, but now I love it. It makes him look like a European intellectual. Especially with that little bit of gray at the temples.

He's in better shape too, fitter than he used to be. He works out at the gym almost every day now, at lunchtime. He has done so for months. A few years ago, he would have turned up his nose at men who did that, but all it took was one particularly unflattering picture of himself in the media, back when he was carrying those extra pounds around his waist.

His features are sharper now, his jaw more defined. Sometimes, in a certain light, I catch sight of him, and I think that he has never been this handsome.

"Sorry, what did you say?" I ask, shaking my head.

"I had it engraved."

He points to it and I take it off my finger to look. It comes off a little too easily, and I make a mental note to have it resized.

I love you more every day.

"Oh, Jim! Thank you, darling."

If I ever had any doubts, then surely this must dispel them. Jim didn't have to do that—the inscription—it's a very nice touch.

"Would you order us more champagne?" I ask.

"Of course." He turns to catch the waiter's eye and signals to him.

I bend down and pull out a soft package from my bag, careful not to flatten its bow, and push it toward him.

"Your turn," I say.

He smiles, draws it closer to him.

"What is it?" he asks.

"You know what it is."

He raises an eyebrow.

"It's my promise." I say this coyly, almost girlish, but the moment is solemn between us. He nods, silent.

"Thank you." He takes the package and puts it inside his soft leather briefcase.

"You don't want to open it?" I ask.

"I don't need to."

"I understand."

"I trust you." He reaches a hand over the table to take mine and squeezes it.

"I'm glad. I trust you too."

"To us," he toasts.

"To us."

The champagne tickles my tongue. It's cold and sweet and delicious. Jim takes a sip, puts his glass back on the table and slowly turns it around, its stem between his fingers.

"So, how is work?" I ask brightly.

"Fantastic," he nods. "We have a new researcher who's joined us, did I tell you? From the World Economy Lab at MIT."

"Really?" It's the first I've heard of it, and I can't help but feel a small pang of unease. I've learned to be wary of Jim's research colleagues. First Allison, an ex-student of his who did some work for him, although he has always maintained there was never anything romantic between them, but then Carol came along, and well . . .

"He's very good," Jim continues. "He showed me some very promising modeling this morning. We're very excited."

It didn't occur to me that it would be a man, and I almost laugh out loud with relief. I only half listen to him after that. I prefer to look at his handsome face while he tells me all about the exciting activities going on at the Forum. That's where my husband works, the Millennium Forum—a groundbreaking economics think tank that advises the government on how to reduce poverty and increase employment and quality of life, through better-funded social services for example, all without increasing taxes. They've got some modeling miracle thing going, supposedly.

"You shouldn't let me ramble on like this, I can see you're distracted."

"No! Not at all darling, I love listening to you talking about all that."

I say *supposedly*, because there's just one small problem with this utopian theory: it's all a lie. Well, Jim would argue that it's not a lie, it's just not quite as refined as he made it out to be, but that every day there's another tweak, and before long, the world will be a better place.

I know all this, because I acquired something, some time ago. I came across some information, which I have kept secret. That information is tangible. Some of it is in notebooks, and some of it is digital and stored on CDs and a couple of USB sticks. If any of that tangible information were to be released into the wrong hands—as in, anyone else but Jim—well, let's just say that his very important career would blow up into a million little pieces. And my husband's career is the one thing, other than me hopefully, that he lives for. It would kill him.

So instead, my husband and I have come to an arrangement. It may not be the most orthodox of marriages, but it works for us. I keep his dirty little secret, and he remains by my side; my loyal, faithful, loving companion.

It hasn't been smooth sailing, but then again, what marriage is? He didn't take kindly to my terms at first. One day, after a particularly nasty fight, when I told him I was sick and tired of his sour face, he asked me to let him go, and frankly, I almost said yes. *Go away. I don't want you either.* But that wasn't true. I did want him. He's my weakness, my husband. I can't help it. I can't let him go.

So I said no. But I told him to take a few days off and have a good think about how he wanted to handle our situation, because one thing we both agreed on was that we couldn't go on like this. "You have to be here, and you have to be happy," I told him. And he looked at me as if I had grown two heads.

And he did go away. I suspect he was happy to do that, but I don't know what happened. I guess he did have a good think, because when he came back he said, "Emma, let's start over. For real. Let's make this work."

I proposed that we go to couples therapy.

When I suggested it, he burst out laughing, but I didn't. I just stared at him. So he said therapists and counselors were not recognized professionals; that anyone could buy a marriage counseling qualification over the Internet. *La-de-dah*, and on and on.

Anyway, since I wanted us to go to couples therapy, we went. And it was wonderful. He *had* to listen. At first, it felt like hacking at a block of ice with a toothpick. But with each session he melted a little until finally he heard me. He understood how I felt, and what I needed from him. At that point, I may have had all the power in our relationship, but the balance has shifted since. I could say we've fallen in love again, but I never stopped loving him. I'm obsessed with him and that's never wavered. But I've watched him fall in love with me again, and if only for that, I regret nothing.

But even arrangements such as ours need a little give and take. And so, as a show of good faith, I made a pledge to him that every year, for our anniversary, I would return to him a part of what I have in my possession. It will take ten years, I decided, for me to return the entirety of my proof. I figured that after ten years of being happy together, he wouldn't want to leave me anymore. I'm delighted that it hasn't taken anywhere near that long for Jim to come to his senses and realize that he truly, truly loves me—and only me—and ever since, I have lived inside the happy ending of a fairy tale.

Today, I have kept my promise, and the beautifully wrapped package I handed him contains one notebook and one CD.

He half stands and leans forward to kiss me. His lips taste of champagne.

"Shall we go to dinner?" I ask.

"Let's do that. I'm starving."

"Me too."

Jim motions to the waiter, who brings the bill. As he pulls out a few notes from his wallet, he frowns.

"Remind me to get some more cash. That was the last of it."

"Why don't you put it on your card?"

"No, this is fine."

We get up together and he helps me with my coat, always the perfect gentleman, and when I walk toward the door on his arm, I am dizzy with a sense of pride. I'm so lucky, I remind myself, as I gaze down at my finger. Jim holds the door for me, and just before I step outside, I spot Charlotte Harper waving at me from the corner table. I nod my goodbyes to her.

"God, I had the most awful dream last night. I just remembered," I say, taking hold of his arm as a shudder runs down my back. I squeeze my shoulders.

He rubs my hand gently. "What was it?"

"More like a nightmare. I was in—I don't know, a courtroom, with a judge, a jury, the works." I shake my head at the memory. "It was awful. I was a has-been, passé."

He laughs. "That's the nightmare?"

I shake my head. "You were dead."

"There, there," he jokes, patting my hand. "I'm not dead. No one died."

Well, that's not strictly true.

"How did I die anyway?" he asks.

"They said I killed you."

◆　◆　◆

It's a little chilly when we leave the bar, but I don't mind. I just wrap my coat around me more tightly.

"Let's take a taxi," Jim says, looking up at the dark clouds gathering above us.

"Really? We're only five minutes away, Jim. We should be fine. I don't think it'll rain."

He puts an arm around my shoulders and shudders a little against me. "I'm freezing! I'd rather take a cab, if that's all right with you."

"Sure. Of course."

We walk to the edge of the sidewalk, both of us looking up and down the busy street. I wish it were a clear night, because then we could be looking up at the stars, but instead I hear the sound of thunder, and any minute now we'll be running for shelter.

Jim lets go of my arm. "Where are you going?" I ask.

He points to the ATM we just passed. "I'm just going to go and grab some cash."

"I'll come with you."

"No, you stay here, see if you can get us a taxi. That would be great."

"Okay. Why not? I'll do that." I make a mock salute and we both chuckle.

Maybe it's because it's our wedding anniversary, but I'm feeling a little sentimental, and as I watch my handsome husband walk to the ATM, I can't help but reflect how far we have come together.

I'm not completely stupid. How long is that going to last? I've asked myself that question many times. But what's the point of that? He's here, we're happy. Why would I waste the best years of my life worrying about a future that may never eventuate?

The rain starts, and pulls me out of my reverie. Jim is still at the ATM, and I turn around and face the street. There's still quite a bit of traffic at this time of the evening; the streets are a little crowded, and people are rushing around me as they try to get out of the rain.

There's a bus shelter next to me, and I move to wait under it, but then I see her. It's just a flash, but it's unmistakable. She's there, watching me, and the next moment she's gone. Now there's only me, looking at my own reflection.

14

I stand still, waiting for the anxiety to pass as I talk myself down. *You're not seeing ghosts, Emma. It's not Beatrice. It was just a reflection of yourself. You know that.* Except I don't know that, since it's not the first time. In fact, Beatrice is showing herself to me more and more. *No, she's not showing herself anywhere. She's been dead for almost two years. Don't go crazy.*

So I don't go under the bus shelter. I just tighten my coat again, and stand on the sidewalk looking out for a taxi. Should I see someone about this? Is this a sign of an impending nervous breakdown? How could it be, since I feel fine, I am happy; happy enough, anyway.

I catch sight of a taxi in the distance, and before I have a chance to hail it, I feel something behind me. At first it's a movement of air. I think it must be Jim, and I want to turn around, but I don't have the time; the pressure is too strong against my back. I start to say something, but there's a screech of tires, and someone shouts, and before I know it I'm on the road, as if I'd flown forward.

I am lying face down, my cheek hard on the asphalt, my head exploding in pain. Just before I close my eyes, I see the tires, an inch from my face. I try to lift my head, but the pain that shoots through my skull won't let me, and everything goes black.

3

"Darling, I'm sorry, but I need a favor. Do you have time to run an errand for me?"

Time is all I have these days, but am I going to say that to Jim? No, of course not. As far as he's concerned, I barely have time to breathe. I am a busy professional, run off my feet.

"I—have a meeting with Frankie. What do you need, darling?" I don't have a meeting with Frankie. I don't have meetings with anyone. I do nothing all day but roam the rooms of this apartment, bored out of my mind. I will run this errand for Jim because, for one thing, it will distract me. But I don't want him to know how truly lonely I am. Jim doesn't like people who complain.

"It's just that I'm an idiot. I forgot to get my jacket this morning from the dry cleaners, and if I don't get hold of it, I'll be in shirtsleeves this evening," he chuckles.

"Well, you know, that's not a bad look for you, actually," I laugh.

"Are you flirting with me?"

"Never!"

But he doesn't want to banter, he's busy. Of course he is. He's always busy. He has very important things to do all day, every day. Especially today, since this evening we're going to a very important function, where the Forum will introduce its new program, or something like that. So instead of laughing with me, he says, "Seriously, Em, can you help me out?"

And I can.

"Of course, my love, I'll bring another one with me. What about your navy blue one?"

"No, if you could just pick it up from the dry cleaners, that would be better. It's the jacket with the dark lapel. That's the one I need for tonight."

"Oh, okay, but why don't you call them? They'll drop it off for you. Or I'll call them if you prefer. Shall I do that?" I'm already looking forward to the task; I can make a phone call and use up, oh, let's see, ten, maybe fifteen whole minutes.

"Tried that. They can't drop it off in time. But if you're too busy, don't worry. I can make other arrangements."

"No, don't be silly, I'll do it."

"You're sure?"

"Of course."

"I left the ticket by the front door I think, on the table. It's at the place near the Forum."

"Oh, I see! Not the one on Third. Got it. I'll pick it up on the way."

"Thank you, darling. You're a lifesaver."

I laugh. I like doing little things like this for Jim.

◆ ◆ ◆

There's a line of people waiting to be served when I get there. I feel silly all dolled up in my glamorous outfit. Maybe I should have picked the jacket up earlier, but it was on the way. I'll meet Jim at the Forum, and we can go together to the Capitale. These are what my days feel like now. Hard work. Everything is too complicated; there are too many variables. Do I have the time to do something? Or should I wait until this other thing happens? In the end I do nothing.

My shrink says it's because of the accident, but I try not to think about that anymore. Not if I can help it. It's been months, and the scar above my eye is almost gone. That's the only tangible sign that I have of it. I part my hair on the left now, so that it's mostly hidden anyway.

I could have died. I almost did. That's what they said when I came to in the hospital. They said I was really lucky that the motorcycle slid on the wet road. It slid all the way to the bus, which came to a screeching halt, inches from my head. The motorcycle driver got off with just a couple of scratches. He was lucky too, even more than me, apparently.

The first thing I asked Jim when I came to was: "Did you see him? Did you catch him?"

"Emma, love, calm down."

"Did you catch him?"

"Who?"

"The guy who pushed me! Or at least I think it was a guy." Maybe it was a ghost. "Someone pushed me, Jim. Didn't you see?"

We must have had that conversation fifty times. *Didn't you see? Someone pushed me, you must have seen it, Jim!*

But he always says he wasn't looking. He was coming back from the ATM, and must have been distracted. He saw me fall, he says, he tried to catch me, but it was too late, and there were so many people rushing around, getting out of the rain, getting taxis like I'd tried to—if someone pushed me, he might not have seen it. But he doesn't believe me. It doesn't matter how many times I tell him. I can tell. He thinks I'm confused, I hit my head, I'm imagining things.

"But did you see me fall?" I'll ask for the umpteenth time, watching his face trying not to betray his frustration.

"Yes. No, I just—you were there, and then you weren't! I wasn't looking exactly, Emma. It was raining. There were people everywhere!"

At first I was obsessed. In my mind, I would go over and over those few seconds before I found myself on the asphalt in the middle of the street. I would close my eyes and recall the feeling on my back; the swoosh, and then the pressure. I could remember it physically at first, but as time went by, it no longer made sense. I couldn't tell if I was making it up. It is possible that in the shock of the moment, I did get confused. Maybe I did trip when I turned and tumbled. I don't know anymore. Then I stopped thinking about it. Except when I see the thin scar above my eye.

"Can I help you?"

That's the other thing since the accident. I'm always distracted, in my own head; I don't realize people are talking to me until they're three sentences into it.

"I'm sorry, yes, here."

I hand my ticket to the woman, and lift my bag onto the counter. She returns with the jacket in its protective plastic wrapping, and lays it down carefully as I look in my wallet.

"God, sorry, I was sure I had some cash on me."

"Don't you hate that?" says a male voice behind me. I turn to look. Christ, there's a line of maybe fifteen people waiting. Of course there would be.

"I can't think what I spent it on, but never mind, I'm sure it will come to me," I say, turning back to the woman.

"Something special, I hope," he says behind me.

I need to get on with it. Get my credit card and pay for the jacket. Not everything has to be difficult. I tell myself to hurry up before everyone gets annoyed with me, then I tell myself that it's fine, it doesn't matter if people get annoyed. *Relax, breathe.*

"I'm sorry, I'll put it on my card if that's all right."

"Of course," she says.

I smile my apologies for holding everyone up, and go to pull out my card, except it's not there. I don't have my credit card. This is ridiculous. I only carry one card in my wallet. When I had the accident, my purse was stolen, and with it, my cell phone and my wallet. I had to get everything replaced. After I got my new credit cards, I figured it would make more sense to carry one only.

I give her a quick smile and try to remember, as I pull everything out more and more frantically, a little shakily. *Let me think. I took out the card yesterday to pay for something online, but I'm sure I put it back.* I can see myself doing it.

I rummage around inside my bag in case it fell out of my wallet, even though what are the odds? The woman behind the counter is pursing her lips; no longer so accommodating. I can feel the shuffling of feet behind me. My neck is reddening with embarrassment. Everyone wants to go home.

"I'm really sorry, I—I don't know what to say, but I don't have my card or any cash with me. I'll have to come back. I'm so sorry."

She makes a face as if to say, *Thanks for nothing*, and I want to cry. I put my head down and shift across all the things from my bag I've left on the counter, so as to let the person behind me get on with it.

"Allow me." A man moves forward to right next to me, puts his hand on the counter and smiles at the woman, who smiles back much more pleasantly than she did with me, I notice.

He's holding up his ticket. "I'll get both, thanks." I'm about to protest, but he turns to me. "Don't worry, you can pay me back later."

I have no idea who this man is. I'm slow, sluggish—this is me now—so by the time I manage to say something, he's paid for his items and Jim's jacket, and he's leading me outside by the elbow.

◆ ◆ ◆

"Thank you." I put a hand on my chest.

"Are you all right?"

"Yes, I'm fine, thank you so much, that was—oh, you know—embarrassing."

"It happens. Nothing to be embarrassed about, I assure you."

I look at him more closely, trying to work out if I've ever met him before, but I don't think so.

He's a bit older than me, probably in his early forties. A good-looking man, with his crinkly eyes and his light brown hair, but not really my type. God! What's the matter with me? Why am I even thinking about whether he's my type or not?

"Thank you, really. I'll pay you back, of course."

He smiles, a sweet, boyish smile, like he's a friend.

"I don't know how to thank you," I continue. "My husband really needs this jacket"—I check my watch—"in about an hour, so I'll get your details and—"

"Have coffee with me."

"Excuse me?"

"I'll give you my details, as you call them, at the same time. What about over there?" He points across the road to a coffee shop. "It's a nice place."

"Right now?"

"Why not? Otherwise how will you find me again?" he smiles.

Is he flirting with me? I don't know what to say, how to behave. I turn my ring around my finger.

"It's beautiful," he says, looking down at it. "Is that what you spent your missing cash on?"

"No, God, I—"

"I know, I'm teasing you. Even I, who wouldn't know a ruby from a sapphire, can tell it's worth more than whatever cash you'd carry around in your purse."

I laugh. "I hope so, it's an anniversary gift."

"Then I'm sure it's very expensive. So, I still have to give you my details, and I could use a cup of coffee. What do you say?"

I hesitate. "It's just that I'm expected, and . . ." I lift Jim's jacket, wrapped in its plastic cover, to illustrate the point.

"Just one. Please."

Then he pauses, and says something I didn't expect.

"I know who you are, Emma Fern. I can't begin to tell you how much I admire you. So meeting you like this, and you talking to me—I don't want to sound weird here, but it's a wonderful moment. If you would let me buy you a coffee, then my life would be complete. You don't need to pay me back, by the way. In fact, I'm buying the coffee. What do you say?"

Should I? I have no idea what to do. I am rooted to the spot, over-dressed and holding up a tuxedo jacket, considering going to Starbucks or whatever that place is.

"Come on." He puts a hand below my elbow, and gently guides me to the crossing.

I let myself be guided, since that's the kind of person I have become, but I stop two steps back from the curb, then I look behind me. It's what I do now. Every time. Once I know there's no one there, I can step off the sidewalk.

4

"So, first things first, let me get your phone number before I forget."

I've recovered myself and we're sitting at a corner table near the window. I am rummaging through my purse, looking for something to write on. I notice we both take our coffee black and strong, European-style.

"Well, my name is Sam Huntington."

I write that down on my scrap of paper. "Sam Huntington . . ." I pause and he reels off his phone number, which I quickly note down. "Thank you. What's the best way to do this? We could meet back at the dry cleaner's tomorrow, same time, I can pay you back then. Would that work?"

"You don't need to pay me back. I told you."

"Of course I do. Why wouldn't I?"

"Let's have our coffees first, and then if you really insist, we'll make some other arrangements. But right now, I'm just thrilled to meet you in person." He beams.

"Thank you. And it's nice to meet you too, Sam."

I can't help feeling a little awkward. This complete stranger has just bailed me out of a tight spot, but now it turns out he's some kind of fan, and I feel obligated.

"I'm a great admirer of your work, I really am," he says.

"Thank you, Sam, it's good of you to say so." That's the other thing since the accident that I'm so sick and tired of: people giving me too much attention.

"What about yourself?" I ask. "What do you do?"

"Promise you won't laugh?"

"I can't promise that," I tell him. "What if you're a professional circus clown? Or a lion tamer? Or one of those workers who pick up dog poop from the street?"

"Do they do that? That's a job?"

"So I've been told, but I don't know if it's true."

"I must look that up immediately." He pulls out his phone.

He's really charming, Sam Huntington. There's something about him that makes me feel that it's okay to relax. I'm starting to enjoy this little detour.

I laugh. "Okay, so what do you do?"

"I'm a professional circus clown."

Now I really laugh. "I don't believe you."

"Nor should you. I tell fibs for a living."

"That's funny," I say, cocking my head, "so do I."

He raises his cup of coffee in a mock toast. "I'd like to say 'great minds,' but that would be untrue. I am nothing like you."

"Don't say that," I chide, but I'm starting to enjoy myself enormously. I initially went along with this to be polite, but now, I'm glad I'm here. "So, what does telling fibs entail, from your end?"

"I'm a ghostwriter."

I burst out laughing. "No! You're not! Now you're making fun of me."

"I'm not making fun of you. Wait, look." He fishes a business card out of his wallet and hands it to me.

"Sam Huntington, Ghostwriter," I read out loud. "People put that on their business cards? You're serious?"

"Yes, I am. Completely and utterly serious. There's my website." He leans forward and points to the URL on the card.

"Isn't that like saying, 'Sam Huntington, Professional Burglar'? Not to suggest you're stealing anything."

"You're hurting my feelings, Emma Fern, Professional Novelist."

"Sorry, but it's hard to take it seriously." And as I say it, I chuckle, which turns into a great big laugh, which is completely inappropriate, but I can't help myself.

He smiles as I recover, wiping tears of laughter from my eyes. "You're not a dog poop picker-upper pretending to be something else, are you?" I ask.

"What, like a professional bank robber? Nope, I'm a ghostwriter. It says so on the card, so it must be true."

"Well, that's amazing. I've never met a ghostwriter before." I almost blurt out that I've met a few ghosts, or at least one of them who stalks me on a regular basis.

"Or maybe you have, but you didn't know it." He winks and I bring myself back to the conversation. Ghostwriters. That's what we're talking about. "You'd be surprised, Emma Fern."

"Okay, I believe you. So tell me about it. It sounds fascinating. Is it?"

"Yes, it is." He leans back in his chair and makes himself more comfortable, clearly in his element. "I started writing essays for students. Most people in my field start out like that."

"Isn't that illegal?"

"I have no idea. Probably."

"Then what?"

"Then I graduated to writing about other people's lives. Lots of people want to pen their memoirs, but don't know how. And lots of people have fascinating stories to tell. That's the best part of the job. That man sitting over there"—with a nod he points me in the direction of a man in his sixties or thereabouts, wearing a dark coat—"he might seem perfectly ordinary to you, but who knows where he's come from? What he's been through?"

Sam leans forward, his forearms on the table.

"I had a client once, who ran away as a child," he says. "Not from an abusive situation, but on impulse. He wanted to make a point, because he felt he'd been unfairly punished. He got on a train and went as far as he could, then jumped on another one, then another. No one stopped him; no one asked him where his parents were. After one whole day he was ready to go home, but he didn't know how. He didn't know his own address; he barely knew how to read, because he was five years old. And this was in Eastern Europe, by the way, whatever that means. Anyway, his family was frantic, but they didn't find him for two months. And in that time he'd met an old man who played the violin in the street. The old man looked after him and taught him to play. By the time his parents found him, he could play the violin. He has never forgotten the old man, or how to play the violin. Then he emigrated here, and now he sells shoes."

"That's an amazing story. Is it true?"

"Yes! The search for him was well documented, and he does play the violin."

"How old is he now?"

"Early fifties."

"Wow!" I stare at the man in the dark coat, wondering what tales he carries along with him.

"My story didn't use to be interesting. It is now." I smile. "But for the first thirty years or so, it wasn't interesting at all."

"Everyone is interesting. You just need to ask the right questions."

"I bet you're very good at that."

"I haven't asked you anything yet."

"Somehow, I suspect that will come."

"I hope so," he says, surprisingly genuinely.

"So that's what you do now? Write about people's lives?"

"No, I write fiction now. I write for authors just like you."

"Not just like me, surely."

"You'd be surprised."

"So you keep saying. Okay, try me. Who have you ghostwritten for?"

"Ah, that would be telling." It's such a nice smile. Slightly crooked. "But I can tell you that writers, well-known writers, sometimes have writer's block. It's not unusual, and they just need a little help. Sometimes they're under pressure, maybe they have a deadline. And sometimes, they are so popular and sell so well that they literally can't write fast enough to meet the demand."

"You're like an artist's assistant."

"That's right."

"But don't you resent—"

There's a buzz on my cell: Jim wants to know if I've remembered to pick up his jacket.

". . . someone else getting all the glory?" He finishes my question for me.

"I have to go. Thank you, Sam Huntington, it was great to meet you."

He stands. "It was my pleasure, Emma Fern, I hope I can see you again."

"Of course. I owe you money, remember?"

"No, you don't. You had coffee with me, remember? That was the deal."

I gather my things and he holds the door for me.

"I'll call you, Sam Huntington the Ghostwriter. Thanks again."

◆ ◆ ◆

"Thanks, sweetheart," Jim says as I lay the jacket on the back of a chair. He's fixing his tie in the small mirror he keeps in his office. Usually in a drawer.

"You won't believe what happened picking this up."

I take him through the whole story of me not having my credit card, which I seriously hope is at home somewhere, and not having any cash, and being rescued by a knight in shining armor. No, I leave that last bit out. But I say someone paid for it for me, and I've got their details to pay them back.

"I think I should call the bank about my card, just in case."

"Your credit card? I saw it last night on your desk, near your computer."

"Really?" I try to recall when I took it out again. "I'm going crazy. Oh well, that's good, anyway. It hasn't been stolen."

"You're okay?" he asks.

"Yes, I'm fine, why?"

"Just that I've noticed you've been forgetting things lately."

I laugh, because he's the one who forgot his jacket and I think he's making a joke, but he doesn't laugh with me. He puts a hand on my cheek and just looks at me.

I bristle. "No I haven't! What are you talking about?"

"Never mind, sweetheart." He leans toward me and kisses the top of my head. "I'm glad you haven't lost your card."

I shake my head. I'm trying to think of something to say, but I don't understand what the problem is, so I mentally brush it off.

"You know," he says, putting the jacket on, "people always complain about this city, but then things like this happen. It warms the heart."

I watch his expression, straightening his tie for him.

"You're making fun of me."

"No, I'm not, I mean it." He does a quick flick of the wrist, and checks his watch. "We should go," he says.

I put my hand in the crook of his arm.

"You look very beautiful, Mrs. Fern."

"Thank you, Mr. Fern. You look very dashing yourself."

Tonight's gala dinner is another fundraiser for the Forum, at an extravagant amount of money per head. I used to love these events.

Recently I've found them difficult to navigate. I get nervous. But not tonight. Tonight, I feel great, and I'm happy.

◆ ◆ ◆

The room is breathtaking, with its Greek columns and the magnificent curved ceiling. The tables are beautifully laid, with tall candles and flowers arranged in the center.

I reach for the first glass of champagne that sails past me on a tray, and knock it back, so that by the time the waiter comes my way again, I can swap my empty flute for a full one.

I wonder how much all this cost. The Millennium Forum has never had a gala fundraiser like this before. Normally it's more of a cocktail party in an art gallery—still swish, mind you, but not on this scale.

Jim puts his arm around my shoulders. "You're all right, sweetheart?"

"Yes, of course, why?" *What did I forget this time?* I almost ask.

"I just want to make sure you're having a nice time." He takes my hand in his, lifts it up. "You still like your ring?"

"I love it. It's beautiful."

He pulls me close, and I rest my head on his shoulder. He presses his lips to the top of my head. "You smell of vacations," he says.

"It's my hair product," I reply, nestling into his neck.

"Exotic flowers and white beach sand."

"Is it? I can't smell anything."

"That's because your hair's too short."

"Hey, you two, get a room!"

I know that voice, and I'm already smiling when I look up.

"Hello, Emma," Terry says, smiling back at me.

"Hello, Terry, it's nice to see you." I kiss him on the cheek and he blushes a little.

Jim puts a hand on my back. "Sweetheart, excuse me a minute. I just spotted Patrick Plummer."

29

"I was wondering how long it would be before you went to work the room. Isn't that why we're here?" Terry says.

"Correct. You want me to find an important person for you to talk to?"

"I found one," Terry replies, his chin pointed in my direction. I laugh.

"Good man." Jim clasps Terry's shoulder as he walks away, and we watch him go.

Terry turns to look at me. "You look lovely, Emma."

"Thank you. You look very fine too."

"Really? I feel dreadful. I've that bug, flu, or something; everyone at the lab has come down with it, except Jim, of course." He smiles. It always amuses me that Terry, and Jim for that matter, call their workplace "the lab." These days, work at the Millennium Forum takes place in boardrooms and offices; it's more about backroom deals with government departments than test tubes or Bunsen burners, yet they still can't help referring to themselves as mad scientists.

At the mention of my husband, I find myself looking down at my ring again.

He follows my gaze. "Very nice. Is it new?"

I nod, a little coy. "Not new, but recent."

"A present?"

"Wedding anniversary."

"That's nice. I'm really pleased to see you and Jim like this. I never got the chance to tell you, but I've wanted to. I was worried about you two there, for a while."

"Were you?"

"Of course! He was so stressed. Work was . . . well, you know, you were there; it was touch and go for a while. The two of you didn't seem to cope well, for a time anyway."

"No, we didn't, did we?"

There was no point in prettying it up. Terry had witnessed that terrible scene in the restaurant way back when, where I made a complete fool out of myself by being fall-down drunk and definitely disorderly, and Jim had been brutally cruel to me, in front of everyone. Not one of our finest moments.

"And then I thought, with Carol, you know, I wasn't sure—oh Christ! Why am I talking about this now? Sorry, Emma. I don't know what's wrong with me. Blame it on the flu."

"It's all right, water under the bridge," I say brightly, patting his forearm. "But I agree, let's not talk about it anymore, Terry. It's a long time ago, thank the Lord, and as you say, things are different now."

Carol. And here I was having such a nice time. The last thing I want to think about is Carol fucking McCready, who worked with my husband and screwed him behind my back. They almost ran away together, for Christ's sake.

I shake the memory away. All that was before I got him back. No need to reopen old wounds.

"I don't know why I said all that," Terry says again.

"It's fine, really." I lean forward and kiss his cheek, then lift my glass in a toast.

"To happy days," I say.

He brings his glass close to mine so they touch.

"Oh, and to tonight! May it be a great success! Well, it already is, but may the coffers be full!"

"Please . . ." He raises his eyes skyward and puts his hands together in prayer. "It has to be."

"Why do you say it like that?"

He frowns. "If we don't get a big cash injection, we're going to be in some trouble. Didn't Jim tell you? That's why we're doing this." He extends an arm around the room. "On top of that, we've got an audit in progress. We're a for-profit think tank, and we're not a startup anymore. So it's not that easy to get people to part with cash in return for, essentially, a good meal. We had to pull out all the stops."

"Well, everything looks amazing, and it's packed too. But no, Jim didn't say. I wish he had."

"He probably didn't want to worry you, especially after the accident. Show me your scar."

When Terry visited me in the hospital, I was not in a good place. I almost told him about what I thought had happened. I didn't, but his gentleness to me then deepened our friendship, and I know he's asking because he cares. I lift the hair that falls across the side of my face. He brushes the scar softly.

"Almost gone," he says.

The sound system spurts out loud popping sounds, and we turn to see the MC tapping the microphone. "Ladies and gentlemen . . ."

I turn back to Terry. "I don't know where I'm seated. I should go and ask the nice man over there with the clipboard," I say.

"I think we're at the same table. Come with me."

5

"You're up early." It's the first thing Jim says to me this morning, and no wonder. It's not even eight o'clock. I'm always still asleep at this time these days. But today I even made coffee.

"I just want to get some things done. Did you sleep well?"

"I certainly did," he replies. I can feel his breath on the back of my neck as he puts his arms around my waist. "You hungry?" he asks. "I can make some eggs if you like."

I turn and hand him a cup of coffee, smiling at the sight of him, all clean and pressed. "Really? Thanks, Jim, that would be lovely. I'd love some eggs."

"Coming right up."

I sit at the kitchen table as he fetches the eggs from the refrigerator and goes about the business of beating them.

"Great success last night. Congratulations again, my darling."

"Thanks." He smiles. "Yeah, I think we met our expectations. I'll find out more today."

"The food was wonderful," I say.

"Wasn't it? Everyone said so. I knew the night would turn out well when I saw Plummer was there. And you know who else . . . ?"

I've stopped listening. I'm busy watching Jim make us scrambled eggs, a smile on my face.

"Terry must be pleased," I say when he serves them up for us.

"I'm sure he is." He picks up his cell and starts to scroll through his messages and emails, already back in work mode.

"Everything all right at the Forum?" I ask.

He looks up. "What do you mean?"

"Terry mentioned things have been a bit slow, financially."

"Really?" He puts his fork down on his plate, attentive. "What did he say exactly?"

I take a moment, casting my mind back to the conversation. "Nothing too specific. Just that you could use the cash, basically. He said something about an audit too." I shake my head. "I can't quite remember, to be honest."

"Well, I have no idea what Terry's talking about," he says dismissively, and goes back to his phone.

"Really? He was surprised that you hadn't mentioned anything to me about it."

He looks at me, but doesn't reply.

"You know, if you needed some money, to tide you over while things are slow, you could always draw some from the savings account. I don't mind."

I am at the kitchen counter when I say this, refilling my cup from the coffee pot. He doesn't say anything, and I turn to look at him to make sure he's heard me.

He's staring at me, frowning. Didn't he think I would do this for him?

"The savings account?"

"Yes! That's what it's for, isn't it? For a rainy day?" I smile.

There's a pause, before he asks, "When was the last time you checked the account, Em?"

"Oh, I don't know." I try to remember. "I haven't made any big purchases for a while, so I've had no need to check, and I never open the statements. I let Jim do that. "Maybe last December, when we drew on it to go to St. Barts, I think."

That wonderful vacation, just the two us. I'd never seen sea that color, somewhere between turquoise and green. And the sand, so pale and—

"Sorry, darling?" Something Jim says pulls me back to the present.

"There's no money left in the savings account, Em. I can't believe you don't know that."

"Don't be ridiculous," I scoff, "of course there is. That's where the royalties from my book are deposited. Every month."

"There are no royalties, Emma. There's hardly anything going into that account these days. You should take a look."

And then he laughs. Not a big laugh; more like a chuckle. As if I'd said something silly, when all I'd meant to do was to offer him some money, to help him out, unprompted. He goes back to his phone. He doesn't even notice how shocked his words have made me. He's too busy scrolling through his emails.

"What are you up to today?" he asks, distractedly, as if that other conversation no longer matters.

"Not much, just—" I was about to say shopping, but that doesn't seem wise anymore. "A few calls, talk to Frankie, work on my new book."

He gets up and wipes the corner of his mouth with two fingers.

"I have to get going. I'll see you tonight, darling." He leans in and kisses me, and I sit a moment longer, sipping my coffee, listening to the sounds of my husband going to work. Coat, keys, door, elevator.

I wait a little while after he's gone, attuned to the silence in the apartment. I sit and wait, and listen, in case he's forgotten something and comes back. It's nice to just listen sometimes. It can be very relaxing, very settling, to be still and just listen. However, this is not one of those times. I am upset, trying not to let it morph into anger. There's no money? *When's the last time you checked, Em? I can't believe you don't know that.* I hate that tone he takes with me sometimes. I really do.

35

The first thing I do is go to my office, to my desk, and check if my credit card is there. I can't see it. Just as I thought, it's not there. I shouldn't have listened to Jim. He must have seen it on a different day, and now Lord knows how much money has been stolen before I get to cancel it. The stress is making me clench my teeth. I'm more annoyed at him than anything else. That he stopped me from reporting it.

And then I see it, just the edge of it, jutting out from under the keyboard. I press my finger down on its corner and slide it out.

That's good, obviously, in a way, but it worries me nonetheless. I feel like I'm losing my grip on things. *I can't believe you don't know that, Em.*

I fire up the laptop and check my bank account online, and sure enough, there's just under ten thousand dollars in the savings account. Not quite the riches we have gotten used to. This apartment, which I frankly dislike more and more, is costing us so much money it's not funny. It seemed like a good idea at the time—just like everything else we did together—living through the past year or so as if the money would never end.

I get up and go to his office, where the documents are kept. Where Jim meticulously files all our bank statements.

I never go in there. I have no need to. It's a nice enough room, with a desk and a small filing cabinet. There are a multitude of books on economics on the shelves covering the walls, and a plush armchair in the corner with a little side table next to it. I put it there thinking he would like a comfortable corner to sit and refer to his books, and read his papers, but I don't think he ever uses it. Everything he does is on the laptop, which is right there, on the desk.

I try the filing cabinet. I don't know what I'm looking for exactly, but since Jim *can't believe* I don't know that, maybe I should find out more about the state of our affairs. Except it's locked, Lord knows why.

That was actually incredibly generous of me, to offer to help him—yet again, I might add—out of a tight financial spot. It's all very well starting a business about economics research—how about running it like you know what you're talking about? Now there's a novel idea.

Because, let's face it, why Jim thought the Forum would ever be successful is anyone's guess, considering the whole thing is built on a lie. It would have taken a miracle—and here we are, not a single one of those on the horizon. So, no. Jim, Carol, Terry, and the Forum have not set the world on fire. Surprise, surprise. And yet does this knowledge stop me from trying to help? From believing in him? Certainly not. For better or for worse, I didn't just memorize those words and recite them by rote, I took them to heart and made them my motto. I am always happy to step in and offer to help my husband in any way I can.

I sit in his chair, trying to remember the last time I did that, without success. I run my hands over the surface of his wooden desk; not a speck of dust. Then I turn on the computer, and I am greeted with a password field. That I can understand. Anyway, since I don't know the password, I shut down the laptop.

Then I call Frankie.

◆ ◆ ◆

"Well of course, it's what happens, Emma. You had a good run, but no writer is going to stay on the bestseller list forever—"

"Did anyone tell J.K. Rowling that?"

"—with only a single novel under your belt. Emma, don't be like that. You should be writing the next one. I keep telling you that. I've asked you a hundred times to give me another novel."

So it's true, there is no money left. I wonder how long we can keep this apartment if that is the case. Jim's salary is substantial, but not enough to keep us in this lifestyle. That part has been down to me. Although I can't say I'll be sorry if we have to give it up. I miss my little house in Woodhaven. It was fun playing grown-up and getting this massive, elegant apartment in Midtown Manhattan, sure, but it doesn't delight me the way that little house did.

I sigh. "It takes time, Frankie, surely you know that."

"You always say that. What's taking you so long?"

"Stop saying 'so long,' please, Frankie! It's not that long!"

"It's long enough."

I love Frankie. He is my publisher, my agent, and most importantly, my friend. He took a chance on me when I brought him my little man-uscript, and he took it on and gave it everything he had. And I mean everything. He turned me from would-be novelist to prize-winning author, and I turned him from the brink of bankruptcy to the top of his game. So what we have is a symbiotic relationship. He needs me as much as I need him. But right now, he's driving me crazy. I need him to stop harassing me about *writing the next one*. At least he has the decency not to bring up the fact I'm under contract and behind the deadline.

It's funny really, but I always forget that I didn't write the first one. I'm so used to being known as its author, I've come to believe it myself. I couldn't write a novel to save my life. I stole *Long Grass Running*—accidentally, mind you—but that's another story.

I chuckle to myself. Maybe I should have thought of this predica-ment before I killed Beatrice, the real author. She's not there to write another one, is she? Maybe that's why she's stalking me in my dreams; why she appears wherever she can. She's probably laughing at me. Oh well, at least I'm still here, and she brought it upon herself anyway. But now I'm stuck with Frankie breathing down my neck about *the next one*.

"What about the movie rights?" I blurt out. "How's that going?"

There. Put *that* in your pipe and smoke it. Why don't *you* do some work too? It's not just down to me, buddy, you're the agent/publisher, after all. We've been talking about those movie rights for long enough. Almost as long as *the next one*.

"Progressing very nicely. Still waiting to hear back on a couple things, but we're close."

"Really? So that's good news, right?"

"Fingers crossed. I could have a nice surprise for you real soon."

"Seriously? Soon?"

"Maybe. Now go away and write something, Emma, please. Otherwise we'll both be out of business."

It's not like I haven't tried to write another novel. I did try, sort of, but it's no use. I am inspirationally challenged. I can't think of a story, or a plot, or a character that I would want to spend any time with, so now I don't bother anymore. I vaguely assumed something would turn up. I have no idea what, or why I'd even think that was a possibility, but I thought I had more time at least.

"Well, who knows? Maybe the *New Yorker* piece is going to rekindle sales," I say, hopeful. I am to be interviewed: they're doing quite a big profile, in fact, for their Poulton Prize winners series. Next week, I think.

"Rekindle, probably not. You'll get a few from that, yes, but it's not going to solve your problems. Just go and write that book, Emma, okay?"

6

Just go and write that book, Emma, okay?

How am I supposed to do that, Frankie?

There's no doubt it was an interesting coincidence that someone in my position should meet a nice ghostwriter. Just like that.

Until now, the only idea I had was to steal another novel. And how would I do that? That's the question that has been occupying my mind these past few months. There was one possibility that I thought "had legs": I could get a job teaching. Not to become a teacher, obviously, but because I figured that creative writing courses teeming with bright young minds writing bright novels would love someone like me to give them a hand. I even researched the various colleges and writing centers in the area. I had no doubt I could teach a summer school and that I'd do very well at it. I may not be able to write, but I know what makes good writing.

Anyway, I didn't get this far, because I didn't think I would need to so soon. I thought I'd have more time. But apparently not.

My evil plan was to offer a creative writing course. Something like "Dust Off Your First Draft with Emma Fern, winner of the Poulton etc., etc." I figured there'd be lots of sign-ups, and I would keep my fingers crossed that one of my students had a masterpiece tucked up his or her sleeve. Then I'd steal it, and give it to Frankie. *Et voilà.* Problem solved.

Of course, the weak link here is the student, and that's the part I hadn't quite figured out. If I killed them, which at one point in the not-too-distant past would have been my first reaction, then that would mean snuffing out a young life, and, frankly, I'm not a monster. Also, I was concerned it would make me a serial killer. I've killed two people in my life already. Does that make me a serial killer? I don't know. I don't think it should, but it probably does. It's like those languages you hear about, Inuit or something, where they only have words for "one" and "many," but never just "two or three." So I guess killing is the same. You kill one, or you kill many, but there's no in-between.

But killing a young person—I assume all students are young, which is stupid of me, but never mind—who has done nothing to harm me, whose only crime is to have written something I want for myself? I don't think murder is justified there, try as I might.

No, I thought money might be the answer. But therein lies the slight problem—that I don't have much money anymore, so that's out now, isn't it? Surely young Hemingway is going to want a piece of the pie, and that slice is going to have to be significant before they're prepared to part with their baby. And I know what I'm talking about, when I say *part with*. It's what got me into trouble in the first place.

So no, I haven't put that plan in motion, for all the reasons stated above. But God is my friend, the Lord is my savior, and I am blessed. Thank you, Lord, for bringing me Sam. I know that now. The timing is too good. It's perfect. This is the hand of God at work. Which is why I call Sam.

"Hey, Emma Fern," he says brightly after I've told him it's me. "Are you calling me to meet up? You realize I don't want your money for the dry cleaning, but maybe if I don't tell you that, you'll meet me again for more coffee and conversation. What do you think?"

I laugh. "What happens when I try to repay you?"

"Oh, I'll make sure to distract you, then by the time you get home, you'll have to call me again to set up another meeting."

"Well, let's start with coffee and conversation and I'll see where it gets me."

"You have a deal," he says. "What are you up to right now?"

"I'm looking at your website, as it happens. Very informative."

"Is it?"

"Definitely. Eleven *New York Times* bestsellers in the past five years!"

"Thank you for noticing. And of those eleven, six are fiction by the way."

"I saw that. Very impressive! Which titles would these be?"

"Now, now, Emma Fern. That would be telling."

"Still, it says here your books have been published by HarperCollins, Simon & Schuster, Random House, and the list goes on and on!"

"Wow, Emma, I'm really flattered. You're reading my website back to me. I don't think anyone has done that for me before. Except maybe my web designer."

I laugh.

"What do you think of my 'About Me' page?" he asks.

"Let me take a look. Ah! I knew it. It says you're forty-one years old."

"How old did you think I was?"

"Forty-one years old."

"I don't believe you. I don't look a day over forty."

"It says here you were born in Austin, Texas, and that you studied Literature and Business."

And that his office is in Midtown. Which is where I live, so that's an added bonus. Or another divine sign.

"Okay, stop it," he says. "You're embarrassing me now. I'm going to take my website down if you keep going."

"Sorry. I'm impressed, though."

"Thank you. So when can we meet for coffee?"

I sigh. "I'm a little busy at the moment. Can we say in a couple days?"

"That long? You owe me money, remember?"

I like this man. He really makes me laugh. I hope we can be friends.

"I'm good for it, Sam, trust me."

"All right, I believe you, Emma Fern."

After I hang up, I google other ghostwriters and it's amazing. It's becoming clear to me that ghostwriting is not the realm of the loser, the would-be writer who can't string a sentence together, the pseudo-intellectual who can't do his or her own research; the untalented, the unwanted, the great literary unwashed—i.e., me.

No, this truly is a revelation. There are statistics out there that point to fifty percent of books in one's local bookstore being ghostwritten. That seems high to me, so let's halve that, and we still have a nice twenty-five percent.

I am elated. Thank you, Lord, for the helping hand you have given me.

But should I find someone different? The fact that Sam knows I am Emma Fern worries me. Maybe I should work with someone else, under a pseudonym. But then I wonder, can people do that? Sign a contract under a pseudonym?

While I'm pretty close to making a decision, I decide to sleep on it. Next time I see him, I can find out more about the process. Under the guise of "just talking" about his work. And if it does feel comfortable, then I think I would like to work with him. That's what it is: working together. People do it all the time, work with a ghostwriter. People on the *New York Times* bestseller list. At least eleven of them in the past five years.

So I spend the rest of the morning doing research, and because I feel better, having had the most productive day I've experienced in a while, I go shopping and make Jim a delicious dinner. Spaghetti with scallops in champagne and tarragon sauce. Easy to make, very nice to eat.

"How was your day? Any feedback from the function yet?"

He has his fork in one hand, and his phone in the other. "Mmm?" he replies, eyes on the screen, scrolling with his thumb.

I think I've put too much tarragon in the sauce. I take another bite.

Jim looks up at me. "Sorry, darling, so much going on. This is delicious."

I've barely touched my food and he's almost finished. He hasn't touched his glass of wine, a sure sign that he'll be going back to work in his office as soon as we're finished eating.

"That's okay," I say.

Jim stopped working at home every night long ago, but lately it's been creeping back. I guess there's a lot going on at the Forum. But he helps me clean up. I talk about my day. I tell him about the piece the *New Yorker* is going to be doing. He's impressed, I can tell. At one point he asks, "How's the new book going?"

One day, soon, I will not have to answer this question anymore. Because *the new one* will be out, nicely displayed on the shelves of our local bookstore, and he can go get his own copy if he's so interested in it. I long for this day. However, since today is not this day, I reply, "Not too bad, pretty happy about how it's going."

Because the more I think about it, the more I wonder, who am I not to follow the hand of God?

7

My cup runneth over.

I slept late this morning, as I usually do, and when I got up around ten, I saw a missed call from Frankie, but there was also a text:

> Come for lunch today, tell me you're free, I want you to meet someone. At L'Ambroisie 1pm okay? Please be there! xo

If the clouds had parted just then and the sun had streamed through my window, warm and bright, I would have thought it was for me. It feels like the tide has turned, thank God. I've been waiting long enough.

I love L'Ambroisie. Beatrice and I used to go there all the time, back in the days when she was nice to me. I don't remember the last time I went there, but if Frankie picked it, then I know it's special, and I know who and what that means since he already told me, in his coy way. So I spend the morning pampering myself. I put on the Givenchy dress that I love. It's very flattering and very modern, and the color is nice against my skin. When I get out of the taxi, I have butterflies in my stomach at the prospect of meeting the producers who will be making the movie of *Long Grass Running*.

I'm a little early, and Frankie is already there. I can see him in the distance as I walk into the restaurant, talking earnestly to someone whose back is to me. He looks so excited and animated. *Wait for me,* I want to shout. *Don't start without me!* And I walk quickly between the tables. Even then Frankie doesn't see me; doesn't register that I'm here until I'm standing right by his side.

He looks up at me and gives me a beaming smile. "There you are," he says, standing up, and we put our arms around each other warmly.

"That's me. I'm here," I giggle, and Frankie puts a hand on my back, then extends his other arm to the man at the table, who is also standing and smiling.

"Emma Fern." I shake the hand proffered to me and he bows. "It's an honor."

I smile back at this man, who is much younger than I expected, but then what do I know about producers? As long as he's old enough to sign his name on my contract, that's all I care about. But I have a flicker of recognition, there's something about him that looks vaguely familiar.

"Emma, this is Nicholas Hackett," Frankie says with a little flourish. He looks so happy, and I'm grinning so much my face is starting to hurt.

"Call me Nick, please," he says, and we all sit down.

Frankie starts to say something. "Nick is—"

But Nick speaks at the same time, so Frankie stops abruptly.

"I can't tell you how wonderful it is to meet you, in person. I'm in awe of your talent, Emma. Oh, is it all right if I call you Emma? May I?"

His face is so open, so earnest. He looks almost scared, with his eyebrows arched, like he's really worried he just committed the ultimate faux pas. It makes me want to pat him on the hand. *There there.*

I smile at him, reassuringly. And I realize where I've seen him before, with his black-rimmed glasses and his youthful appearance. In fact, I've never seen him before, but he's the spitting image of that documentary maker, Louis Theroux.

"Of course, Nick. Please call me Emma," and I am more than a little gratified at his little gushing display.

"Shall we order first?" Frankie picks up his menu and Nick and I do the same. *Good idea*, I think, *get the small stuff out of the way*. I order the first thing on the menu, and there's a bit of activity with glasses being filled and waiters taking our orders, but then it's just the three of us again, and Nick says, "I'm honored that we now share the same publisher, Emma. That's why I picked Frankie, you know, because of you."

He looks at me with his big guileless smile and I think he's waiting for me to say something.

"Pub—publisher?" I stammer.

"Yes!" Frankie pipes up brightly, and then he puts his hand on mine. "Do you remember the article in the *New York Times*? About Nick?"

I turn to look at Frankie. I'm still smiling, but it's a little forced. Frankie is looking proudly at Nick, even though I'm pretty sure he was addressing that question to me.

"The article?"

Nick puts both palms up in a mock gesture, as if to fend off all the attention.

"Please, let's not talk about me, it's too boring. I want to hear all about you, Emma."

Frankie chuckles. What on earth is the matter with him?

"We'll get to that," he says, "but first let me explain. You've seen the article, haven't you? About the bidding war for Nick's novel?" At last, he is looking in my direction.

"Oh, that was crazy, crazy stuff," Nick interjects, flapping his hands. And what's the matter with him too? Is he drunk? He has the strangest mannerisms. But then again, so does Louis Theroux.

"There was a bidding war for Nick's novel. Wait till you read it, Emma, it's something else, let me tell you. It's like you, you know? That feeling I had. I can't wait for you to read it."

47

"Frankie, stop it!" says bashful Nick, and Frankie laughs.

"Anyway," Frankie continues, "I put in an offer, but I wasn't in the running. As good as you've been to me, darling Emma, I couldn't compete with the heavyweights. This was way, way out of my league. But you know what he did?" He points his chin at Nick in a gesture that is so familiar, it's almost rude. But Nick seems unfazed. He's rearranging breadcrumbs in a little pile next to his fork, all the while smiling at the white tablecloth.

"No," I say finally, because Frankie seems to be expecting me to say something, and at this point I have no idea what the heck he's talking about, or who he's talking to, or who Nick is, and this better be good because I am having a great day, and the tide has turned, and the hand of God is guiding me. And now I do remember the article, and I remember Nick's guileless face staring out from the page, and funny, I didn't notice then that he looked just like Louis Theroux. But I do remember something about the promising young writer who'd written a masterpiece, put it up for auction, and then didn't take the highest bidder, which was unheard of—unethical almost, if you ask me. But what I don't understand is why we're talking about that, and when do we start talking about my movie rights?

"He chose us, Emma. We're publishing Nicholas Hackett, aka the most promising writer of his generation. Can you believe it?"

What is it with Frankie? He's talking to me, he's saying my name, but all the time he's looking at Nick like he's a lovestruck puppy, and Nick is playing with his breadcrumbs. Am I supposed to say something now? Something other than *what the fuck*?

I look around quickly, because suddenly it occurs to me that maybe they're playing some kind of prank on me. There's someone out there filming my reaction, and then we'll all crack up and forever be saying things like, *Do you remember the time we signed with Nick the producer, but we tricked you into thinking you were meeting Nick the most promising writer of his generation?* And we'll roll over laughing. But somehow, I don't think that's happening, not really. That's not Frankie's style.

"You're embarrassing me, please stop it," Nick keeps saying, with a modesty so genuine he must have practiced it an awful lot.

Finally they remember I'm here and they turn to me, smiling expectantly.

"Wow," I offer, that being the best I can come up with.

Frankie gets us a bottle of champagne, and we toast the most promising writer of his generation, no less, and I am wracking my brain, because how could I possibly get this so wrong? Did Frankie actually say we were meeting with a producer? No, of course not, but he hinted at it—didn't he?

I'll have a surprise soon for you—isn't that what he said? *Come for lunch today. Please be there.* I'm sure that's what he said.

What does Frankie think I've been waiting for? He knows full well what I've been waiting for. For him to do his job, for one thing. He is my agent-cum-publisher and he's been peddling my movie rights for almost two years now. Why on earth does Frankie think I'm going to be so excited to meet this . . . dork? And now he has eyes only for Nick, like Nick's walking on water, like he's in love. I know that look. That's the way he used to look at me.

"But tell me about you, Emma—really, enough of this. I loved *Long Grass Running* so much. You are an inspiration to me, to many of us aspiring writers."

Frankie beams again. "I'm so happy you two have met," he says.

"What's your novel about?" I ask, even though I already know, since I did read the *New York Times* article and it's all coming back to me in big, bright, neon signage.

"Oh, let's not talk about my novel anymore, tell me what you're working on. There's so much anticipation since the Prize!"

"Well, I . . ." and from the corner of my eye I can see Frankie's face has frozen in place, because he doesn't like that question any more than I do.

"Emma did write something since then: a memoir, of her friendship with the writer Beatrice Johnson Greene," Frankie says. "Did you read it?"

"No! I didn't know about that. I'm so sorry!"

Which is no surprise, of course, because that book tanked.

"Nonfiction is not an easy switch to make. It was more of a personal testimony to a dear friend," I say, to no one in particular.

"Oh, so nothing in the works for you? I would have thought that you'd be on the verge of publishing by now. But what do I know? I'm such a novice," Nick says, and I stare at his fork, picturing myself lunging for it and sticking it in his neck, or should I do Frankie first?

"I'm sorry?" I ask, realizing Nick is saying something else.

"I said it can't be easy after winning the Poulton. It's not like you can hit that note twice, surely." He presses his lips together in an apologetic smile, and it occurs to me that Nick is not as guileless as he seems.

This is not my lucky day.

I decide to walk back from the restaurant. I'm too agitated and frustrated to go home yet. I'm so angry with Frankie, I'm almost shaking. How could he choose that preppy little fake over me? How could he do this to me? I'm the one who won the Poulton, for Christ's sake. I'm the one who put Frankie and his pitiful little publishing company on the map. And this is how he repays me? There would be no Frankie, no preppy "Nick the Prick" if it weren't for me. I made Frankie, and now Frankie is going to make Nick. And what am I? A has-been? Is that what he thinks? I can walk into any bookstore in this city, secure in the knowledge that my novel, my Poulton Prize–winning novel, will be on the shelves, prominently displayed.

I'm feeling so rattled that I keep walking, and now I'm downtown, so I take a detour to that little bookstore I like on the Lower East Side. I'll go and check, and I'll bet anything they still stock my book. It will make me feel better; maybe I'll even buy a copy. Maybe I'll buy them all. Get them to order new stock. But I get there, and it's all boarded up. I'd forgotten, even though it's been like that for months. They say something terrible happened here, but I don't believe it. It's just gratuitous gossip as far I'm concerned. I think the man who looked after the store has simply moved on. Bookstores are not exactly thriving businesses these days. Still, it's a shame. We chatted once or twice and I liked him. What was his name again? Joe. I wonder where he went. I thought he was—I don't know—simpatico.

I sigh, and walk away. I'm never going to read Nick's book. And what about my movie adaptation? That's what I want to know. I bet Nick gets his movie made before mine, and if that happens, I will fire Frankie, and then I will kill Nick.

I don't want to go home yet. I walk in the direction of the Forum, and when I'm a block away, I take out my cell phone and call Jim.

"Hi, Em, what's up?"

"Nothing much, just . . ." I hesitate.

"You're okay?"

"I'm fine, really. I was wondering, do you want to have a drink? I'm not far from your office and—"

"Now?" he asks. "It's what? Three o'clock in the afternoon and you call me to have a drink?" He sneers on the word *drink*. "No wonder you're so vague, Em."

"Oh! I thought it was later than that. Sorry, darling."

"I'm really busy here, Em, I'm at work. Was there something you wanted?"

There are voices in the background and Jim says something that sounds muffled, as if he has his hand over the phone.

"No, I—sorry, no," I say, stuttering, "I'll see you later."

I put the phone back in my bag, keeping my eyes down. I shouldn't have mentioned having a drink. I feel a flush spread across my cheeks. I wish now I hadn't called. Really I just wanted a hug from him. Sometimes Jim is incredibly attentive, and yet it's surprisingly difficult to ask him to be there for me. I know he's busy and he's at work, but the abruptness of his tone just now stings and I start to cry. I feel ridiculous, rooted to the spot, unable to move. I put my hands over my face, waiting for the sobs to subside.

"Emma?" I hear beside me, a woman's voice I don't recognize, and a hand now sits on my shoulder. "Are you okay?"

I take my hands away from my face and look up.

"Carol?"

8

"What happened? Are you all right?"

I just stare at her, in mild disbelief. Carol. Jim's Carol? Carol, who tried to take Jim away from me? Carol, who worked with Jim at the Forum and pretended to like me, all the while engaging in sordid trysts with my husband?

Carol McCready?

I shake my head.

"What are you doing here?" I ask finally, hiccupping a little. She still has a hand on my shoulder, rubbing it gently. As much as I hate myself for it, I don't want her to stop. It's surprisingly comforting.

"I just had a meeting," she says vaguely, "then I saw you. Are you okay?"

"With Jim?" It comes out a little more abruptly than I intended it to.

"Jim? No! God no."

But I burst into tears again. I don't know what's wrong with me. It's this horrible lunch with Nick. It's made me feel hopeless.

"Come with me. Let's go and sit somewhere," she says.

"I'm not going with you." I shrug her hand off my shoulder. She cocks her head slightly, gives me a look that says, *Don't be like that.*

"And anyway, don't you need to go? Surely you have work to do."

She shakes her head. "Nothing that will miss me. I could use a drink, to be honest. And it would be nice to talk."

"Why?"

"Why not? Come on, I know just the place," she says, gently grabbing my elbow.

I don't know if it's the mention of a drink, or if it's because I'm so angry about Nick that I just want to tell someone, or if it's that I wonder what on earth Carol thinks *would be nice to talk* about that makes me follow her. Maybe it's simply the sympathy in her voice that does it. Or maybe it's the thought of what Jim would say if he could see me now. *See? If you hadn't been rude and dismissive, I wouldn't be here, chatting with your ex-lover.*

Who knows? Either way, against all odds, I let myself be led.

It is just the place, she was right. It's dark enough, with soft music playing, and at this time of the day it's almost empty. I order a Scotch and Carol surprises me by doing the same.

I take a breath. "Thank you."

"What for?"

"For being kind." I give her a small quick smile. "You didn't have to do this."

"You looked a bit lost there, Emma. I didn't want to leave you like that. But you're welcome."

We take a sip of our drinks. After a moment, I ask, "What do you do now? For work?"

"Still economics, of course, but I'm based in D.C. now, at the Department of Labor."

I nod. "Is that where you went after . . ." I let the question trail since we both know what I'm talking about. *After you had an affair with my husband and I had to blackmail him into ending the relationship.*

"Yes, the opportunity came up, I needed to move on." Carol drums her fingers against her glass, her gaze down. I take a better look at her. She hasn't changed much, but she looks good. She's lost a few pounds, and her dark hair is longer than it used to be, or maybe that's just my memory. It suits her, this hairstyle: thick and shiny over her shoulders. She's still ordinary looking, really, but with her nice, fitted suit, she looks very professional. I become aware I'm clenching my teeth.

"I bet Jim gave you an excellent reference."

She looks up at me, startled.

"Sorry, it just came out."

She shakes her head. "I understand, of course. Those were hard times, Emma, for me as well as you. Honestly, I'm so glad that's all over."

"Do you ever see him?" I ask.

"No."

"Your paths never cross?"

"Once or twice, from a distance, at the odd conference, something like that maybe. We just avoid each other when that happens. The Department has dealings with the Forum, but not through my section, thank God."

"Do you miss him?" I hear myself ask. I don't dare look at her though, and it's me who stares into my drink now.

There's a beat of silence, then she says, "I miss the feeling sometimes. The feeling of being so head over heels in love with someone. Being obsessed. Not wanting to think about anything or anyone else. But do I miss *him*? No. He wasn't for me, Emma. He's too selfish, too much the narcissist." Our eyes meet. "Sorry."

I blink the apology away.

"I fell for him hard," she continues, "for his grand ideals and his genius. But he never loved me, you know. He just loved the fact that I loved him. I realized that pretty fast." She sighs.

It's interesting hearing her say those words, not least because I've wondered about myself over the years: whether what Jim loves most about me is that I put him on a pedestal. Although I don't think about that so much now.

"Being found out is the best thing that happened to me. I've moved away, I love my new job. I travel the world for my research, I have a great place in D.C. and new friends. And I've got some perspective on a relationship that was pretty toxic, if I'm honest. I'm glad to be out of it."

It's funny, because I don't know anything about what their relationship was like. In my mind, it was excruciatingly perfect, they were so well suited. To hear the word *toxic* to describe their affair is a revelation.

"Anyone special now?"

She gives me a little smile. "Maybe. Too soon to tell, but it's promising."

"That's nice. I wish you all the best, Carol. And thank you for being honest."

She clinks her glass against mine.

"To the future."

"And is that what brought you back here today? Your work, I mean?"

She nods. "I've been asked to host a seminar at NYU, on law, ethics, and economics. It's become somewhat of a specialty of mine."

"Wow." I can't help but be impressed. For a surreal moment, I am flattered that she's here with me, having a drink.

"But you," she says, "what a great couple years you've had, winning the Poulton Prize too. That's amazing, Emma. You're incredible."

I feel myself blush at the compliment.

"Thanks. Yes, it's been quite a time."

"And you're happy? You and Jim?"

I nod. "We are. It wasn't easy, but I'm happy to say we made it."

"I'm glad," she says, patting my knee. "I truly am. The two of you belong together. Things are exactly as they should be." We fall silent, each in our own private world, and then she says, "I never had the chance to apologize to you, Emma. But I've thought of you many times over the past couple years, and of what I put you through. Looking at it from this angle, after all this time, I can't believe I behaved as I did. Having an affair with a married man. I'm truly sorry, Emma. For all the hurt."

Her words are so unexpected that my eyes fill with tears, and I'm going to start crying again, but she gets hold of my shoulder and says, "No! No! Please! Not Niagara Falls again! I've run out of Kleenex!" and I crack up, and she does too, and we're both laughing so hard that people are looking at us, but it's such a relief. Then we hug, and she tells me again how sorry she is.

If anyone had told me that I'd be having a drink with Carol; enjoying her company, I wouldn't have known whether to laugh at them or punch them. And yet here I am, and it's nice. It reminds me how I used to like her. I want to tell her I came to see Jim today because I was feeling fragile; I needed him, but he was so abrupt and dismissive that I felt even worse. I'm sure she would listen, and understand. But I don't dare.

We order another round, and she asks me about Terry; the "lovely Terry," as she calls him, and she wants to know what it's like winning the Poulton Prize. She's fascinated by my life. She says she wishes she had my talent; that I'm so lucky, which is funny to me since she's one of the smartest people I've ever met.

◆ ◆ ◆

"So? What did you think?"

"How about, 'Good morning, Emma, you look lovely today, how's my favorite author doing?'"

"Sorry. Good morning, you look lovely, Emma, and what did you think?" Frankie says, kissing me on the cheek.

I smile, all wide-eyed and innocent. "About what?"

"Well, Nick, of course!" At last he extends a hand to indicate the chair for me to sit in. If I am to sing Nick's praises, I'm allowed to do it sitting down.

"He looks an awful lot like Louis Theroux."

"Who?"

"You know, that documentary maker, the English guy. He's on BBC America—*Louis Theroux's Long Weekends* or something."

He cocks his head at me. "I have no idea what you're talking about."

"Well, it's your loss. It's amazing. They could be twins."

He waves both hands in front of himself, as if to say, *Stop it already.* "I'm not asking about what he looks like. What did you think of him as a person? As a writer?" and when he adds, "You must have been impressed," I tell myself to breathe, to concentrate on a spot just above his head, and that I should look up that meditation app I read about last week.

"Yes, Frankie, I was very impressed."

"He couldn't wait to meet you, you know. He's in awe of you."

"And I of him."

"No, Em, seriously."

"Frankie, as much as I'd love to wax lyrical about young Nick, that's not what I've come for."

"I know. Okay. Here." He pushes a couple of sheets of paper across the desk toward me.

"What this?"

"Your publishing schedule."

I pick up the pages and quickly read through them.

"Very funny," I say.

"What?"

I point to the top of the first page. "The working title. *I'm Working On It.*"

"I'm glad you think so," he says. "But don't forget, I have a team of people waiting for you. Cover designers, editors. It's all in there." He points at the document.

I scan through the details until I find the part I dread. I have six months to deliver the draft. I have no idea how long it takes to write a novel. I wonder how long it would take Sam.

"Okay. That's fine." I hope.

"It should be. You're eight months behind schedule."

"I was hoping you wouldn't say that."

"I want you to meet Waleed. He's going to be your main editor, and he'll be coordinating everything from now on. Whenever you and I speak, it will be about where to go for lunch, okay? He's fantastic. You'll love him. He's heading up our new imprint."

"You have a new imprint?"

"We have a number of new imprints. Thank you for noticing."

"Wow, things have really changed around here."

"You bet they have!"

"Can I ask a question?"

"Of course."

"How much are you giving young Nick?"

"I can't tell you that, Em, you know that."

"Why not?"

"It's confidential, just like your terms."

"Did I get more?"

"Yes, you did."

"Okay, good." I reach down for my bag. I just want to get out of here.

"You're ready for this afternoon?" Frankie asks.

"The *New Yorker* interview? Of course I am. Why shouldn't I be? Or maybe you'd rather Nick did it? There's still time to switch, I'm sure," I say, pretending nonchalance.

"Stop it. Go away. Call me after."

9

Of course I'm ready. And I woke up early and cleaned the entire apartment, even though I know they'll only see the living room.

"So, where would you like me?" I giggle. I'm so nervous I'm overcompensating. My movements are jittery as I set down the carafe of water and tray of glasses on the coffee table. I would have preferred "coffee or something stronger?" but they turned it down with a "maybe later, but some water would be nice if that's all right."

Of course it was all right. It also gave me a little time to calm myself. I haven't done one of these in a while and I just need to get back into the swing of it.

My interviewer, Alex Gonski—"call me Al"—is quite charming, if maybe a little younger than I expected from checking out his byline picture last night. I thought he'd be in his late forties, at least.

He turns to the photographer.

"Sofia?"

Sofia is crouched on the floor getting her equipment organized. She points her chin in the direction of my Nella Vetrina plush Italian couch. "There's good. The light is nice."

"Okay."

Al extends his arm, inviting me to sit down, as if he were the host and I the guest. I do as I'm told and cross my legs at the ankles, prim and proper, then change my mind and cross them at the knees.

Al settles himself in the armchair opposite me and pulls out his notebook, and a small recording device, which he sets on the glass coffee table between us. The click he makes with his pen brings up a flash of another interview moment, in very different circumstances, when Detective—who was it?—Carr, I think, and the other one, harbored disturbing suspicions that I might have been involved in a murder.

I mentally shoo the image away and concentrate on my interviewer.

"So, Emma Fern. It's very nice to meet you. Thank you for agreeing to this."

"Not at all. The pleasure is all mine."

"I'd like to start with the interview, and Sofia"—who by now is standing quietly, framing me in her lens—"will take pictures. Is that all right with you?"

I nod.

"Once you and I are finished here, we'll take more pictures. How does that sound?"

"Great."

"Okay, let's begin. What's it like to win the Poulton Prize?"

Oh good, an easy one.

"It's a dream come true, Al. It's everything you could imagine— humbling, shockingly unexpected."

"Did it change your life?"

"Oh God, yes." My gaze wanders around the room as I say this. "It's changed my life."

"Okay, great." He makes a couple of notes. I'm aware I should say something else.

"It's a big confidence booster for my writing career, too."

"What was it like working with Beatrice Johnson Greene?"

Frankly, I'm getting mind-numbingly tired of that question. I should never have written that stupid book in stupid memoriam of my friendship with Beatrice. I'd meant to set the record straight, but as a result, I get more questions about that than about *Long Grass Running*.

"Well, that's very well documented. As you may know, I published a short memoir of my friendship—"

"Yes, I read it. It was touching."

"Thank you."

"But in your own words?"

Whose words do you think it was in? I want to ask. I take a breath. Let's get this part out of the way, then we can get back to me.

"Beatrice was . . ." I look out of the window, as if losing myself in the recollection, which I'm not, but I always find this is a good look, and I give him my spiel about Beatrice having adopted me as the daughter she never had, and how she believed in me, *la dee dah*, such a tragedy, *la dee dah*, and frankly I can go on about this for hours if I have to, and finally I wear him down.

"Thank you, that's a lovely recollection. I was more—I'm also interested in the writing process. I appreciate how important her support was to you, but as you point out, you've written about it in your memoir. I'd like to talk about her contribution to the writing of *Long Grass Running*."

I actually recoil at the question, and my hand flies to my chest, palm open.

"Beatrice's contribution? What does that mean?"

"I didn't mean . . ."

The gesture was a little too dramatic. He'll think he's offended me, and that's not where we should be going. So I cough a few times, my hand still flat on my chest.

"Sorry," I manage in between coughs. He hands me a glass of water from the tray and I take it gratefully, swallowing small gulps.

"I'm sorry," I repeat. "Dry throat. Thank you. I've had the flu, but I'm fine now. Where were we?"

"Discussing the collaborative process with Beatrice Johnson Greene."

"Ah yes, well, you have to understand that Beatrice and I did not write in the same genre. If I'd listened to Beatrice, *Long Grass Running* would have ended up as a cozy mystery!" I chuckle and he smiles, but doesn't move on, so I continue. "But in terms of, maybe, structural elements? Yes, certainly, or after reading a draft chapter, she would say something like, 'What about the older sister? I liked her. Why isn't she part of this scene?' And I would then see the scene through her eyes, and therefore my readers' eyes, even though they came later, of course, and I would consider her advice. It's very helpful to know what your readers think of your characters; which ones they like best, that sort of thing. So yes, that's the sort of contribution she made toward the novel."

I'm quite pleased with that. I smile. Benignly. He goes back to his notebook, takes a moment to read something, then he looks up at me.

"In your email, you said you wanted to make certain admissions about the part Beatrice Johnson Greene played in the writing of *Long Grass Running*. Maybe it's better if you tell me in your own words."

I smile at him. A thin, tight smile.

"In my email?" I ask finally.

"Yes, let me see, I have it here. The one you sent yesterday. You wrote, 'I want to make certain admissions about Beatrice's role in the writing of *Long Grass Running*.'"

I look away. The silence between us is going on for too long, and the panic that fills my chest is making it hard to breathe. I take a small gulp of air and turn back to him.

"The thing is, Mr. Gonski—"

"Please, call me Al."

"Al, the thing is, I miss Beatrice very much. And you writing this profile of me, in a magazine as prestigious as the *New Yorker*, makes me want to share and acknowledge Beatrice, and the incredible friendship we had. I thought we did that already. Didn't we?"

He blinks. "But the word *admissions* . . ." he says.

"What about it?"

"Well, it implies something different than, say—"

"Recollections? Because that's the word I meant to use. I wanted to make certain recollections about Beatrice. The phrasing may have been awkward, but that's what I meant. Can we move on now?"

I have both hands on my knees; my knuckles are white from their grip to stop myself from shaking.

He blinks again, quickly, and then he says, "Of course. So, next, which is your favorite Poulton Prize–winning novel?"

Is this a joke?

"Well, *Long Grass Running*, obviously."

I breathe again. The energy in the room is back to normal, and I am so relieved that I burst out laughing, but then it strikes me that he thinks I'm the one who's joking.

But it's the truth, and it's everyone's truth too. *Long Grass Running* is everyone's favorite book. But I can't tell him that, so instead I nominate my next favorite Poulton novel: *The Dollhouse*, it's called. It's beautiful, and I tell him why. He thinks it's a good choice. I can tell.

"So, the question on everyone's lips, Emma, is are you working on something new?"

"Ah-ha!" I wave an index finger at him. "The million-dollar question."

I pause for a moment, ready to spill out one of my many platitudes, but then I think back to my conversation with Carol.

"This Nick guy sounds like a complete jerk," she said. "Did he really say that? That you won't be able to hit that note twice? That's just—nasty."

"I know, and in front of my publisher—our publisher, unfortunately—to boot."

"You know what you have to do, don't you?"

"What?"

"Hit that note twice."

I laughed. "Easier said than done."

"Just write something brilliant. Then watch him squirm."

It inspired me, her saying that. Why couldn't I hit that note twice? Well, plenty of reasons, obviously, but still, just thinking about it makes me chuckle.

Al coughs softly.

"Well, yes, Al, as it happens, I am working on something new."

"Really? Wonderful. Can you tell me about it?"

"It's a—" I raise my eyes skyward. Usually, I say yes out of habit, and I've lost count how often that happens. *Just write something brilliant.* "It's about someone," I begin, "who is observing someone else, you know?"

He doesn't look as if he does, so I try again.

"This person is observing; following someone, but only in reflections."

We're not making any inroads.

"This person is trapped. They only exist in reflections, is what I mean: in mirrors, in water, in glass. They're trapped, you see."

That's quite good, actually, and I'm warming to my subject.

"So this woman—no, this man, sorry"—I can't make it about Beatrice's ghost or I'll never get another night's sleep as long as I live—"this man, who can only exist in reflections, is in love with a woman and follows her, through bus stops—"

He cocks his head.

"I mean, the glass panes on bus stops, you know the ones? They're reflective; at night anyway. And puddles, rearview mirrors, and other mirrors, all sorts of mirrors . . . That's all I can tell you at this stage. I mean, that's all I'm prepared to tell you. At this stage."

He nods thoughtfully. "Thank you, that's really interesting, it sounds fascinating. I can't wait to read it."

Neither can I.

"It's too soon to tell how it will turn out yet." I smile.

"I'm even more flattered that you shared it with me, then."

"And your millions of readers." I point at the pen in his hand that is scribbling everything I just said.

He smiles.

"You don't keep your books here?" he says now, looking around the walls.

I do the same. "My books?"

"I usually find when I interview writers, particularly accomplished ones such as yourself, that they have floor-to-ceiling bookshelves. At some point in the interview, I always like to take a look at what's on those shelves, see what they're reading. It's very helpful, to find out about someone, more than you'd think."

"Really? Well, no. I don't keep my books in the living room."

He waits for more.

"I keep them in my library."

"You have a library?" His eyes open wide, almost as wide as his mouth. It's kind of charming, really.

"No, of course not!" I slap my thigh. "I was joking. I mean who has a *library* these days, right?" I laugh, rocking my head back.

"At a guess?" He counts on his fingers. "Claire Messud, Woody Allen, Karl Lagerfeld, George Lucas—"

"Isn't he dead?"

"George Lucas? I don't think so."

"Maybe I was thinking of the other one."

"Philip Pullman, Neil Gaiman—"

"All right, I believe you," I say, gaily, a hand raised to ward off any more names. "People still have libraries. Well, I don't. I have a Kindle. Do you want to see it?"

"No bookshelves? Really?" He's disappointed.

"I keep books in my bedroom."

"Ah. Could I take a look?"

"Certainly not. My husband wouldn't like it."

"Of course."

I'm not sure Jim would care, actually, but I don't want these people in there. It's just a pile of paperbacks on my bedside table: a couple of crime fiction authors and one or two romance novels. We are not going in there.

"And in my room. My office, I mean."

"You work here? In this apartment?"

"That's right."

"Can we see your office?"

I hesitate just a second. "Sure, why not?"

He gets up and beckons Sofia with his index finger. I lead them to my office and show them in.

"You're very organized."

He's looking at my desk, my beautiful, large, expensive, and pristine desk, upon which I have a small pile of leather-bound notebooks—unopened, neatly stacked—a pen holder, with a couple of nice pens in it, and a small dish for bits and pieces like paper clips or rubber bands, except there's nothing in it.

"I pride myself on that," I say. "But I work on my laptop, here." I pull open the wide shallow drawer below the desktop, in which my laptop lives.

"Ah, nice. All right if we take pictures?"

"Go right ahead."

Sofia snaps away and Al takes a look around. The desk stands against the far wall, and hanging above the desk is a large corkboard. I was going to put my index cards on that, for my ideas, but it's become a receptacle for odd pieces about me, cut out from newspapers and magazines, or things I print from the Internet. The corners of the various pages are mostly curled up; they've been there a while.

I show him my office bookcase. It's mostly copies of *Long Grass Running*, actually, in a multitude of languages, but there are a few other interesting novels and books on writing, from that half-hour way back when I thought I'd "give writing another go."

When they're done, we return to the living room and do a quick photo shoot, the part I've been looking forward to. I spent a good hour this morning doing my makeup, and I'm pleased with the way I look.

I stand where I know the light is most flattering. Sofia asks me to turn this way and that, and I put on various expressions—pensive, thoughtful, thinking, creative—which obviously all look the same, but I know the difference.

"Thank you, Emma, I really appreciate your time," Al says when we're finished. He has a warm handshake and a nice smile. We're outside the door of the apartment.

"No, thank you," I say, graciously. "When does it come out?"

"The fifteenth."

"Of this month?"

"That's right."

"I look forward to it."

I'm about to ask if he thinks I'll make it onto the cover, but I think better of it.

After they've gone, I sit on the nearest chair and put my head in my hands. I thought they would never leave. But I feel okay, and I'm pretty sure I rescued the situation when Al brought up the business about an email, but I don't understand. I didn't send that email. This is the kind of thing that keeps happening to me. I feel like I'm losing my mind. I need to go and take a look at my emails, but first I call Frankie.

"How did it go?"

"Really well, I think. A bit slow at the start, but we got there in the end."

"Great, well done!"

"I told them all about my new book."

"You did?"

"Yes, I think they really liked what they heard."

"Oh, Emma, that's fantastic! Next time, run it past me before you give interviews about it."

"Why?"

"Because I don't know what it's about. And now I can buy the *New Yorker* and find out."

I chuckle. "You're right, sorry. I'll tell you all about it next time I see you. And it's going really well!"

"Music to my ears," he says, and I laugh.

10

But I'm not really laughing. I'm confused, and I go to my laptop to check my emails. Did I really send this? Was I drunk? What did he say again? That I wanted to make some kind of confession? I scroll through my sent mail folder, but there's nothing remotely like that in there. I sit at my desk, pinching at the skin on the side of my thumbnail. I don't know who to ask, or what to do. It's a relief when I hear the front door, and I know that Jim is home.

I walk into the living room, expecting him to be there, or at least to call out for me, but all I see is his coat thrown across the back of an armchair, which is a little odd, and not like him. He's very particular about his clothes.

"Darling? Where are you?"

"I'll be there in a minute, Emma."

I go to his office. The door is closed, so I knock quickly and open it. He's staring at his computer screen, his back to me, hunched over. There are a couple of folders on the floor, the contents spilled onto the carpet.

Lately I've noticed he seems to have moved most of his office—his other, outside office, that is—here, to our home. There are cardboard boxes piled high, dangerously leaning in some cases.

"Everything okay?"

He turns. "I said I'll be there in a minute, okay?"

He's got that red patch again, just above the bridge of his nose. The telltale sign that Jim is stressed.

I walk in and bend down to pick up the papers from the floor.

"Leave it! Please!" He says this so loudly that I stand quickly and almost stumble.

"What's happened?" I ask, as gently as I can, as if he's a dangerous animal.

"Nothing, really, I'm sorry. I have to work, okay?"

There's a spreadsheet open on his laptop. It takes up the whole screen, numbers all over it. A line graph in a corner.

"Emma, please?"

"Okay, sure," I say, somewhat petulantly, as I turn around to leave. I'm annoyed too now.

"Thank you, darling. Sorry, I'm really swamped here," he says.

I smile quickly and retreat. Part of me wants to ask him about the email. I want to know what he thinks. But I don't dare. I know he's going to say something about me being vague again. Or losing things. Like my mind.

I fix myself a drink, and consider offering him one, but then I change my mind. He can get his own drink.

Maybe it was a misunderstanding. Maybe Al was thinking of a different email. Maybe Frankie said something about my memoir concerning Beatrice to Al. Yes, that's what it was. It must be.

I flick through a magazine, determined to keep it out of my mind. What should I be making for dinner? If I still had money, I think I'd consider hiring someone to cook for us. I do love it, but some days, like today, not so much. I try not to think about Nick, but I can't help myself. The more I think about him, the more convinced I become that he's a fraud, a phony. A poseur. I bet his book will be awful. Why would Frankie court someone like that? He was literally dripping with adulation for this man. I just don't get it.

"Okay. All done," Jim says as he comes over and sits next to me on the couch, putting his arm around my shoulders. My annoyance dissipates immediately.

He closes his eyes and we lean back together. "Sorry about before. Big day."

"Everything all right?"

"Sort of. It'll be okay. Just work stuff."

I move away from his embrace, so that I can face him, look at him. "You can talk to me, you know?"

"I know." He smiles briefly, but there's a flash of something behind his eyes. It's so fast I almost miss it. I lie back against his chest.

"How was your day?" he asks.

"Great, I had the *New Yorker* interview today."

"That's right! Congratulations. It went well?"

"Very well. We talked about my new novel . . ." I let the thought trail as I recall my conversation with Carol. *Just write something brilliant. Watch him squirm.* I wish Jim had said that to me. I wish I'd had that conversation with him.

Should I tell him? *I had a lovely afternoon with your ex-lover yesterday. I can see why you liked her so much. She's really nice!*

"That's good," he says. And for a moment I wonder whether I spoke out loud. "What did you do yesterday, by the way? After you called me. I forgot to ask."

I sit up. "Nothing much, I caught up with an old friend," I say, flicking through my magazine again.

"That's good. Who?"

"Jackie," I lie.

"So you did have a drink."

"No, I didn't. We had coffee."

"How is Jackie?"

I pick at the lint on my skirt. I don't even know why I brought her up. Jackie who used to run the store with me. My home decor store that I loved, until I published *Long Grass Running* and I sold the business to her.

"She's good. She looks very well, happy."

"That's nice. And your book? It's going well?"

I sit up again, look at him. He still has his eyes closed. "What does my book have to do with Jackie?"

"Nothing, I know it's on your mind, that's all."

"Are you worried about it? That I won't be able to write another book?"

"Don't be ridiculous. Of course not."

"Maybe I want to go back to the store, with Jackie."

I lean back against his chest and feel him twitch beneath me.

"Why on earth would you do that?" he asks.

"Well, it was an easier life, in many ways. Less pressure, for one thing."

He puts his arms around me, over my shoulders. It's a lovely feeling. I kiss his hands and feel his lips on the back of my neck.

"You're not going back to work with Jackie. That's the most ridiculous suggestion I ever heard, so drop it. You've been working very hard on this new book. You talk of nothing else," he continues, "and I am so proud of you, sweetheart. Your success, what you've achieved, it's incredible. Just today I was telling my clients all about you. What you do. How amazing you are."

"Really? Why?"

"Because you're the most interesting thing about me."

It's so unexpected, hearing Jim say those words, that my eyes well up. I think it may be the nicest thing he has ever said to me.

"Don't give up, Emma, you must believe in yourself. This is your destiny, Em. It's our destiny."

I sigh. "If you say so."

"I say so. You won't think about this again, okay?"

"Okay."

"I mean it."

"It's all right, I wasn't actually thinking of doing it."

◆ ◆ ◆

I couldn't sleep. Neither could Jim, I suspect, from his tossing and turning about whatever was keeping him working at home last night. Were the Forum's finances really as tight as Terry had said? Or was it something completely different?

But that's not what kept me awake last night. No. Me, I was fantasizing about my next novel. The brilliant one. It's not going to be *Long Grass Running*, obviously. Part of me thinks nothing will ever be that good, but just the thought of not having to listen to Frankie going on and on every five minutes, saying, *Go write something, Em*, fills me with joy. He'll give me a break. He'll tell me to take a vacation. Shame I spent the advance already.

Armed with my morning coffee, I sit at my desk—now preserved in photographs for all to see—and open my laptop.

I say it out loud: "I'm going to write something brilliant." The phone rings? *Sorry, can't take it, I'm writing.*

I pull out one of my beautiful notebooks, and open it to the first pristine ruled page, and take a pen from the pen holder.

The man in the mirror.

Now that sounds familiar. I cross it out.

Reflections of . . . something.

Look at me.

I see you.

Through the looking glass.

That one's a joke.

Echoes.

Maybe.

I leave the "what's the title?" exercise for now, and start to jot down what my story will be about. I'm sure I have the thread of something here. I just need to get hold of the end of it, pull gently, and let it unravel itself into a story.

So I begin.

It's about a man, who is trapped in the reflections of—anything, really. Mirrors, obviously—all the other things I told that Al guy—and this man, he's in love with a woman. He follows her around, from one reflection to another. When he can't see her—because wherever she happens to be, there are no windows/mirrors/puddles of water—he is devastated, longing to find her again.

Then I write more, gibberish mostly, and after an hour or so, I reread what I've got, and because I'm so impressed with what I've come up with so far, I then write things like: *What the fuck is this guy doing there in the first place?* and *In the category of really stupid ideas, the envelope please . . . the prize goes to Emma Fern for* Echoes of Imbecility. *Thank you very much. I'd like to thank my pea-sized brain, first and foremost, and secondly my appalling education. I couldn't have done it without you both.*

◆ ◆ ◆

"Sam Huntington."

"Sam, it's Emma Fern."

"Hey, Emma Fern!"

I can hear the smile in his voice as I start chatting. Small talk. That I still owe him money for the other day, and I'm glad to see his website is still up, when all I want to ask is: *Are you really as good as you say you are?*

"Did you find your credit card? I meant to ask last time we spoke."

"Yes, I did, under my wireless keyboard of all places."

"That's where most of my things are, I think. I'm afraid to look under there. There's bound to be an overdue notice from the IRS or something equally unpleasant."

He makes me laugh. But I need to get on with it. I have business to attend to here, so I take the plunge.

"I know we said we'd get together for a coffee, but I wonder if we could make it a more professional meeting."

"Sure, what do you have in mind?"

Deep breath, Emma, deep breath. "Will you ghostwrite with me? Or is it *for* me? What's the term?"

There's a pause, and I close my eyes tightly. Did I say the wrong thing? Did I give something away about myself? Am I a complete idiot?

Then he says, "Work with you? Yes, I would love to work with you, Emma."

And my breath comes out finally, the breath I hadn't realized I was holding. I'm relieved he didn't say, *But why? What's the problem? You're a Poulton Prize winner, for goodness' sake! You don't need the likes of me!*

I also like that he called me Emma, not Emma Fern. I expected the "Fern" to come after the "Emma" when he said he would do it, because that's what he calls me, and I was already cringing. I don't want to be reminded that I am Emma Fern, because invariably, Emma Fern is followed by "bestselling Poulton Prize winner," and for the first time in my existence, I don't want to hear it.

He makes it very easy. It's like making an appointment with your doctor. Which is what he is, after all, a kind of doctor. He's going to fix me up.

"Great. Thank you," I say. "I'm free this afternoon. Can I come over to your office?"

"This afternoon is fine. I just had a cancellation."

"Wonderful."

I'm so relieved. There's a future ahead of me and it's bright and happy, and there's a novel at the end of the rainbow.

11

It's a nice office; much nicer than I expected, although I hadn't expected anything, so I don't know why I'm surprised. But if I had thought about it, I would have pictured an executive suite, very impersonal. Lots of glass, gray carpet, concealed lighting, tall potted plants in the lobby. Like a law firm, I suppose.

"Do you have an assistant?"

"No. In my business it makes people nervous. The fewer people who know about my clients, the better. That's how it is."

We're in a converted warehouse, and the curved windows remind me of Beatrice's apartment—but I'd rather not have to think about Beatrice or her apartment if I can help it, so I shake off the memory. Anyway, that's where the similarity ends. The space is way smaller than Beatrice's penthouse, for one thing. It's divided between an office area with a desk, a workstation-type space, and a sitting area. The walls are white. It's bright in here, warm and friendly. There are flowers in vases; the floors are polished wood, the color of honey. It makes me think of a wedding planner's office, but since I've never been in one of those either . . . Maybe if I went to one I'd find it was all glass and chrome.

There are no personal photos though, I notice, but books and books and books in tall shelves against the walls. It's got a nice feeling, this place.

Sam indicates the couch for me to sit on and he chooses the armchair. On the coffee table is a copy of *Long Grass Running* with bits of paper sticking out; place markers, I gather.

"So," I begin, "how do we do this?"

"We talk, that's all. Do you mind if I take some notes?"

He already has a notepad on his lap.

"No, that's fine. But I haven't decided yet. Not exactly."

"I know. Tell me what's happening. Let's start with that. How are you feeling?"

"Did I come to the wrong office? Should I be lying on the couch?"

"You'd be surprised. But no, not right now." He puts the notepad on the coffee table and leans forward, resting his forearms on his thighs.

"You see, Emma, the more I know about what you want, and how you feel, the easier it will be. It's the consultation stage. You can decide not to go ahead at any time."

"All right."

I'm very nervous. My chest feels a little tight.

"I haven't been able to write, basically," I say. "My friend, you see . . ." I take a big breath. "She died, but she's the one who helped me write . . . this." I point to the book on the table. "Without her, I haven't been able to finish anything."

"That seems perfectly normal to me. You're talking about Beatrice Johnson Greene, aren't you." It's not a question.

"Yes." I feel my eyes water a little, which is a neat trick I've mastered. Like Pavlov's dog. I've had to do so many interviews where I've been asked about poor dead Beatrice, that I've trained myself to think about the day my mother died in response. That always makes me sad. I'm so good at this now, I don't even need to think about my mother. The trigger works on its own.

"I imagine her death was very hard on you," he says gently.

"So we *are* having a counseling session." I smile.

"We don't have to. But I just wanted to say that I understand how you must feel."

"It's just that I miss her, and I also feel a little—how can I explain?—guilty. She mentored me, you know."

He nods.

"Anyway," I sigh, "what else can I say? I'm stuck. I have writer's block, I guess."

"You know what I think? I think you're afraid."

"Of not doing as well without her? Of course I am."

"No. Afraid of doing just as well without her."

Okay, I did not see that coming. I take a moment to think about this. I like this man. I already like where we're going with this.

"Well, either way, I don't think I'm going to solve the problem by myself, so that's what I'm here for. I need some help, Doctor Sam."

"And that's what *I'm* here for. And another thing, Emma. It's very common to be stuck, as you put it, when you've already had one big success, especially when you've won a prestigious prize, as you have."

"Have you had—what do you call them?—cases like this?"

"Clients. Yes, I have."

"Did they win a prize?"

"No." He smiles. "I can write a very good book, but I can't perform miracles."

"Pity," I say, then I change gears. It's time to get down to business. "Sam, as you can imagine, I have a bunch of questions. I'd like to start with those if that's okay with you."

"Shoot."

It takes a while. I want to know everything, I need to. What about confidentiality? What are the contract terms? How long does it take? When I ask how much it costs, he tells me that in my case, it's expensive. For a moment I think he's making a joke, but his face says otherwise.

"Why?"

"Because my fee is different depending on who is publishing the novel, how important the author is, that sort of thing."

"How much?"

"Two hundred thousand dollars."

I raise my hand to my chest. "You've shocked me. There's no way I can afford that much money." I stand up, pick up my purse. "If I'd known, I would never—"

"Sit down, Emma. There are other ways."

I look at him, then slowly I sit back down.

"You can give me a share of the royalties. There are many writers who choose that option."

"I see. But everything still remains confidential?"

"Of course, that's no different."

"How big a share?" Although I don't know why I ask, it's not like I have much of a choice, but the number he quotes is not unreasonable. Let's say that it doesn't make me stand up and leave.

I nod. "Okay, I can work with that."

"You can shop around, but you'll find my terms are standard."

"I believe you."

I sign the contract right there and then. He's surprised, shocked almost. He says I should take it away with me, show it to a lawyer; at the very least to someone I trust, like my husband. "No need," I tell him. "I'm here now. Let's do it."

"As you wish," he says, almost shrugging.

"Can we begin right away?" I ask.

"Of course. But first I need some coffee. You want some?"

"Coffee would be good, thanks."

He gets up, goes through a door that I assume leads to a kitchen of some sort. I pull out my notebook but then I change my mind and put it away. I want to tell it, not read it from my notes.

Sam returns with two steaming cups on a small tray. He settles down in the same armchair as before, notepad ready. He looks at me.

"Now, I'd like to talk about *Long Grass Running*, which I've read, of course, but I'd also like to get a fresh sense of your style, your idiosyncrasies, so to speak, and I have—"

"No. Stop right there."

"Okay." He raises an eyebrow.

"I want to write something completely different. I don't want to revisit the past. And I definitely don't want to write something that takes place there. In the past, I mean. I want to write something modern and original. That's why I've been having such trouble, in fact."

"Okay. But if you're going to change the style and time and space, then it would still be good to keep your voice in there; the more I can read of it the better. Do you have anything of yours I can read? Other than this?" He points his chin to the book on the table.

"No. There's nothing I'm prepared to show you, put it that way."

"You're sure?"

"Positive."

He looks away, as if trying to decide what the next step should be.

"But I have a story," I say.

"You do? That's good. Let's hear it."

I center myself, close my eyes.

"You don't have to start at the beginning, if that helps," he says.

"It's all right. I got it." And I do. I dive into my story. My hands fly around as I describe the rain-splattered sidewalks, the windowpanes and glass doorways; how the character easily slips from one reflective surface to the other; how the woman he is following has no idea of his presence. Sam takes notes, nods, and sometimes he interrupts me to ask a question. We talk about the point of view. We discuss the symbolism of the imagery. I come to think that my story is about being madly in love, but trapped, not being heard or seen. Living beside the object of your desire, but being invisible. He talks about surrealism in literature, the juxtaposition of reality and the imagination. I'm not interested in that. I just want it to make my heart beat. I interrupt him. We explore the directions the story could take, talking over each other. It's exhilarating, so excited are we by the ideas we're having, and when he leans across and puts his hand over my mouth because he wants me to listen, I fall backward in laughter. His enthusiasm is contagious—or is it mine that infects him? I begin to really love my little story. It now sounds unusual, unexpected, and engaging at the same time.

12

It's not even five in the afternoon when I get back, and as soon as I open the door, I know something is wrong. It's just a feeling, like a false note. I see Jim's bag in the hall. I'm about to call out for him when I hear him whisper.

"Emma!"

I gasp, look around, but I can't see Jim. But I can still hear him.

"Emma!"

"Jim?"

"Ssshhhh! Emma, over here!"

His head appears through the doorway on the other side of the living room; the doorway that leads to a small corridor, and then to his office. I hurry across the living room, somewhat baffled by his hand signals, which alternate between *Come over here!* and *Be quiet!*

"What's wrong?"

"Sshhh!" he hisses.

He takes my hand and holds me close, then he says quietly in my ear, "Can you look inside, but be careful, so they don't see you, okay? And tell me if there's a green dot on my laptop screen."

"I don't understand what—"

"Shh! Shhh, Emma! Quiet, please. Come over here, look inside the office, and tell me if you can see the green light for the webcam! At the top. Is the webcam on?"

He smells of sweat—and something else, acrid. I realize with a start that he's not well, but I nod and do as he says, and he takes hold of my arm and makes us swap positions, so we do an odd little dance. Now I'm next to the door to his office, my back against the wall, and I slowly turn my head to peer inside and—

"OH MY GOD WE'VE BEEN BURGLED!"

He pulls me back, but I shake him off and walk in, and there's stuff everywhere. Papers, books, files, boxes open and spilling out, all over the floor, all over the chair, all over the desk.

"Is the light on? The computer webcam on top of the screen. Is it on?" he asks sharply from the doorway.

I'm in shock. Everywhere I look there is chaos. "When did this happen? Is anything missing?"

"Emma!" he calls out again. I look at his computer screen, I can see the dot, but barely. It's not lit up. I go closer and peer into it.

"No. It's not."

"Are you sure?"

"Yes! I'm sure!" I slam the laptop shut. "Jesus, Jim, what's happened here? Did we get robbed? Have you checked the rest of the house?"

He comes in now, shakily. He looks closely at the laptop, even though it's shut.

"Jim!"

"No no no no, we didn't get robbed. I'm working. That's all."

I wait for the rest of the sentence, expecting something more. Something about coming home to this, or the police are on their way, but he doesn't say anything else.

"This is you?"

"I have a lot on, Emma."

I look around the room, and I'm getting scared now, because I really think Jim has lost his mind.

"You did this?"

He tries to explain, but falters.

"What's going on?"

"It's . . . work. I'm being watched."

"What?"

"They're filming me, or watching me. I'm sure of it."

"Why? Who?"

"Oh, don't you worry about that." He waves a finger at me. "I have a very good idea who's doing it."

"So who?"

He looks around, as if he's only just noticed the mess in here, and he bends down quickly to retrieve the files and papers scattered around. I touch his shoulder and he shakes me off.

"Stop! Jim! Who is watching you?"

"They want—it's because of the—oh fuck, Emma, my work is competitive, okay? If someone steals our algorithms, then we're screwed. Okay? You get that?" He stands and pokes the side of his head really hard and he repeats it: "You get that?"

"Jim, stop, calm down."

I move closer and look into his eyes. Is he on drugs? I can't tell. I've never seen him like this before. My heart is beating fast in my chest, and I take a deep breath, force myself to calm down. If Jim needs help right now, I need to be in control.

I take both his hands in mine. "How did it start?"

"They're—it's our research, you know? Someone is trying to mess with it; with me. That's why I have to work from home." He looks around, fast and furtive at the same time, he's like a trapped animal.

"You've been here all day?"

"No. Yes."

"Okay, listen, let's tidy this up. I'll help."

"No!" He quickly gathers some of the papers on the floor, haphazardly. Piles them up in a mess on the desk.

"Jim, stop. Come with me. Let's go in the living room."

I crouch and take his arm, but he flings me off. I do it again. "Leave it!" he says. But I won't leave it, and eventually, after a few tries, he lets himself be coaxed and I gently guide him to the couch, holding his hand. We sit down and it's as if he can barely see me.

I pull him to me and we sit a while, his head resting against my shoulder. I stroke his hair until finally I feel his breathing slow down. My thoughts tumble over each other. Is Jim being paranoid? He certainly shows all the signs, but maybe it's true what he's saying. He's being spied on. That would explain why he's been spending more time working at home. Still, something isn't right.

"I'm going to make us something to eat, okay?"

He pulls himself away and nods, runs a hand over his face.

I help him lie down on the couch, and put a cushion under his head. I look at him. His eyes are closed, and he seems comfortable. When I look up, I catch her in the window behind the couch. Beatrice. One side of her mouth raised in a half smile; a smirk. I turn and go to the kitchen.

I put both hands on the rim of the sink and bow my head. In the past few days, Jim has been acting more and more strangely. I did believe him, when he said it was work that made him stressed. Maybe it is about the money, what Terry said that night. Could it be? Even that wouldn't explain what I've just seen. I'm scared that he's having some kind of nervous breakdown. I run the faucet and pat some cold water onto my face.

I get some eggs and ham from the refrigerator. I'm going to make us an omelet. He needs to eat, that's the problem. He's probably got a bug of some kind. Terry said everyone was falling ill at the Forum; that's undoubtedly part of it. Jim hasn't been well, but he hasn't stopped working—the opposite in fact—and he hasn't been eating enough.

I reach for the milk and spot the bottle of white wine in the refrigerator door. I pull it out and pour myself a glass. I deserve it. I need it. It will calm me down.

I cut the ham, beat the eggs. I force myself to concentrate, watching the butter sizzle and foam in the pan. A small hot spurt lands on my hand and I lick it off. Surely he's concerned about the data; the fake data. He must be going out of his mind about it. What are we going to do? I can't get my thoughts in order. By the time I serve the omelet on our plates, I'm surprised to see the bottle of wine is empty.

◆ ◆ ◆

"You don't know what I'm going through, Em, the pressure I'm under," Jim says, as I put our plates down on the coffee table. His tone is gentler now. He sits up, runs a hand over his face.

"I know, darling."

"You don't. You have no idea." He sighs, and says something I never expected to hear from his lips. "Maybe I should move on. Give up the Forum. We could start again, you and me, move, do something different, together. You and me."

My heart makes a leap. I stare at him. He still has a hand over his eyes. He moves it across his face to wipe what I see are tears.

"We can, darling. We can do anything we like. I'm here for you. We can do this together." I'm slurring my words.

"You don't know what it's like. The pressure, the secrets . . ."

I don't quite catch the last words, but I think it's "the fear."

Neither of us says anything. All I can think is that Jim has no idea what I've been through. None.

"Won't you eat something?" I ask, but when I look back at him, he's asleep, his breathing slow and regular. I lean back, put my head on his shoulder.

"I know about secrets and fear. And guilt," I murmur. "You think I don't, but I do."

I'm drunk, I shouldn't say it, but I can't help myself.

"I was there, you know, when she died. God. It was awful."

I wait, expecting some kind of indication that he heard me, but he's asleep, his hand over his eyes, snoring softly.

"Beatrice. She's everywhere. She scares me. She haunts me." And then softly, very quietly, I put my lips to his ear and I whisper, "I killed her, you know."

"Hey."

I open my eyes. Jim is gently touching my cheek. He's smiling at me. His hair is still damp from his shower. He's freshly shaven and his clothes are neat and pressed, and for a moment I believe that I dreamed the whole "Jim has gone crazy" thing.

No, I didn't. I sit up in bed.

"Hey yourself. What time is it?"

"Seven thirty. You don't mind that I woke you? I have to go to work, but I wanted us to talk."

"No, of course. I'm so glad you did!"

I take his face in my hands and look into his eyes. They're a bit red, a bit bloodshot, but I think he's going to be okay. We're going to be okay.

"I'm sorry, Emma, I really am. Here."

There's a tray on the bedside table, with a steaming cup of coffee, a fried egg on toast, a glass of orange juice, and a cutout paper flower balancing in a small glass.

"I couldn't get a rose at this time of the morning. I hope this will do?"

He puts the tray on the bed, over my lap.

"This is—unexpected," I say. "It's wonderful, thank you. Did you sleep okay?"

"I did. Thanks for not waking me up. That's what I needed, a full ten hours' sleep, uninterrupted."

"The couch comfortable enough?"

"It must have been, I slept through the night until half an hour ago." I laugh.

"I'm really sorry, Emma."

"I was so worried. What's going on? What was that all about?"

He takes a breath, looks at a point over my head. I resist the urge to turn around to see what's so fascinating. His eyes come back to mine.

"There's been some . . . developments, let's say, at the Forum, that make me uncomfortable."

"What kind of developments?"

He takes a moment to formulate his reply.

"I'm telling you this in confidence, okay?"

"Of course."

"We're going through a review of the processes in place. It's because of the government contracts we get. We have to meet certain quality-control standards."

"Okay."

"And I think that some unknown people are using this process to conduct industrial espionage."

"Really?"

"That's why I've been working from home a lot."

"Oh God, are you sure?"

"Ninety percent sure. But I don't want to take any chances."

"Of course! Can you go to the police?"

"If I can prove it, yes, of course. It's a crime. But I need more time."

"So, with the . . ." I hesitate.

"With the webcam? And my overreacting?" He smiles. "My home laptop is connected to the internal network, so technically, everything on it can be accessed and also operated, remotely. I was working, reviewing the data, when I saw the webcam light come on."

"Seriously? You saw it come on?" My jaw drops. "So someone is really watching you?"

"It looks like it, but it was only for a second. Em, it really freaked me out. I'm already on edge, you know that. It's a really stressful time. I—we could lose everything if our competitors get hold of our models and algorithms. It would be the end of everything I've worked for. I don't know if I imagined it, the webcam coming on, but it scared me. I thought they'd taken it to another level."

Strange as it may sound, it makes me feel better to hear all this. Sure, it does have a touch of conspiracy theory, but then again, who knows? What if they—whoever they are—really are using the process to access Jim's secrets? Which one would Jim be more afraid of? That they get his algorithms or whatever they're called? Or that they discover it's all bogus? I think we both know the answer to that. I don't want Jim to be put under all this stress, but I'd rather his behavior was real and justified than evidence of something seriously wrong with his health. Like going insane.

"What does Terry say?"

"Not much. I don't think Terry understands the seriousness of the situation."

"I see."

"You'll keep this between you and me, right?"

"Of course, darling."

"I'm sorry, Em—that I overreacted. I'm going to make sure I get plenty of sleep and that I don't overstress myself." He smiles, caresses my cheek.

"Can I ask you something?" I say.

"Sure."

"Does this have anything to do with—you know . . ."

There's a twitch, just above that spot between his eyes.

"With what?"

"You know, your research. Your data model. Are you scared they'll find out? You know, the problems you've had with the results—"

He moves away from me, almost falling off the bed. "Fuck, Emma! What are you saying?"

His tone is so forceful, I feel like I've been punched.

"Are you threatening me with something?" he asks.

"No! I'm sorry, oh God! I'm really sorry. I shouldn't have said anything."

He's getting up, but I put my arms around him, awkwardly.

"Don't. I'm sorry. Stay. Please."

His body is rigid in my arms, but after a short while I feel him relax.

"Sorry," he says, finally.

"You should go to the doctor, Jim, get something to calm yourself down, if you're so stressed."

"I know, you're right, I'll do that."

He caresses my cheek again. "I love you, Em. I really do. I'm sorry. You were there for me."

"I love you, Jim."

"I know. Now eat your breakfast and let me go to work." He stands up. I let him go. Reluctantly.

"Will you be home for dinner?"

He looks at me, one eyebrow raised. "I'll do my best, but I'll be late. It's my Boston meeting today, remember?"

"Boston?"

"You know, we talked about it."

"Oh, right. Well, I'll keep something for you if you're late."

He shakes his head. "Don't. I'll grab something on the way home."

After he leaves, I put the tray back on the bedside table, chuckling a little at the cutout paper flower. I push the covers back and swing my legs to the side of the bed, feeling the soft carpet beneath my feet. I don't remember anything about Boston. It's been like this since the accident.

I'm the one who should go to the doctor. I forget things. Maybe I really am going crazy. Maybe I'm the one having a nervous breakdown. I would have thought if you had a nervous breakdown, you'd know it. But maybe not.

I get up and grab my robe from the back of the door, go straight to his office, and I gasp.

It's pristine. I take a closer look, try to open the filing cabinet, which has been locked again, everything on the shelves is back and neatly stored. I look at the laptop on the desk, open it, and turn it on. There's a whizzing sound while it wakes up, and then the password prompt. But I'm not trying to check the contents of his hard drive, I just want to take another look at the webcam.

There's a piece of packing tape stuck over it.

13

As I step into the shower, I tell myself that it's going to be okay. I'm not going to think any more about forgetting things and nervous breakdowns. I'm going to concentrate on Book Two, or the Book of Sam. We had such a great session yesterday and the story is coming alive in my mind.

I get dressed quickly, I can't wait to go to work. I can't remember the last time I felt this good about starting my day.

My phone rings from somewhere in the living room, where I left it last night. I go to pick it up. It's a blocked number.

"Mrs. Fern?"

"Yes?"

A male voice says something, but it's muffled and I don't quite understand. He's in a busy place, like a train station or something.

I press my hand over my other ear.

"Can you speak up, please? I can't hear you."

"Sorry. Is that better? I'm Dr. Johnston. I'm calling from the New York Presbyterian Hospital, in Queens. Do you know Frankie Badosa?"

"Frankie? Yes! Is everything all right?"

"I'm sorry, Mrs. Fern, but Mr. Badosa has been in a car accident. He's in Emergency. His office said you were listed as the person to contact. Can you come now?"

It's true, what they say. When you get news like that, everything changes in an instant.

My vision blurs. My legs wobble under me. I grip the back of the nearest chair. "Yes, of course, I'll come now," I manage to say. I ask the question I'm afraid of. "Is he going to be all right?"

"We're doing everything we can, Mrs. Fern."

Oh God! Not Frankie, God, please. Please, please, please God. I stumble. I rush to get my things: my keys, my bag, my coat. I close the door behind me and step inside the elevator, which is still on my floor. Dr. Johnston's words echo in my head over and over again. *We're doing everything we can.* It's bad.

Dennis is the regular doorman in my building. I like Dennis. He's a big man; tall and stocky, the type of man you expect to see outside a nightclub. He would be more at home as a bouncer than in livery. He told me recently that he was saving to study acupuncture. I looked at his hands when he said that, and I was surprised to see how delicate they were. If I had to get needles stuck into me, I would be okay with Dennis doing it.

"Are you all right, Mrs. Fern?" he asks now.

"Would you help me get a taxi, please, Dennis?"

He does.

It took forty-five minutes to get to the hospital in Queens, and I cried and prayed for the entire journey. I saw the driver watching me in his rearview mirror, an anxious expression on his face. He didn't ask me if I was all right. When you take a taxi to the Emergency Department of a hospital, you don't have to explain why you're upset.

I ran to Admissions, but it's chaos in those places, and I didn't get to speak to someone right away. Then I told them I wanted to see Frankie; that I had to see him now. I told them I was the next of kin, you can call his office if you don't believe me, I said. I told them I wanted to speak with Dr. Johnston immediately.

Another twenty minutes went by before Dr. Johnston arrived at reception to see me. He sat next to me in one of those plastic chairs, but I stood up, and said to him, "I'm here, where's Frankie? Can I see him? Will he be all right?" And he told me the same crazy thing that the attendant in Admissions said earlier.

"There is no patient by that name here."

"But you called me," I said. "You told me to come."

"I didn't call you, Mrs. Fern. You have the wrong hospital."

He left and I put my hands on my head and wanted to hit myself, because that's when I got it, finally. I wanted to tear my hair out for not even thinking of the obvious.

Call Frankie.

So I did, my fingers trembling. I called his cell phone and he said, "Hey, Emma, what's up?" and I said, "Nothing, I'll call you later," and I hung up.

◆ ◆ ◆

It's raining when I get out of the taxi at my building, and Dennis kindly meets me with an umbrella. My whole body is aching with tiredness, and all I want to do is have a bath and go straight to bed, but I know that's not going to happen.

"How is your friend, Mrs. Fern?" Dennis asks.

"My friend is not nearly as sick as I first thought, thank God. Thank you, Dennis."

"I'm glad to hear it, Mrs. Fern."

"Me too, Dennis, thank you."

When I turn the key in my door, I know that something is different. It's difficult to put my finger on, but it's like a presence in the air. I almost expect to see Beatrice sitting on the couch, waiting for me. The silence feels ominous nevertheless, and I find myself tiptoeing inside my own apartment.

The first thing I notice is the large abstract painting in the living room. It's slightly crooked. I stare at it for a while, wondering why that would be. It's not as if we move it regularly. We don't have a safe behind it.

A safe. Did we get robbed? I look around the room quickly, but everything is here, except it's a little different. The two armchairs on either side of the couch have been moved, leaving small depressions in the carpet.

I walk quickly from room to room, and it's the same thing. Some drawers are not closed flush. Almost, but not quite. The tall vase in the corridor has been moved around so that a little of its central pattern now faces toward the wall. Everything in my closet has shifted slightly, as if picked up and put back with care.

Even the kitchen hasn't escaped. There's a trace of a white substance on the floor tiles that looks like flour.

14

I spend the rest of the afternoon curled up on the couch, trying to understand what's happening to me. Nothing makes sense. I want to talk to Jim. I think it must be true, what he said about being spied on. I want him to come home and tell him about Frankie, but why Frankie? They wanted me out of the house, yes, but why Frankie?

It's almost eleven when I hear the key in the door, and I jump off the couch and rush to meet him.

"Hey," he laughs. "So you missed me, then?"

"Oh, Jim, something terrible is happening. You—"

"Hold on, let me walk in first." I nod, and he looks at me. "You're okay, Em?"

"No, I'm not. Come and sit down. I have to tell you something." I take him by the hand. "You know what you said, about being—"

"Wow, slow down. Let me get us a drink first, look what I got." He brandishes a bottle of expensive champagne, as if we don't already have enough of that here.

I shake my head quickly, shuddering. "Okay. Sorry, sit down, and I'll get glasses for us. We need to talk, Jim."

"No, you sit, Em. Relax. I'll do it," he says, removing his jacket and laying it on the back of the chair. I curl up on the couch again, listening to the sounds in the kitchen. I wish he'd hurry up.

He comes back with our glasses and sits next to me, puts his hand on my thigh.

He frowns at me. "Okay. What's going on with you? Are you ill? You're being a bit strange."

I sit up and I take the glass he offers me. "I don't even know where to begin."

He nods, sagely, as if pondering over what I've just said.

"You know what you said this morning? About being spied on?"

"Yes?"

"Because I think—"

"Emma, stop. Slow down. Drink up, it'll relax you. You're being intense."

I tell him about the call, about Frankie, about the small details that had changed around the place by the time I got back. But then I notice a strange shadow pass over his face, almost as if he's trying to contain his joy, or is it triumph?

"You're not saying anything," I say.

He refills my glass. I hadn't realized it was already empty, which explains why I'm feeling a little lightheaded suddenly.

"What do you want me to say? I'm listening to you."

Something is not right. I put a hand on my cheek. "Is it hot in here? Or is it just me?"

Jim just smiles at me and sits back in his chair.

"Why are you staring at me?" I ask, but he doesn't reply. "What is it, Jim?"

"I'm just listening to you, that's all."

I take a deep breath, but it doesn't quite reach the bottom of my lungs.

"I don't know what's wrong," I say. "I think I ate something that didn't agree with me."

I lift a hand to my forehead, but even this gesture is surprisingly difficult, heavy. It's like my muscles are working in slow motion. My skin feels clammy. Something is wrong, very wrong. I'm starting to feel scared and my heart is beating too fast. I think I'm having some kind of attack, a panic attack? Or a heart attack or—my God!

I try to sit up a little straighter, but I can't move.

"Jim, help me. I don't feel well."

"I love you."

It's such an incongruous thing to say right now, I would laugh if I could.

"I love you too. I wish this awful feeling would pass, though."

He chuckles. "I said, I *loathe* you."

He's smiling, but there is no kindness in his face. He's watching me with narrowed eyes, and I wonder if this is all just a bad dream.

"What did you say?"

"You heard me."

"I don't understand." My words are slurred, my jaw is slack. "I'm— I'm hallucinating, Jim. Oh my God, it's Beatrice. Jim, help me, please! It's her! Please help me!"

In my hallucination, Jim is laughing at me. It's awful. I'm so frightened.

"I'm having a heart attack, Jim! Please, I beg you, help me!"

"No, you're not."

"I really think I am. Can't you see? I can't speak properly. I'm going to pass out."

"Not yet you won't. Eventually, yes, but not right now."

"What are you saying?"

He has an awful smirk on his face. It's horrible. It's her. She's done something to us. I've slid down on the couch, so that my back is half across the seat and half across the back. I have one arm on my chest and the other has dropped by my side.

"Listen to me, Jim."

"No, Emma. You listen to me."

Oh my God. Something in his tone. "Did—did you put something in my drink?"

"Yes."

"I don't understand."

"I hate you." He leans forward, his eyes hard, boring into mine. "You have no idea how much I hate you. I've wanted to tell you that for a very long time and now I can. The very sight of you makes me sick. Did you know that? No. Of course not. How could you? You're completely delusional. Do you really think this little charade you've been playing is real? That we're *happy*?" He sneers on the last word like he's disgusted. "You really thought you could blackmail me into this happily married couple, crazy scenario you've dreamed up, for ten years? For ten fucking years of my life? Do you have any idea how crazy you are, Emma?"

I thought you loved me, I try to say, but it doesn't work; it doesn't come out properly. I am screaming in my head: *Don't you see? I thought we were going to make it! I thought you would learn to love me again and that you would be happy too! I thought you understood!*

"I tried to kill you once, you know that? I pushed you into traffic. There's a way to do that, you know, to maximize the chances of killing someone, and doing it so fast and so discreetly that no one would have known it was me. It's all in the shoulder." He jerks his shoulder forward, puts his hand to it. "Then you extend your arm and pretend you were trying to help. Of course you have to time it correctly, which I did. That bus—it was supposed to kill you. It wouldn't have stopped in time. But you got lucky, the driver saw the motorcycle and he anticipated it losing control. Crazy, hey? How lucky you got."

He stands up and does something I have never seen him do before: he pulls out a packet of cigarettes from his pocket and lights one. At that moment, I think maybe I'm having a nightmare and that I will wake up and everything will be all right. But the smell of cigarette smoke is real.

"I have spent the past year trying to find a way to get rid of you," he says. "I still haven't found the documents you stole from me; your little blackmail stash. Today was my last shot at it. Yes, that was me, the whole 'Frankie accident' interlude. I just needed to get you out of the house, Em. Do you have any idea how hard it is to get you out of the house? I don't know what you've done with those documents. I've looked. Believe me. I've looked everywhere and I can't find them. But I'll tell you one thing I found. Okay, not found, I stole it."

He pauses and looks at me. He's stopped pacing. He's smiling, and I'm terrified.

"I have waited a long time for this moment, Em. All this time, you've had something on me, and now I have something on you too."

He sits back down. I'm so frightened I'm shaking. I don't understand what's happening, but I'm afraid of what he's going to do to me.

"Your cell phone. I took it after I tried to kill you and you didn't die. I took your bag that night. I knew I couldn't risk trying to kill you again, not that way. I had to come up with a new plan. Anyway, I stole your cell phone and I read all your texts. Every single text."

My texts. I already know what he's going to say.

"Especially the very interesting texts you exchanged with your dear friend Beatrice."

Oh, dear God.

"The ones where you discuss the publication of *Long Grass Running*. The ones where she calls it *my* novel, and I knew. I always knew. Reading those texts just crystallized it for me. You didn't write a word of that book, did you? After Beatrice read the review—that big review in a big publication, remember?—she texted you: *They loved my novel.* I knew when I saw it that you didn't write it. She just gave it to you. I don't know why. But you know what, Emma? It did make me feel a lot better. I never believed you could write like that, and for a while, I thought you were much smarter than you seemed. But you're not. I was right all along. You're stupid, and I wish I'd never met you. Did you like my email to the *New Yorker*, by the way?" He laughs. "I wish I could have been a fly on the wall when they asked you about that one."

There's sweat trickling into my left eye and I can't move my hand to wipe it off.

"To be honest, I didn't think it was enough proof. She wasn't explicit enough. It was close. Most people would agree that it was likely she wrote it, not you. But I wanted something else."

I did it for you! I scream in my head. The words come out, but they're garbled moans. *Don't you understand that? I did it so you'd love me more, so you'd respect me more, so you'd want to stay with me.*

"You were never going to come up with another novel, and let's face it, you didn't even try, so I set you up. Just to see how quickly you'd take the bait. I think we can both agree you took it lightning fast. I sent you to the dry cleaners, made sure you had no cash or card to pay, and that nice man who helped you out, who just happened to be a ghostwriter, one of the best in the world? Let's just say Sam wasn't there by accident. And you—you stupid, imbecilic, worthless excuse for a human being—you fell for it."

I'm crying. He's killing me, slowly so that I can hear all this. I wish it were over. I wish I would die.

"I have a copy of a contract that was sent to me two days ago, that bears your name and the name of the ghostwriter you hired."

He stands up, and I want to recoil, but I can't. He stubs his cigarette out on the coffee table. Straight onto the glass.

"But wow! Emma, I take my hat off to you. Even I never thought you had it in you. Killing Beatrice? Oh boy. That's a whole other level. Wouldn't you agree?"

There it is. He said it out loud. I woke up this morning, hung over, confused, tired, but vaguely happy. Then I remembered what I'd said to him, but I thought it had been a drunken dream.

"Yes, I know, you thought I was asleep, or delirious. Here I was, trying to get something on you that would stick! I thought you stole the novel! I was going to blackmail you about that!"

He laughs, sits down again, and brings his chair closer to me.

"It begs the question though. If you killed Beatrice, why did her agent Hannah write a confession? Before killing herself?" He peers at me, eyes narrowed. "Do you want anyone asking that question? Do you want any of this to come out? That you stole the novel from Beatrice? And then you killed her? And now you're hiring someone to write the next one? I have all the cards, Emma." His face is inches from mine. "So tell me. Where is it? Where's the research you stole from me?"

I shake my head, it barely moves. My lips form the word *no,* but I don't know if the sound comes out right.

"Tell me!" he roars. "Speak! Now!"

I can't. I want to scream. I can't speak. I can't move.

"Fuck! I gave you too much. I have no idea what you're saying."

He gets up again, runs a hand through his hair. He paces back and forth in front of me, mumbling to himself. He stops, faces me.

"You won't die. You'll just have a nice long sleep, and when you wake up I'll be gone. But I'll be in touch, Emma. You got that? Is that a yes? I can't tell, but it better be. If you say anything to anyone about me, if you show anything in your possession to anyone, I will destroy you. I will go to the police. I will tell everyone what you did. Do you hear me? Everything. You. Did. Do you understand?"

My eyelids are fluttering. I don't know how long I can stay awake.

I'm so frightened. Don't leave me. Please. I will die here. No one will find me. Please don't leave me like this. I will give you everything you want. Please don't let me die.

And the last thought I have in my mind, when I see Beatrice's face floating behind him, is: *I'm sorry.*

15

When I come to, I don't know where I am or what the time is, or what happened to me. My limbs are cramped, and the pounding in my head is making my vision blurry. At first I think I must have been in some kind of accident, but I'm in my own apartment. I am still on the couch. I don't know how long I've been here, but from the quality of the light that is streaming through the windows it must be morning. Gingerly, slowly, I shift my muscles, almost one by one. I manage to hoist myself up, so that I'm in a sitting position. My clothes feel damp; from sweat, I suppose.

I need water. I manage to stand up, make it to the bathroom, and gulp water from the faucet. I don't have the strength to turn away before I vomit. *I hate you, I loathe you, I will tell everyone what you did.* I walk into the shower, turn it on, and stand under the cold spray for what must be an eternity. I only have the strength to cry.

After the shower and a handful of painkillers, I go to my bed and collapse into sleep. I fall in and out of strange dreams, and when I'm not asleep, I am crying.

I wouldn't say it's a thought I'd had every day since our wedding, but I asked myself often enough: *Why did he pick me?* We have one framed wedding picture in our bedroom, and in it Jim is looking down at me and I'm smiling at the camera. He's smiling at me, but it's not a smile that says, *I am so ecstatic I could burst*, it's more of a "Happy?" aimed at me.

When we were engaged, we used to see his parents occasionally, before they moved to Florida, and I remember one of the early family dinners when I was helping set the table. I went to the kitchen because we were one plate short, or maybe it was a fork, and I overhead his father asking Jim if he was sure I was the right person for him. Not unkindly; more out of a fatherly desire to make sure his son was as content as he could possibly be. Still, it hurt me deeply, and I stood there afraid of hearing Jim's answer, but desperate to find out.

"Yes," he said finally, and my heart sang, but then he added, "because she will always do whatever I say," or words to that effect. I don't remember exactly, maybe it was "because she will always agree with me," but the gist of it was that I would never interfere with anything he wanted. If he wanted to move abroad, I would do it. If he wanted to have ten kids, I would procreate.

His response hurt, but it also rang true. I would agree to anything he wanted. I would never challenge him, or demand that my needs be met ahead of his. If that's what it took, then so be it.

And me? What did I see in him? He made me feel *worthy*, that maybe I wasn't as ordinary as I thought. That there was something special about me. There must be. But as a result, I was always walking on eggshells, because if he left me, should he one day decide that I wasn't the one for him after all, then I would become *unworthy* with the stroke of a pen on the divorce papers. I have spent most of my adult life making sure he believed he had made the right choice.

I sleep again. I wake up. In the bathroom, I am shocked at my own reflection, but there's a sliver of lightness creeping in. It's a strange feeling, like taking hold of the edge of a revelation and trying to hold on to it.

I'm free.

No, I'm not. Who am I kidding? My psychotic husband is out there with my old phone and those text messages. That's the part that worries me. The late-night confession? He made it up. Never happened. That's what I'll tell anyone who wants to know. Anyway, that case is closed. Beatrice's agent, Hannah, killed her. Everyone knows that.

Oh God. If only. The only way I'll keep him from telling anyone is if I never give Jim his research back.

◆ ◆ ◆

"Emma! Hello, did we have an appointment?"

I step inside Sam's office and I push him with all the strength I can muster. He stumbles backward, knocking over a potted plant in the process.

"Hey!"

"How dare you?" I shout in his face. He's sprawled on the floor, his arms raised to deflect any blows I might inflict. "Who do you think you are? Is this what you do for kicks? Set people up? You're a sick man, Sam Huntington."

I stand still, get my breath back. He gets on his knees, never taking his eyes off me—to make sure I won't pounce, I suspect—and slowly, he stands up again.

"I don't know what you're talking about," he says, sullen. I don't bother arguing with the lie.

"Why? Just tell me that! What did I ever do to you?"

His mouth twitches and he runs his hand over his face, and then slumps down on the nearest chair.

"Okay, sit down," he says in a tone of resignation.

"I'm not sitting down."

"Listen, Emma, I thought I was doing the right thing, okay?"

To think I ever liked this man. "I'm going to report you. You're sick."

"He said you were struggling."

"You know, Sam, coming here, I wasn't even sure it was true. I thought there must be some other explanation. You've just told me that it *is* true."

I'm shaking. I sit down.

"Don't be angry, please."

"Oh, for Christ's sake! Sam, it's a little late for that, don't you think? Just tell me what happened. How did it start?"

"He—he called me to set up an appointment."

"When?"

"A few months ago. Five or six."

"Six months?"

"Yes. I'm a busy man, Emma. I didn't have the time to take the project on right then and there. I needed to clear the decks."

"If only you'd stayed *busy*, Sam. How did he find you?"

"I don't know. He didn't say. But he wanted the best; someone with a proven track record, that's what he said."

"But why? Why would you go along with this—this awful setup? I've never done anything to you. I didn't even know you existed until that day. Why would you do that to me?"

"It's not like that. He said you were struggling, that it was really affecting you and that he wanted to help you. I told him that you should contact me directly, but he said you'd never do that. You were a professional. It wouldn't occur to you to contact someone like me."

"A ghost."

"A ghostwriter."

"Did he pay you?"

"Of course he did, to meet with you. He set up a scenario where we could have coffee and a chat. He said that was all that was required of me. I really like you, Emma. I loved your book, and I understand how someone in your position could be struggling."

I jerk back. "Someone in my position?"

"Prize-winning author. It's not unusual. I told you that. I was flattered that he'd asked me to help. Sorry, but you're Emma Fern. Who wouldn't jump at the chance?"

"So he said to have coffee with me, and then what?"

"That I should introduce myself, give you my card. Whether you'd want to follow it through would be up to you. That's all. He said if you didn't contact me, that would be the end of that."

I scoff. "Of course."

"It's the truth, Emma."

I lean and point my finger in his face, so close I could take his eye out. "You don't get to talk about the truth, Sam. Don't even say the word."

"I'm sorry."

"Then what?"

"Then nothing, that's it. You contacted me and we worked together, and it's great, Emma. It really is. Everything is fine, isn't it?"

"You must be joking."

"But I—"

"Shut up. I'm asking the questions. I took the bait—"

"It wasn't like that."

"What did he want you to do, then?"

"Just to send him the contract."

"Why?"

"He said he wanted to go over it, to make sure the terms were favorable to you. He said that since he instigated the transaction, he felt a responsibility to protect you."

I laugh. Then I remember Jim's little spiel about how proud he was of me, all those lies that night. How I should never give up being a writer, *blah blah blah.*

I stand up.

"Emma, please stay. Let's talk."

"I never, ever want to see you again." I extend a hand. "Give me my contract."

"Don't. Emma, listen—"

"I said, give me my contract. All the copies you have." My jaw is trembling. I will hurt this man if I have to.

He stands, deflated. He walks over to the filing cabinet and pulls out a file. Hands it over to me. I flick through it quickly. There are notes, and the copy of the contract I signed. I take them out of the folder, and drop the rest on the floor. Then I proceed to tear up each page, one by one.

Sam just looks at me, his eyes pleading—for what, I don't know. I wonder if he's going to cry. I hope so.

"Our agreement is null and void. You are never to reveal that you ever even met me. Do you understand?"

"I genuinely believed I was doing the right thing, Emma."

"You should have told me the truth."

"You're right. I'm sorry. I really am."

And just as I'm about to slam the door behind me, he says, "It's worth a shot, you know. We did good the other day. I think we could work together. I really think—"

I turn back.

"Fuck off, Sam."

◆ ◆ ◆

I shouldn't. I know I shouldn't. But I don't care. I'm so angry, I go straight to the Forum. To tell Jim he won't get away with this. I don't care what he says to the world about me. I will never, ever return his material. I am going to ruin him, even if it ruins me in the process. He will regret the day he met me. No, he will regret the day he *crossed* me. This abuse ends here and now.

I am running through the conversation in my mind, and when I push the main entrance door to the Forum open, I do so with such violence that the glass door almost bounces off the joints.

I rush up the stairs to Jim's office, and there's a woman at the reception desk. It's not Jenny. I don't know what happened to Jenny. Jim probably fired her because she wasn't pretty enough, or young enough, or didn't look up to him enough.

"Excuse me? Can I help you?" she asks, a little alarmed.

I don't answer. I go straight for the door of Jim's office. You want to spill the beans on me, Jim? Go for it. Be my guest. I don't care. I won't be the first person to hire a ghostwriter, and I sure won't be the last. No one will believe your tale about Beatrice after I publish what I have about you. Jim thinks he's won, he thinks he's got me backed into a corner. He's wrong, and he's about to find out.

I shove the door open, and it slams against the wall. It's only two long strides to the desk, and I'm already there by the time the man on the other side has stood up, almost knocking his chair down behind him.

I've never seen him before.

"Where's Jim?"

He jerks his head, as if he's looking for an escape. "Who are you?" he asks.

"Emma!"

I turn and see Terry standing in the doorway, the receptionist craning her neck behind him. Safely behind him, I might add.

"Emma, what are you doing here?"

"Where's Jim?"

"He's not here."

I spin back around to the man standing behind the desk. "Who are you?"

"Jim's not here, Emma," Terry says again. He's standing beside me now. I feel his hand on my elbow. I shake him off.

111

"Where is he? When will he be back? I'll wait. I don't care." I sit in a chair. The man behind Jim's desk is still standing. He looks from me to Terry and back to me again.

"Come to my office, Emma," Terry says. "We'll talk about it."

"No thanks, Terry. I'd rather wait."

"He's not here."

"So you said."

"No, you don't understand. He's left. Jim doesn't work here anymore."

16

"Come in, please. Sit down. Can I get you anything? Water? Coffee?"

"No, I'm fine, thanks."

Terry sits at his desk and I take the only other chair, on the other side of it. I give him a moment to gather himself because he seems a little nervous. Anxious, even.

"What happened?" I ask.

He puts his elbows on the desk and rests his chin on his crossed fingers.

"I've been meaning to call you."

"Have you? Why?"

"I need to find Jim. I need to speak to him. Do you know where he is?"

"Ha! That's funny. You don't know—of course you don't, but Jim—" I was going to say, *Jim has left me*, but something stops me. "We've separated. We've decided to go our separate ways."

I expect Terry to be shocked, but his face remains blank.

"Did you know?" I ask.

He contemplates that, then he says, "Jim said that things haven't been good between you. That you haven't been well." He's about to say something more, but instead he adds, "I'm sorry."

"Don't be. It's mutual. Anyway, he doesn't live in the apartment anymore."

He nods. "I didn't know he'd moved out."

"When did he resign?"

"Three days ago."

Oh God!

"So you don't know where he is either," I say, then I catch myself. "No, of course you don't; you've said that already."

"I have no idea. But I wish I did. I can't reach him. He's not replying to my calls or emails."

"If he resigned, why do you need to find him? You're making it sound important."

"We're having problems with the audit."

"Ah."

He sighs, runs a hand over his forehead.

"I don't know if Jim told you, but we've had some significant investments, as you probably know. The thing is, we haven't exactly delivered"—he flashes a quick, apologetic smile—"and now the investors want to know why. A significant amount of that money has come from the government. It's a mess, I don't mind telling you."

"Money's gone missing?"

"I'm not sure. Our record-keeping hasn't been as thorough as it should have been. Even if there is money missing, it's not as much as you might think. But yes, some questions have come up in the audit." He sits back in his chair. "The biggest problem we're facing is that the results have been so poor so far, from all the implementations of our recommendations, even on a small scale, that our investors and clients are starting to think we sold them a lemon, so to speak."

I understand now why he looks so awful. He's got bags under his eyes, like he hasn't slept in weeks. He's lost weight too.

"When did the audit start?" I ask, watching various pieces of the puzzle coming together in my head, fitting like Lego bricks.

"Four months ago, but we've known about it for at least six months now."

Six months. According to Sam, that's when Jim first contacted him. So he's been planning to run away ever since he was told that an audit would take place. He had to come up with a way to get his documents back from me before he was found out. Except he messed that up. He messed up a lot of things, now that I think about it. And he really did have a nervous breakdown. That business about unknown people spying on him to steal his industrial secrets, he really believed that. What Jim did to me wasn't just because he *loathes* me, as he so charmingly put it, but because he's completely lost his mind.

"I'm sorry, Terry. It sounds like you've been landed with the problem."

"Well, let's not get carried away. Jim's probably taking some time for himself. When did he move out?"

"If I hear from him," I say, standing up, ignoring the question, "I'll tell him to call you."

I don't want to be caught unprepared. I could tell Terry that, frankly, the likelihood of Jim getting in touch with him is somewhere south of zero, because he's left Terry and me to pick up the pieces of his phenomenal screw-up and he has no intention of dealing with the consequences himself.

We've both been had.

◆ ◆ ◆

I hate being here, in this apartment. I hate everything about it. Sometimes I'm even scared of my own reflection, because I never know anymore if it's me, or her.

I walk around, trying to figure out what Jim took away with him, and it's not much. I begin with our bedroom and his clothes. We have a large walk-in closet that is split between his clothing and mine, and, looking at his side, I see he's left quite a few items. Most things, in fact. He's taken his nicest clothes, however—a coat, at least two suits, the leather jacket I bought for him last year, and some basic items. It's as if he's gone for only a few days instead of forever. Next I check his home office. The door is closed, and when I open it, I'm surprised again to find it perfectly tidy. But the drawers of the filing cabinet are gaping open. I flick through the files with the tips of my fingers, but I can't tell what's missing. His laptop isn't here anymore, obviously.

I move from room to room, looking at the artwork on the walls. I paid so much money for this stuff. What was I thinking?

I should call Craig, and ask him what I should do with it. He'll help me sell it. He'll know what to do.

Craig is a sort of friend, an "on the outer rim" type of friend, although the inner rim of my circle of friendship is completely bare, except for Frankie, and maybe Jackie, if she still considers me a friend, given how long it's been since I've contacted her.

I met Craig through Beatrice and we've kept in touch very occasionally, often because we run into each other at gallery openings, and we'll organize a catch-up for lunch, or he'll invite me to one of his notorious parties, but Jim doesn't like him much, so we never go to those.

I am not going to let this man destroy me, and since he's destroying himself, all I have to do is—nothing.

I'm going to pull myself together for real this time. The first thing I'm going to do is go grocery shopping and stock up with healthy food. I'm going to start an exercise regime and build my strength back up. I'm going to stop drinking. I will throw away all the alcohol I have in the house. That's been part of my problem. I've let things get out of hand with my drinking. I will buy a juicer.

I will get myself an attorney and begin the process of divorce, and come to think of it, I should do that sooner rather than later. I know nothing of our finances, as it's been made clear to me, and I better make sure that I bear no responsibility for whatever financial mess he's gotten himself into. Separation of assets—all that fun stuff.

Sam calls, but I don't answer. Then he calls again. And again. I don't answer any of those calls. I want him to go away. He'll get the message eventually.

So when the phone rings again I groan, ready to turn it off, but it's Frankie.

"Hey, Em, it's me." It does me good to hear his voice. Last time I heard it, I was checking that he wasn't smashed into a million pieces.

"Hey back, Frankie. What's up?" Funny, that's what he usually says to me, but my tone is wary. *Please don't talk to me about Nick, or about my book.*

"Where are you?"

Something about his tone makes me stand up straight. "I'm home. Why?" I walk into the living room, the phone cradled in my neck. "Something happened?" I ask, closing my eyes in silent prayer.

"I'm looking at your Twitter account."

"Okay . . ."

"You posted something just now."

"No, I didn't," I say quickly. "I never post to Twitter, you know that. That's what you do."

"Fiona does, actually."

Get to the point, Frankie.

"She's here with me in the office. I'll put you on speakerphone."

"Hi, Emma." Fiona's voice comes out loud and crackly, and I have to take the phone an inch away from my ear.

"Hi, Fiona, what's up?" I say chirpily, the feeling of dread already forming in my stomach.

"There's a weird tweet from your account. It came through just now. We just want to check if it's from you."

"What does it say?"

"*I killed her.*"

I'm going to be sick. My stomach lurches, and I press the palm of my hand against my forehead, trying to relieve the pressure that is building against the back of my eyes.

"Are you there?" Frankie asks.

It's hard to breathe. "Yes, I'm here," I manage, finally.

I can hear another call coming through. I pull the phone away from my ear and look at the screen. I don't recognize the number, but I know I have to take it. I have to know.

"Just wait a sec, Frankie. I have another call."

He says something, but I don't let him finish.

"Hello?"

"Emma Fern?"

"Yes?"

"This is Ann Kennedy from *USA Today*, is this a good time?"

"Why?"

"Hmm, right. Regarding your email? This is Emma Fern?"

"What email?"

"That you have something to confess."

I burst out laughing. "Seriously? It's a prank email, whatever your name is. Okay? I didn't send you an email, for Christ's sake. Do you believe everything you read? Jesus! Goodbye!"

I end the call. Then I hear Frankie. "You're still there, Emma?"

"I don't know what's happening, Frankie." My voice is wavering. "That was a reporter. What's going on?"

"I know. We've had a couple of calls too. It's everywhere. I'm sorry."

When the room starts to tilt around me, for a moment I can't tell if it's because I've fallen over. But I haven't.

"What's 'everywhere'?" I hear myself ask.

"It seems someone is sending emails on your behalf, and posting to your social media, that you killed someone. You killed a woman."

"It's bullshit!" I shout. I almost bounce in position. "I didn't kill anyone! Do they say who I'm supposed to have killed?"

"Emma, we're going to take all your social media offline, okay? Until we get to the bottom of this."

"Don't do that. It'll look like I have something to hide," I wail.

Frankie sighs. "Do you know anything about this?"

"Do I know if I committed murder? Seriously, Frankie? Hmm, let me think. No. Nothing springs to mind."

Fiona's voice comes through again. "That's what the tweet you sent says."

"I know that's the tweet, for Christ's sake! And I didn't send it."

I must be imagining it, but it's as if they both recoil from the phone. I almost hear the whoosh.

"Listen, Frankie. I didn't *tweet* this. I don't *tweet*. Okay? You do the tweeting. You know that."

"Okay, I hear you."

"We got hacked, Frankie. Jesus! *I killed her?* What's that supposed to mean?"

"I don't know. We'll figure it out. We'll change the passwords."

"Do that. Right now, please. And this tweet: pretend it's a publicity stunt gone wrong. Say that it's to do with my new novel. That'll work, right? We're whetting the reader's appetite."

"Don't worry about it. We'll take care of it." Frankie says.

My head hurts. That's how he did it, with the *New Yorker*. He has all my passwords. Of course he does. I'll need to change them. Right away.

When the text comes, I think it's going to be Frankie with more bad news. But when I pick it up, I feel like I'm going to faint. Like a physical reaction. It's Jim.

Can I have my stuff back now?

My fingers are trembling so much it's hard to hit the right buttons, but I manage all the same, and I send a reply, one that I already know I will regret but I can't help myself.

119

Fuck you.

Nothing else happens for a few minutes as I stare at the screen, shaking and afraid to look away. Then, just as I finally put the phone down, there's another one. And there's a moment, as the screen goes blurry, that I am transported to another time, and another place, and for a split second I wonder whether I'm wrong about Beatrice being dead. Because that text is from her. She sent it to me a long time ago, before we put her in the ground, before I won the prize, when we were still friends and I had agreed to be the author of her book.

Emma my love! We did it! She LOVES my book!

17

Every time my phone rings or I get a text, my heart skips a beat. I'm anxious, all the time, and I don't understand why I haven't heard anything else from Jim. It's been almost two weeks now and it makes me nervous. He's up to something. I know it. Sometimes I'm convinced that I'll wake up and my face will be plastered over the front page of the newspapers.

POULTON PRIZE WINNER CONFESSES TO MURDER!

The anxiety I feel about Jim has become a weight in my chest. I don't know what to do, but I will think of something. Today, I decide I'll go for a run. I haven't gone running in, Lord, two years, I think.

It's hot outside, almost steamy. I start by walking briskly. I should have brought earbuds, and something to listen to.

"Emma!"

For a moment, it's as if the ghost of Beatrice has spoken to me, and I slam my hand against my chest. I'll ignore it, I decide. I'm going to ignore that ghost and maybe it will go away.

"Emma!"

I turn then, and look at the woman who has appeared from nowhere and is now standing beside me.

"I have to see you. You have to help me," she says, quietly.

"Carol?"

She's wearing dark sunglasses and a gray baseball cap with its wide brim pulled low. I recognize the Dodgers logo.

"Jesus, Carol! You gave me a fright! What are you doing here?"

"It's Jim."

She speaks so softly I can barely hear her. I move closer. Her chin trembles.

"Carol, if something has happened to Jim, that has nothing to do with me anymore. We've separated. Everything has changed since I saw you last."

"I know."

"How do you know? You said you never saw him anymore. What's going on here?" I look around quickly, confused. "Is he here?"

"Oh God, no! Emma, Jim's not with me! He doesn't know I'm here." Her tone is urgent, pleading. She takes hold of my sleeve. I look down at her fingers grasping the fabric and resist the urge to peel her off me.

"Can we talk?" she whispers.

I take her hand away. "No. I'm sorry, but I don't want to know, okay? I told you. It's nothing to do with me anymore."

I move around her, determined to get away from her.

"Please, Emma, wait, I meant—I'm frightened," she sobs. "I'm really, really frightened. I don't know what to do. You have to help me. You're the only one who can help me."

I have my back to her, and I could take a step forward, right at this moment. We're in the middle of a busy street. What could she do to stop me? But I don't take that step. I can hear the desperation in her voice. Do I feel sorry for her? Yes. But mostly, I want to know what Jim's done now. And there's also a small part of me, not the nicest part, that experiences a tiny pang of satisfaction that it's not just me he loathes, it seems.

I close my eyes for a second, and turn around.

"Do you want to come up to my apartment?"

She looks around. "No. Not here."

"I was just going to go for a run. Do you want to come with me?"

She jerks her head like I just said something bizarre.

"No."

"Then I'm all out of options, Carol."

She leans in closer to me, and says, "Meet me at Gramercy Park. East side. Near the gate. In half an hour."

Her head is bent. She removes her sunglasses and raises her eyes to look at me, pleading, and I hear myself say, "Okay, I'll be there."

I watch the relief spread over her face as she gives me a small smile. "Thank you," she says, and turns around, hands in the pockets of her hoodie.

I have a really bad feeling about this.

◆ ◆ ◆

Gramercy Park is only a couple of miles away from here, not half an hour's worth of running, so I take a detour along the East River.

The city is teeming with tourists at this time of year. It's crowded, and it's hot. I'm not as fit as I once was, but I know from experience it will come back, and the pain in my lungs feels good. Still, I know not to push myself too hard. I stop to take a breath and I bend down, my hands on my knees. I see my rings. My wedding ring, and the other one: the one engraved, *I love you more every day*. I quickly tug at them to take them off, and then I throw them as far as I can into the river. Two guys walking past look at me, a question in their eyes. I turn away and resume my run, feeling that much lighter.

Carol is already there when I get to Gramercy Park. She's sitting on the low concrete wall that supports the fence, still wearing the shades and the baseball cap.

"Here." I hand her one of the paper cups I'm carrying. "I got you the same as me, black, no sugar."

She takes it from me, slowly. Her hand is shaking. I pretend not to notice and I put my foot on the fence and stretch my leg, casually.

"What happened, Carol?"

She takes off her sunglasses and looks up at me. Her eyes are red-rimmed from crying.

"Sit down, please," she says, patting the concrete next to her. I wipe the spot with my sleeve and sit.

"Shouldn't you be in D.C.? Why aren't you at work?"

"Jim came to see me," she says, without looking at me.

"When?"

"Two weeks ago. Right after he left you."

"I see. He told you about that? Did he tell you what he did to me? I doubt it somehow." I close my hands into tight fists, trying to keep control. "I thought you didn't see him anymore? How did he find you?"

"I'm not hard to find. He was waiting for me, outside my office building."

"What for?"

"He's got it into his head that I'm part of some conspiracy to send him to jail, or to steal his secrets, I'm not sure. It's because I work for the department that's investigating the Forum."

"Ah. So you know about that. The audit. Terry is looking for him, by the way. Seems Jim has a few questions to answer. If you see him, you might want to pass on the message."

"It's not a joke, Emma."

"Tell me something. Do you know that he faked the modeling data?"

She looks down at her hands, picking at the skin around her thumbnails. "He didn't put it that way at the time. But there were already some problems at the Forum, when Jim and I were . . . let's say that we both worked to keep some details away from Terry. But I thought it was minor; just some kinks that would be fixed with a few adjustments. I thought he needed a bit more time." She sighs. "That's what he led me to believe. I never got to find out what happened after that. I left. As you know."

I've heard that spiel myself from Jim: *I just need a bit more time. It's just a matter of making a few adjustments to the modeling.*

"You do realize it's a bit more than that, right?" I say. "He totally faked the data, then crossed his fingers, hoping for the best. Essentially."

She nods, wipes a tear with the back of her hand.

"Go back to your story: he was waiting outside your office. Then what?"

"We went back to my place, to talk. We talked all night. He told me that he left you because he wanted us to have another chance at love."

I burst out laughing. "Another chance at love? Seriously?"

She looks wounded. I just shake my head, trying to suppress the laughter that won't go away.

"And I suppose you forgot all about how *toxic* it had been," I say, "and how him leaving you was the best thing to happen to you. Am I wrong?"

"It's hard to explain."

I stand up. "Well you know, Carol, I couldn't care less how it is, he's all yours. Enjoy."

She grabs my arm. "He thinks I'm spying on him, Emma. He's gone crazy. The last forty-eight hours have been the most terrifying of my life. He accuses me all the time. I can't breathe. He says that if I really loved him, I would prove that I'm not working with them, whoever they are. The people who are going to put him in jail."

That sends a shudder through me. "Go back a bit. Jim declared his undying love for you. What happened after that?"

A flush spreads across her cheeks.

"He was very convincing. Very apologetic about how he treated me."

I can't help raising an eyebrow. She notices it.

"I know, I was in the wrong. Can we not go over that again?"

"You're the one who brought it up, Carol."

"This was Jim at his best. It all came back to me, how much I loved him. He looks great. He was incredibly loving, incredibly attentive, and I let myself get swept up in that. It may not have been smart, or right, but it's what happened."

She sounds a lot like I used to: in love, charmed, enraptured. It's almost funny to hear it back from someone else, except it's not. It's pathetic.

"Then he started to question me about work. Was anyone at the Department talking about the Forum? Or him? I told him no! It's not my section, it doesn't come up. Then he wanted to know if I had anything to do with the investigation. I don't. I told him so, repeatedly. But he wouldn't believe me. He asked the questions over and over, and frankly it was driving me crazy."

I don't believe for one minute that Jim wanted to rekindle his love affair with Carol. He'd left it too long. When I hear her say he'd missed her and all that, my first thought is that he'd wanted a place to stay. He doesn't have an income anymore; he wasn't going to splurge on a hotel. The master manipulator was going to dump her as soon as he got back on his feet. For the first time, I can't help but feel sorry for her.

"His behavior has been crazy ever since the audit," I tell her. "He's been completely paranoid, like you wouldn't believe."

She scoffs bitterly. "Oh, I would, I do believe it. Trust me."

"Did you? Have something to do with the audit?"

She touches her throat, gives me an incredulous look. "No!" she says. "Christ! Not you too!"

"Hey, it's not as incredible as it sounds. You knew about the fake research."

Carol starts to say something, but I raise my hand, silencing her.

"And you were the scorned woman," I add. "You now work for the very government department that is being cheated by your ex-lover. It's not that far-fetched, Carol, so I'm asking again—and before you answer, believe me, I don't care either way. But I would like to know. Did you? Nudge the audit, so to speak?"

"No. I didn't. I didn't even want to think about him anymore. The less I had to do with Jim Fern, the better. Okay?"

I bend down to rub my calf, thinking it over.

"So then what?" I ask.

"After he moved in with me, he would call me at work, like, ten times a day. If I turned off my cell phone, he'd call through reception. It was starting to affect my job. I told him I didn't want to be with him anymore, that I wasn't comfortable, and I wanted him to move out."

She starts shaking again, squeezing her hands together. I reach across and put my hand on top of hers. She takes a deep breath.

"He threatened me, Emma. He put his hand on my throat and he squeezed. He said that he knew it was me, that I was spying on him, and that I shouldn't go to work until the whole thing blows over."

"Have you told the police?"

"What would they do? Caution him? If I go to the cops, he'll really hurt me. I have no doubts about that."

"So what did you do?"

"I've had to take some leave from work. Jim didn't want to stay in D.C. We're staying on Long Island. My parents have a place in Bellmore, but they live in the U.K. now."

"Nice life if you can get it."

I don't know why I said that, considering I have it too. I raise a hand in apology.

"I don't know what you want from me, Carol," I say. "I can't help you. I've had my own problems with Jim. I want nothing to do with him."

She looks at me, her lips trembling, and I can see it in her eyes. The fear. The desperation.

"He trawls through my emails, Emma. He watches my every move. Last night, I woke up and he was sitting in a chair by the bed, staring at me. He goes from being incredibly in love, saying that he can't live without me, to threatening me. He pleads with me to believe him, that we will be happy together in our new life when none of this is hanging over his head, and then in the next minute, he's suspicious of everything I do or say. Convinced I'm out to get him, or something like that."

"And yet you're here," I point out, and we both look around and behind us at the same time.

"He was asleep. I left a note saying I needed to renew my passport—it has just expired, which is the truth. I made sure I wasn't followed. I was incredibly careful, believe me."

"Your passport?"

"He wants us to go abroad. Start again."

I snort. Where have I heard that one before?

"Where?"

"Tunisia, I think."

"Tunisia? There's a demand for American economists in Tunisia?"

She looks askance at me. "They have no extradition treaty."

It's all I can do not to burst out laughing.

"You could have just called if you wanted to talk to me so badly."

"Are you crazy? He's been checking my cell phone every day: who calls me, who I've called. If your number came up, I'd be . . ." She lets the word float between us.

In trouble? Dead?

For a moment, I wonder if I could get her to find my old phone among Jim's things and return it to me. But in exchange for what? I couldn't help her if I wanted to—what could I possibly do? My gut tells me I need to get as far away as possible from this whole situation.

I stand up. "Again, this has nothing to do with me anymore. I couldn't care less whether Jim gets done for fraud, or caught up to his elbow in the cookie jar. He can fly to the moon if he wants. I certainly won't stop him. Let him go to Tunisia."

She shakes her head. "He won't go without me."

I sigh. "I understand, I really do, but I don't want any part of it."

I turn on my heel, determined to get away from her and her problems. She'd better not contact me again. But then she says, a little too loudly for my taste, "Your friend, Beatrice Johnson Greene. He said you killed her."

And there it is. The moment I've been dreading for days: finding out that Jim has told someone. I stop and turn around and do my best to laugh, my head thrown back.

"He said that?" I ask, once I've recovered myself. "That's a good one!"

She shrugs. "I know. He's losing his mind. But he also said you didn't write your novel, that it was her, Beatrice, and you stole it."

My arms are dangling by my side. I squeeze my hands into fists. "That's just insane. How could I steal something like that? For God's sake! Wow, he really has gone crazy. Off his rocker. I mean, up till now, you made him sound a little unhinged, I'll admit that, but this? He's really lost it, you're right. I mean, of all the stupid, made-up, fantastical stories he could possibly come up—"

"He's going to kill me, Emma. Help me."

I sit back down next to her.

"What are we going to do?" she asks.

I say it out loud, the very same decision I made a few minutes ago, in the privacy of my own head.

"We're going to kill him."

18

Will three make me a serial killer?

We've moved to a small bar near Gramercy Park, my resolution about not drinking having gone the way of the dodo. And anyway, we can hardly have this conversation on the sidewalk, and the park is out of the question since we need a key to get in.

It's an ordinary little "bar and grill" type of establishment, suitably intimate and dimly lit. There are a few patrons, but it's quiet. It's still early for drinking, or so some people might say.

We're sitting in a booth in the corner. Carol won't remove her baseball cap but she does take off her sunglasses. She has dark circles under her eyes, the telltale signs of a sleepless night. Without her hoodie on, I can see she's thinner than when I saw her last.

She starts to cry.

"Carol, please don't do that. Look around, for Christ's sake. We're in a public place."

"I can't kill anyone," she says.

"Okay, I understand. I mean, neither can I."

"I wouldn't even know how."

"Me neither. It's probably very difficult."

"It's not an option, Emma. We can't kill him."

"Okay. Listen to what I have to say, then you tell me if you have a better idea."

So I tell her. Everything, sort of. I tell her what kind of man Jim really is, if she doesn't already know. How he tried to kill me by pushing me into traffic. How he drugged me and tried to kill me again, which is not strictly true, and as I watch her eyes grow wide, and her tears fall, I tell her, in no uncertain terms, that if she wants to stay alive, then we don't have a choice.

"You're in his sights now, Carol. You said so yourself. He's going to kill you. Well, the rest of that sentence goes like this: unless we kill him first."

It takes a long time, but I wear her down and she believes me. So we try to plot ourselves a murder, but everything comes up blank. Where would we get a gun? What if we pushed him off a subway platform, right in front of an oncoming train, pretending it was suicide? Poor, sweet Carol . . . ever heard of witnesses? CCTV cameras? I could push him into traffic; give that a shot. He told me there was a trick to that: pretending you're stopping the person from falling just as you have in fact pushed them to their death.

No. Too risky.

"What about your place?" I say.

She snaps her head around, and stares at me.

"What about my place?"

"Could we kill him there?"

"No! Of course we couldn't! It's my parents' place anyway. And what would I do with the body?"

"Is the house by the sea? Could we dump him in the ocean?"

She blinks rapidly. "How can you be so . . . practical?"

"Yes, I know, but we've established that it's the only solution, haven't we?"

She nods.

"Okay, so." I pour her a glass from the bottle of wine I ordered. This is a bottle-of-wine kind of discussion.

"I don't know if I should be drinking," she says.

"So don't. I don't care. I'll get you some water if you want."

She takes a sip. "We have a boat," she says.

"Really?"

She nods.

"That's good! Do you sail?"

She waits a beat, as if I'll clarify the question, then she says, "A little. I used to when I was younger, with my parents, then again as a teenager. I haven't done it in a while. Why? What are you thinking?"

"I don't know yet, but that's got to be something we can work with. Jim sails too. He took me sailing once, years ago, for my birthday. Tell him you're organizing a day or two out on the sailboat," I suggest.

"Off Long Island?"

"No, in the Caribbean."

Her eyes widen. I raise mine skyward in a silent prayer.

"Yes, Long Island," I assure her.

She bites the side of her thumb, but she's thinking. We put our heads together. Whispering. It's like she's turned her brain on. We both come up with ideas, and throw most of them out. Every now and then she interjects with "I can't do that" or "I could never pull that off," and variations on that theme. It takes a while, but in the end, we nail it; we come up with what I think is the perfect plan.

"I'll find the place to rent the boat from. It needs to be from a marina that would suit our purposes. One of the smaller ones."

Because we've decided we can't use Carol's boat. For various reasons. It's too small, for a start, but also, we need witnesses. Lots of them.

"I'll get all the other stuff we need as well," I tell her. "You don't need to do anything."

"When?"

"Give me a couple weeks."

"I don't know if I can wait that long," she says, shakily.

"Sure you can. Just, you know, pretend you love him, ask him about Tunisia. Bring back some brochures with you."

"No no no! I can't wait that long. He's really unbalanced, Emma. I don't know what's going to happen over the next two weeks. For all I know, he'll have already bought two tickets to Tunisia."

"I understand." And I do. She's right. "Give me your number. I'll let you know when. Just let me do the research first."

"You can't call me."

"OK. Can I text you?"

She shakes her head. "No. I'll get one of those disposable phones on the way back. I'll text you the number."

I help myself to another glass of wine from the bottle in the ice bucket and pause over her glass, as if to pour. She puts her hand over it.

"No, no. He'll smell it on me. I'll get some soda water." She stands up to make her way to the bar and turns back to me.

"Do you mind paying for it? I'm out of cash and I don't want to use my credit card."

"Oh? Okay, sure."

I fumble in my bag for my wallet. I mean to give her some cash, but she just grabs it from me. I find the gesture annoying, frankly. We're not that close. I don't want her to get any ideas that we're friends now, united as we may be in hatred.

When she comes back with a glass and a bottle of Perrier, I grab the wallet back from her and put it into my bag.

"We need to hurry up, Carol. You should think about getting home."

She nods quickly. "I'm not sure I can convince him, Emma."

"Sure you can."

"Maybe I can tell him it's a surprise?"

"No, please don't do that. He'll think you're taking him to the cops. Or getting him committed or something. He's paranoid, remember?"

"I'll tell him we have to make plans, because we need to get away soon."

"Yes. Good."

She takes a few sips of water. "But that we should do it somewhere else, in case we're being watched."

"You're a star. That's great. In fact, why don't you display a little paranoia of your own, when you get back?"

She looks at me sideways. "That shouldn't be too hard."

"I mean, tell him you think you saw the webcam light come on, on your laptop, or on his, if he's removed that stupid bit of tape."

She nods, small ones.

"Tell him you don't feel comfortable discussing your getaway plans in the house. But that you have an idea of where you could go and be really, really undisturbed."

"In the middle of the ocean."

"Well, maybe not the middle, but yes, that's the general idea."

"Do you think it will work?"

"You're doing great, Carol. It will."

19

I've found the perfect place for our assignation. I spent all last night trawling the Internet, looking for just the right marina from which to rent a boat, and this morning I paid them a visit. I've told Carol we can do it on Wednesday. That's in two days. Two days is not a lot of time, and I have an awful lot to do before then. For one thing, it's surprisingly difficult to find men's wigs in this city. Women's wigs? Easy. But for men, not so much. The assumption seems to be that men want toupees or hair implants, and the first couple of stores I visit recommend I go to the type of place where one would need to make an appointment to discuss the root, so to speak, of the problem.

"It's just for a party," I tell the young woman in yet another store that I visit.

"Oh, like a costume party? You could try a party supply store; one of the larger ones."

But that's not right either, I'm not looking for a costume wig. I don't want to look like Louis the Fourteenth. I start to get a little nervous that I won't find it in time.

When I get to the next store on my list, it's the same again. There are rows and rows of wigs on display, in all shapes and sizes, but they're all for women.

I'm about to leave, when the sales assistant asks me what I'm looking for.

"A wig, but for a man. I mean a man's look, but not like a pirate or a powdered, landed-gentry type, just, you know—"

"Yes, I understand, a man's wig," he says. "I don't have too many of those, but come with me."

There's a row of them, on the bottom shelf against the side wall of the store. I hadn't noticed them when I came in, but even from this distance I can tell they're not going to be right. They're not even close.

"Can it be dyed?" I ask, pointing at one, thinking that since it's all I've got, I'm going to have to bite the bullet and find a way to make this work.

"Not these, they're synthetic. Come this way."

I follow him to the back of the store. This part is done up like a hair salon, with large mirrors and styling chairs.

"Over here"—he makes a sweeping gesture—"we do the full service. We fit people with the right wig, and we can cut and color it, just like real hair. Is it for you?"

I'm about to say no, but then I change my mind.

"Yes, I'm in a play, with my local theater group."

"You're playing a man?"

"We're doubling up. We're small. Amateurs, you know how it is."

"Can't say that I do. What's the play?"

"*Death of a Salesman.*"

"Should be fun."

"I hope so."

He pulls out four different wigs, each sitting atop a mannequin's head, and puts them on the counter, one after the other.

"If any of these are close, we can color and cut it, to match what you want. What do you have in mind?"

"Um, Bill Clinton, twenty years younger. Slightly longer hair too. And darker."

"Okaaaay." He draws out the word, as if to say, *Whatever rocks your boat.* "What about this?" He picks up a wig, holds it up for me to see. "If we take out a little here, and set the top there, maybe add a bit of a wave . . ."

"Yes, I can see that. Can we make the sides a bit gray?"

"We can, that's no problem. Let me check the fit. Why don't you have a seat?"

I sit where he indicates and he puts the wig on me, shows me how to tuck my hair up into it. I look ridiculous. This is never going to work.

"It feels a little tight," I say.

"It's supposed to. You wouldn't want it to move every time you turn around."

I tell him what I want, in detail. I pick the color, describe the cut. If he's surprised by the exactitude of my requests, he doesn't show it. I'm paying for it, so why would he care?

"When would you like it by?" he asks, after removing it from my head.

"Tomorrow?"

"Ah no. That's not possible. We have orders already and—"

"I'll pay extra."

We agree on an extravagant amount of money. I give him my name (Jackie Collins—the first name that pops into my head) and I leave a hundred dollars in cash as a deposit. I also pick up a woman's wig, a black bob with bangs: a cheaper, synthetic one for which I pay right there and then. "It's for the other part I play," I tell him.

"Thank you, Ms. Collins. We'll see you tomorrow after three o'clock."

It's such a relief, but still, I'm nervous. I think maybe I haven't given myself enough time to put this plan in motion. I haven't thought the details through, because already, the details are bothering me. The wig: no matter how hard I try, it's not going to be quite right.

I decide to go and buy myself a hat, just in case. And I remind myself that there isn't a lot of time. Jim is a loose cannon right now.

I have to get to him before he gets to me.

◆　◆　◆

Carol wants to meet again, she says; just once more, which is worrying. Does she want to back out? Has she not been able to convince Jim?

I went to the marina again this morning, very early, taking a jog on this sunny day; a perfect excuse, if I do say so myself. There are a couple of runners up and down the pier.

I've picked out the boat. Not too big, not too small, just the right size. A catamaran with an outboard motor, that you can rent out "sans captain"—bareboat charter, they called it—and usually for two people, although they'll accept up to two children as well, I'm told, but only if it's for a day trip. We're not going for a day trip. We're doing an over-nighter. And we're certainly not bringing any children.

We meet at Gramercy Park again. I've spotted a coffee shop around the corner, so I lead Carol there, wordlessly. It's only when we're sitting down that I ask her.

"What's the problem?"

"I don't know, I—"

"You're not bailing on me, are you?"

"No. No. It's just that he's getting worse, fast. He's obsessed, and this plan is making me really nervous. If anything goes wrong, Emma—"

"So don't let anything go wrong! Christ!" I take a deep breath. Getting frustrated with Carol is not going to help at all. I need to keep it together.

She nods. We sit huddled together, our heads close, whispering. She tells me he's been going through her things. He's not even hiding it anymore.

"Give me your phone, the burner one," I tell her, my hand outstretched.

"No! Why?"

"Because it's the only evidence that can trip you up if he finds it. I'll give it back to you tomorrow. By then you won't have to worry anymore. Come on, Carol, give it to me."

It's like I'm her mother, for God's sake! I put the phone in my bag and take a better look at her. She's so anxious, she's almost quivering.

"You need to pull yourself together, please. You'll screw this up otherwise, do you understand? We're almost there, Carol, okay? Just hang in there for another day."

She nods again. I stay with her a little longer, talking to her, talking her down from her panic. I make her recite the plan back to me again.

When we get to the part where she has to report him missing, she blurts out, "I can't be the one calling the cops."

I raise my hands in frustration. "Why not? It can't be me, Carol, you know that! I'm not supposed to see him, or have anything to do with him! It makes no sense for me to call the cops and tell them he's disappeared. He's already disappeared from *my* life!"

"But I'm the one who has to rent out the boat!"

"So what?"

She shakes her head, and there's nothing I can say to change her mind. I start to wonder whether this is too difficult for her. I am actually considering whether to pull the plug on the whole thing.

"What about Terry?" she asks.

"What about him?"

"I could send him an email, from Jim's laptop. Say that he wants to meet him. He needs some time, but he's ready to come back to work and sort this out. Something like that."

"Okay," I say, tentatively.

"I could schedule the meeting for Thursday. Then when Jim doesn't show up, he'll get worried. Maybe you could call Terry on Friday. Prompt him, you know?"

"It's not going to work, Carol. Terry isn't going to report Jim missing. If you can't go through with this, then we need to cancel the whole thing."

She nods, slowly.

"Remember what we said. After we get back to shore, Jim"—and I make air quotes here—"will ask you to drop him off, and tell you he's going to walk for a while, and he'll see you at home later. It's even better, don't you see? It will look like he planned it."

She's still nodding, mulling over what I've just said.

"But I like the idea of Jim contacting Terry. I think you should do that anyway."

"Do you know Jim's password?" she asks. "I think he's got a password on his laptop."

"Sorry, you'll have to figure this one out for yourself."

She starts to pick at the skin around her thumbnail. She's going to come up with excuses, I can tell.

I take her by the shoulders.

"Make it work, Carol. Do you understand me? Otherwise you're on your own. Is that clear?"

She doesn't look at me, but she nods, and takes a deep, resigned breath.

"Okay," I say, "let's go over the plan again."

20

I asked Carol to give me her disposable cell phone because it makes sense. It feels risky for her to carry it around. If Jim finds it, we'll be done for. But as a result, she has no means of contacting me, so we both have to trust that everything is going according to plan.

I get out of the LIRR station a little after 6:30 a.m. I take off my hoodie and put it in my backpack, and put my Dodgers cap on over my ponytail. I look more like Carol now, and I walk briskly toward the marina.

I'm early, and there are a couple of joggers running up and down the pier, but that's it. I'm carrying a midsize cooler. It's just a prop, really; if anyone saw me, and if they were ever asked about it, I want them to think it was Carol getting organized. I've hopped on the boat that she has rented—and I sure hope she has, otherwise I'm well and truly trespassing. I go inside the cabin, where the long seats are. They open, and there's a fair bit of space for storage inside, and I slip in and close the top over me.

It stinks, it's dark and hot, and uncomfortable. I estimate I'll have to wait about two to three hours before they arrive.

After thirty minutes, one arm goes to sleep. It's just in an awkward position, but I can't really move, and I don't want to open the top in case they suddenly arrive. I'm getting a bit nervous. So much could go wrong. They might not even show up, although by now I'm starting to hope that will be the case.

It's hot. I'm sweating profusely in the small space. I check my watch. I've been here for three hours already. They should be here by now. I'm starting to panic. And then I hear Carol's voice.

"Isn't this nice? What do you think, Jim?"

I hear Jim say something, but I can't quite catch it. There's a bit of wind and he's not talking as loudly as Carol. She needs to take it down a notch. She sounds like she's auditioning for a part.

They're walking down to the cabin now. I hold my breath. There's some activity going on—the unpacking of bags, I think. They're so close. I can hear Jim now: "This is great, sweetheart. You're right, it's perfect."

Sweetheart.

"Shall we get going?" she asks. "I can't wait to get out there."

"Give it a minute," he says. "I'm going to take a look around."

My heart skips a beat. I think, *Oh God. He can't find me. Please don't let him find me.* I fully expect Carol to say something like, "No, don't do that, you can do that later," but she just says, "Okay, good idea," and it makes my heart race even faster, but I understand why. It would be suspicious if she didn't. Then she says, "I'll come with you."

I must be as quiet as possible. I must not cough or even breathe loudly. My backpack is a problem; it's nestled against my stomach, but it takes up more space than I'd like.

They're back upstairs now and I can just hear them from where I am. Jim says he likes the boat. He comments on various features. Carol wants to sail it, but he disagrees. They engage in some banter about it, and I mentally take my hat off to Carol for sounding as relaxed as she does.

Carol says she's thirsty. She wants to go downstairs and grab some orange juice. Would Jim like some?

It's too early. I know what she's doing. If he doesn't sail off now, then she can't wait anymore. But it's too early. It's too risky. Jim says no, he's fine, maybe later, and I breathe a sigh of relief.

But they do come downstairs after all, and I press a hand on my chest to try and quiet my heart. There's a bit more activity, and for a moment I think they're going to have sex, right there on top of me, so to speak, and I want to throw up. But Jim goes back to the deck and Carol follows him. After what seems an eternity, I hear the whir of the motor starting, and we start to move.

I knock my head against the side as the boat jerks backward. Eventually, the motion of the boat is smooth again. We're going out to sea and I manage to rearrange myself and get into a more comfortable position.

I can only hear the noise of the motor, for what seems like a long time. But then I catch the sound of their voices. I can just make out what they're saying.

"How far do you want to go?" Carol asks.

"This should be good, I think, don't you?"

It's hard to guess how far out we are by now, but it must be at least a couple of miles.

"I'll put up the sails," Jim says.

"I'll give you a hand."

There's a lot of pulling and swearing, and the noise of flapping. The boat lurches. I can't hear what they're saying anymore because of the wind, but then I feel it again, and we're on our way.

I don't know how long I can stay like this. There's a cramp in my leg and I wriggle my toes, but it brings no relief. The wind has started to die down. I hear them murmuring somewhere above me, and strain to listen.

"I think I'll go and lie down," Jim says. "I'm more tired than I realized."

No, no, don't let him do that, Carol, please. Not on his own.

"Stay here a while. It's nice up here. Please?" Carol says, as if she read my mind.

"I feel a bit woozy. I hope I haven't lost my sea legs," he chuckles. Carol giggles and says something I can't quite make out.

After that I can't hear them anymore, just the sound of the water lapping and the wind snapping in the sails. I want to move my legs, my fingers, but I don't dare.

It's silent for what feels like a long time, but when I check my watch, I see that it's only half an hour. Then I hear something. Footsteps. Someone's coming. They're getting closer to me and I can't tell if it's Carol or Jim. *Oh God, help me!* My heart is pounding and I hold my breath; shut my eyes tightly.

"Emma, are you there?"

I exhale as Carol slowly lifts the top off the seat. She looks as scared as I am. Her hand is on her chest.

"Oh, you're here, thank God!" The relief in her voice is as clear as my own.

"Can I move now?" I whisper. "Is it safe?"

"He's asleep," she replies.

"How long?" I ask.

"Ten minutes."

"Okay, just stay with him. Let me get out of here."

She returns to the deck. I unfold myself slowly from within the seat. My body aches. I'm cold and my limbs are stiff. I bend one leg at the knee, extend it, and do the same with the other. I stand up slowly, and walk up the stairs. I can see the back of Jim's head. The rest of him is obscured by the top of the cabin that juts out from the deck. There's no sound. I can see the shore in the distance. The sun is still high in the sky. We're not quite far out enough yet.

It's too soon.

I stretch my muscles, getting the blood flowing back into them, sensation returning to my fingers. I rub my gloved hands together. Carol comes and stands next to me.

"Everything okay?" she asks.

I put a finger to my lips. *For God's sake! Be quiet!*

I half crouch, and slowly, silently, make my way to the front of the boat. Carol follows right behind me.

"How many did you give him?" I whisper.

"The whole bottle: twenty, twenty-five, I'm not sure."

I nod.

"Are you sure that's enough?" she asks.

"Yes, I'm sure. Trust me." I almost tell her that I've done this before.

I pick up the now-empty glass of orange juice and look inside. There's only a trace of the mushed-up pills in the bottom. Carol did well.

"What do we do now?" Carol asks.

"We wait."

"Shouldn't we tie him up?"

"Don't be ridiculous. We don't want any trace of marks on him."

I remain crouched down while the boat sails on. I can't imagine that anyone could see me at this distance, but why take the chance? It takes another twenty minutes for the shore to recede to a thin line. It really does feel as if we're in the middle of the ocean. The sun is starting its descent, the colors of the sky are changing, and I am longing for the cool of the evening. Salty wind is burning my skin. My eyes hurt.

We don't speak. I help Carol lift the sails so the boat slows down. I take a close look at Jim's face. His eyes are closed, and his breathing is regular. His jaw is slack. There's a thin line of spittle leaking out of the corner of his mouth. I nod at Carol and we begin to remove his shirt and pants and his shoes. We work silently, carefully. Once it's done, Carol goes into the cabin to retrieve the other set of clothes she brought with her. They're more or less the same. The polo shirt is a bit paler, but it will do, and we dress him again. We are both sweating from the exertion, and it's only the beginning.

We sit silently on the netted fabric between the hulls, checking on Jim occasionally, making sure the dose was enough to keep him completely out for this long. I wish she'd waited before giving him the barbiturates, but I also understand her desperation to get it over with. Carol has closed her eyes, listening to the water. We look like twins. We are wearing the same outfit, with the same cap on, just like we discussed. If anyone saw me this morning, they would have seen her instead, preparing for their trip before coming back with Jim.

"Ready?" I whisper.

She nods, opens her eyes, steeling herself. We take down the sails together, then lower the anchor. Then we go back to Jim, positioning ourselves. She takes his legs and I slip my arms under his armpits.

We manage to raise him up, but it's not enough. He's too heavy, so we lay him down on the deck. "It's not going to work," I say. "We need to find another way."

"Let's roll him sideways, push him over the side," Carol says.

I see where she's going, and it's a good idea. We manage to twist his body so that it's parallel to the edge and then we're on our knees, side by side, half sliding, half rolling his body across the deck until finally, with a grunt and all our determination combined, we push him overboard.

We collapse to the deck from exhaustion. Carol lies back, and I watch Jim's body, face down, bob and float on the surface of the water. The light is almost gone. I check my watch, it's almost seven thirty. I look around us: there's nothing. No one in sight. We are completely and utterly alone.

Carol has stood up. She grabs hold of a cable and looks out.

"Can we go, please?" I ask.

She doesn't reply. Finally, she pulls up the anchor, with some difficulty.

"You're sure you can sail?" I joke.

"Just give me a minute, please." She's panting from the effort. "Okay, help me. Here, pull this," she says, and I am more relieved than I can say.

I look out to where we dropped him. I can just make him out in the darkness, or maybe I'm imagining it. The boat lurches a bit as we reset the sails, the wind working to increase the distance between us and Jim.

Bye bye, I think.

I can't say I'm upset.

21

"Let's stop," I tell Carol.

It's completely dark now. We're far enough. I'm not a great sailor, and I'm anxious that we should be able to make our way back.

We take down the sails again, drop the anchor, and the boat quickly stops with just a bobbing motion. There's little wind anyway. Carol peers over the side of the boat.

"I'm going to change," I tell her.

"Okay."

I go downstairs, taking Jim's clothes with me. I open the seat and pull out my backpack. There's a small bed at the back of the cabin. Just big enough for two people. I lie on top of it, flat on my back, my head on the pillow, and I close my eyes, just for a moment.

When Carol wakes me up, I don't know where I am. It's pitch black, except for the small red light above the door.

"Emma, wake up."

"What time is it?"

"Three o'clock in the morning."

I've been asleep for hours. I peer at her, try and make out her face in the darkness.

"Is everything all right?" I ask.

"It's fine, everything's fine."

"Why didn't you wake me earlier?"

"What was the point? You may as well get some sleep."

I swing my legs over the side of the bed, feel the floor with my feet.

"I want to wash my face, get changed."

"Okay."

I turn on the lights and look at myself in the mirror. I pull the wig from the backpack and put it on, careful to tuck my ponytail into it.

I resist the urge to take a shower. I remove my clothes and step into Jim's cargo pants and his polo shirt. The pants are too big, of course, especially around the waist, and I secure them with the belt I brought along. I have some additional padding in my bag, but that can wait.

I go back upstairs. Carol is standing on the bow, looking into the distance.

"It's me," I say, then add, "I've changed," to warn her.

She turns and gasps at the sight of me in Jim's clothes.

"You gave me a fright."

"I tried to warn you."

She looks me up and down, then cocks her head to one side. "I don't know."

"What?" I ask, looking down at myself.

"They're too big on you, his clothes. It looks odd."

I let out a frustrated sigh, pulling at the polo shirt that's at least three sizes too large. "You're not helping, Carol. It's not as if I can do anything about it now."

"Give me a second." She moves quickly to the back of the boat and returns with a bright blue windbreaker. "Put this on."

"What's this?"

"It's Jim's."

I don't recognize it, but that means nothing. She helps me put it on. It's light, and it helps hide the ill-fitting clothes as well as the obviously female contours of my upper body.

"Thanks," I say. "It does feel better."

We sit together, watching the black water that surrounds us; she keeps peering out over the side.

"Stop doing that, please," I implore.

"Doing what?"

"Looking for him."

"I'm not, I wasn't."

"I don't believe you. He's not there, okay? He's at least five miles that way." I point.

"I know."

"Just don't go weird on me. You should get some sleep. I'll stay here."

"Okay."

She pads downstairs, careful in the moonlight. It's almost four o'clock in the morning. I stare out to sea. I'm not looking out for Jim; he's gone. But I see her, just like I knew I would—a fleeting image, like a ghost in the mist.

Get lost, Beatrice. Leave me alone.

It's almost three o'clock the following afternoon by the time we get back to the marina. I've been up since 3 a.m. I feel nauseous with anxiety, sitting on the small bed in the cabin while Carol is outside, securing the boat to the dock. I offered to help but she said it was best for me to stay down here until we're ready to leave. No need to let people take *too* close a look at me. I suppose she's right. I just want to get out of here.

"We've got a problem."

Carol is standing in the doorway to the cabin. She's biting the side of her thumbnail. My stomach clenches.

"What's wrong?" I ask.

"It's the guy from the boat rental office. He's right outside, on the dock. Talking to someone."

151

"Shit." I close my eyes, willing myself not to panic. "The guy you hired the boat from?"

"The guy *we* hired the boat from, Jim and I. And they had a nice long conversation, the two of them."

"Okay." She doesn't need to point out that he'll know I'm not Jim if we run into him out there and he starts chatting to us. "We'll have to stay put for a while."

She looks back toward the dock. "Wait. He's leaving. No, he's stepped onto a boat. Two down from us." She cranes her neck. "He's gone inside the cabin." She turns to me. "You need to go. Now." I stand up quickly, grab my backpack from the floor. She pulls me by the elbow. "Hurry up. And put your hat on. You can take it off later."

I rummage through my bag and pull out the hat. Then I put the sunglasses on. Carol is pushing me out onto the deck and I almost stumble. There are a few people out there coming and going. No one is paying attention to me.

"Aren't you coming?" I ask as I'm about to step off the boat.

"I'll be there in a minute. I want to make sure we haven't left anything behind. Wait for me at the end of the dock." I hesitate. Then I hear her whisper behind me, "Please, Emma. Hurry up, he's going to come back, he'll see you and come over and talk to you if you don't get a move on. Please."

The urgency in her voice propels me forward and I jump onto the dock. I put my hands in my pockets to stop them from shaking. Seeing all these people from the corner of my eye, I'm scared that I'm not going to be able to pull this off.

When I get to the main pier, I stop and turn back, looking for her. There's a wooden barrier along the edge and I lean against it, keeping my head down.

Five minutes go by. I don't understand what's taking her so long. Maybe the guy she saw earlier is talking to her now. *How was your trip? Catch anything?* I hope not. It would be odd for Jim not be there with her. We want as many people as possible to see Jim and Carol return together. That's the whole point.

I keep glancing up to check for her, but after ten minutes she still hasn't returned. I don't understand how I could possibly have missed her. Or her me.

I keep looking at Jim's watch on my wrist. Twenty minutes. I can't stay here. Should I go back to the boat? I decide against it. I walk toward the parking lot, past the rental company's office, where I stop and glance through the glass frontage, but she's not there either. I want to wait for her here, but there's nowhere obvious for me to do so, and everyone around me is walking, so I keep going.

When I get to the parking lot, she's already there, standing beside the white Buick Verano. I join her in great strides.

"Where the fuck have you been, Emma?" she snaps. She's frowning at me, her eyes narrowed.

"Me?" I ask through clenched teeth. "And where the fuck were *you*? I've been waiting exactly where you told me!"

"No you haven't! You weren't there. I looked for you everywhere, Emma!"

"I was on the pier, at the end of the dock, you should have seen me!"

"Well, I didn't, because you weren't there!"

"I looked for you everywhere too! Oh, stop this, Carol, we're here now, okay?"

I'm sweating a little, the wig is too hot for this weather, and I can't wait to get this windbreaker off me. I note that she's already removed her baseball cap. We need to get out of here.

"Let's just go," I say. She opens the passenger door for me. I slide into the seat, drop my bag on the floor.

"Is this new?" I ask, hoping to release the tension.

"I've had it about a year," she says, a little surly.

"You sure look after it." The dashboard is dust-free. The whole car smells clean. "I'm impressed."

Carol checks things in the back while I wait. She puts the cooler away. There's a screaming child just outside my window. I turn to look at the woman pulling him by the hand, looking frustrated as he's yelling at the top of his lungs. He abruptly pulls his hand away and flings himself on the ground, fists thumping. His mother crouches, and after a fair amount of begging and cajoling, the child gets up and she takes his hand again. She throws me a quick apologetic glance. I give her a small nod in return and open the glove compartment, just for something to do; something that would justify me not looking at her. I pretend to look for a map. I fiddle around with my backpack at my feet. Inside the front pocket I spot Carol's cell phone, so I pull it out, drop it in the compartment, and close the door, fiddling with the latch. By the time I look up again, the woman and child have gone and I breathe a sigh of relief.

Carol returns and gets into the driver's seat.

"Let's go," she says, "it's over."

It's over, I repeat to myself.

It's over.

Carol is surprisingly calm, calmer than I expected, whereas I'm vibrating with anxiety.

"What did they say? When you returned the key?"

"They said, 'Thank you. Did you enjoy yourselves?' That sort of thing. Perfectly normal."

"Okay, good."

She glances my way. "You're okay?"

"Yes, I'm fine."

"You don't look it. You look anxious, Emma."

"I'm not anxious. I'm hot and I want to get out of this fucking getup."

I tug at my wig, but she puts a hand on my arm. "Don't. Wait. We're almost there."

"Yeah, I know."

I tell her where to drop me off. It's a block away from the shopping mall where I spent a few hours the day before yesterday mapping out my escape route, looking for the blind spots where the CCTV won't catch me, if anyone comes looking, which would be highly unlikely.

I'm not taking any chances though. When I went there, I wore the other wig, the black bob, and I picked clothes I don't usually wear, from the less expensive section of my wardrobe.

Carol stops the car. We quickly go over the rest of our plan. We expect Terry will call when Jim doesn't show up. If not, I'll prompt it somehow. Something like, *Hey, have you heard anything from Jim? I got a disturbing message, etc.* "I hope he's okay. I'm really worried about his state of mind," I'll say.

Meanwhile, Carol will call the cops and report Jim missing the day after tomorrow. We discussed it, and agreed that if he'd really disappeared, she wouldn't have thought to contact the police before then.

We think his body will wash up ashore eventually. A clear case of suicide if there ever was one. Carol never would have agreed to go on this boat trip with him if she'd known he'd use it to plan his suicide. She'll tell them that, when they drove back after the boat trip, he asked to be let out of the car. He wanted to walk. He needed to think about the work situation. He seemed okay when he left her, but now she thinks maybe he was faking it for her benefit. That was the last time she saw him. She should never have let him go.

And even if his body doesn't bob its way to shore somewhere, then that's fine too. *He's gone. He's been planning his escape. Have a look in Tunisia.*

We go over it one more time. We'll probably never see each other again.

"Good luck to you, Carol," I say. "Have a good life. I mean that."

She gives me a small smile. "You too, Emma." She puts her hand on my arm. "And thank you."

I put my hat back on, pull it low. Between that and the sunglasses, as long as I keep my head down, you can barely see my face.

She lets me out. I lean in, kiss her on the lips.

"See you soon, sweetheart," I say, nice and loud, and leave, closing the car door after me.

I walk inside the shopping center, then to the main department store and straight to the public toilets. The door leads into a short corridor. There's no one there. I open the door to the ladies' room, ready to make my apologies if I need to—*sorry, wrong one*—but it's almost empty, with someone in one of the cubicles, but no one at the sinks. I step inside the other cubicle and change back into my own clothes, and remove the wig. I store it all in the backpack and go to the mirror to check myself. It's fine. I look fine. I look like myself again. A very tired, sunburned version of myself.

I throw water on my face. I hear a toilet flush and a woman comes out to the sink area. She smiles at me in the mirror. I give her a quick smile in return and rinse my hands. After I've dried them, I look in my bag for some makeup. While I apply lipstick, the woman leaves. I purse my lips and make a mock kiss in the mirror.

So, here we are, Jim.

No, wait, you're not here anymore, that's right. How could I forget?

You really underestimated me, you little piece of shit, didn't you? Not for the first time either. And look how that turned out for you.

I apply a little eyeshadow, congratulating myself on a job well done. I feel fantastic.

Does three make me a serial killer?

22

I woke up this morning infused with a lightness I have not felt in years. I'm free, and I'm strong, and I want a new life. I want friends and loved ones around me. I want laughter and good food, friendships, and confidences, and I want to fill the void with people.

I slept surprisingly well last night. No ghosts, no nightmares, just the sleep of the just. I go for a run, and all the time I am running, I have images flashing through my mind, snapshots of Jim and me at dinners, birthdays, vacations, celebrations, of us making love, and all I can think is: *What was I thinking?*

Why did I stay so long with this psychopath? What on earth did I see in him? Flipping through the slideshow of my memories from this new vantage point, all I can see is a pompous narcissist, and then there's me, looking up, prepared to do anything to please him. It makes me run faster. I see a man who was so self-deluded that even after he committed major fraud, he still thought he had come up with the magic formula to solve the world's problems. *No, Jim, you faked it, remember?*

I used to think he was so smart. Now I realize he just enjoyed putting me down to raise himself up. His behavior toward me was bordering on abuse, frankly, and I should have my head examined.

But that was then, and today is a new day, and good riddance to you, Jim.

I change out of my running gear, have a shower, and dress in nice clothes. I look much better now. I feel great. My running routine and healthy diet are paying off. That drab, sad face, those ugly dark circles under my eyes, that sallow look are all gone.

How is Carol faring? Did she sleep? Or did she stay up all night wondering whether it was all a bad dream. Is she relieved? She must be relieved. There's something to be said for not having to look over your shoulder all the time, convinced that the psychopath over there, in your bed, the one who professes to love you and only you, is trying to kill you.

A few months ago, I never thought I would say this, but I quite like Carol now. I thought she showed some guts yesterday. I hardly know this woman. We spent a little bit of social time together way back when, and then she moved away. But she surprised me. Considering what we've shared, I find myself almost regretting that we will never see each other again.

Almost, but not quite.

◆ ◆ ◆

I don't want to stay in that dreary empty apartment, so I decide to go and buy myself a juicer. Now that the new me has emerged, and the new me is getting fit, healthy, happy, eats lots of vegetables, and does not drink so much. I read somewhere that fresh juice every morning does wonders for the skin, and what's not to like about that? So I take myself off to Williams-Sonoma, one of my favorite stores in the city.

I'm wandering around the Homewares department, and I'm looking at a shelving display of dinnerware—very beautiful pieces, in fact—when I feel a tap on my shoulder. I turn to find an elderly woman I do not recognize looking at me expectantly, a thin smile on her face.

"Would you? Please?" she starts to say.

She's short, significantly shorter than me, although not quite a midget. She must be in her seventies I think, maybe late sixties. I sigh internally, rearrange my features into a question and a smile, because it makes me look benevolent—and, I hope, kind. It's usually women of her age that have particularly connected with my novel, although, as has often been said, *Long Grass Running* transcends generations. Considering I've been complaining that people don't recognize me anymore, I should be pleased. But then from the corner of my eye I catch sight of "Nick the Prick," some distance away and walking in my direction. He's checking various items in a desultory fashion. Why, if it isn't the "Most Promising Writer of his Generation." What perfect timing. He hasn't noticed me yet, but he will any moment now, since I'm more or less right in his path.

I smile back at the elderly woman.

"Of course," I say, sneaking another look at Nick making his way toward us. I make a show of opening my purse and looking for a pen. It would have been quicker to ask the woman for one; she probably has one ready, but I want to time it with the moment when Nick reaches us and I need those few more seconds.

"If you wouldn't mind . . ." the woman says again.

"Yes, of course," I repeat. "Here," I say, finally brandishing the pen. "Do you have something I can write on?"

"Excuse me?" she tilts her head to the side and raises her cupped hand behind her ear.

Perfect. She's even hard of hearing. I lean slightly closer to her and say, as loudly and as slowly as I reasonably can, "Do you have a piece of paper? For my autograph?"

Nick must have heard me as he looks up and raises his hand in a big wave, as if I'm a long-lost friend, his face open and beaming as he walks more purposefully toward us.

But the older woman jerks back slightly.

"What on earth are you talking about?" she says in a high-pitched voice, stern as a schoolmistress.

A wave of confusion descends between us. What *does* she want from me, then? A selfie? Really!

Women like her want my autograph. They are—or were, anyway—probably the largest single demographic to have read, and loved, my novel, and when they see me, and recognize me, they ask for something tangible, something that they can take home to their husband and sons and daughters and say, "You'll never guess who I saw today in Williams-Sonoma." I even had one woman beg me to wait right there while she rushed off to the nearest bookstore to get another copy of the novel she already owned, just so I could sign the flyleaf.

The older woman frowns, lifts a papery, trembling finger to point at something behind me, above my head.

"Could you reach the top shelf for me, please?"

I turn around and lift an arm, instinctively, without thinking, my hand extended to the item, and I should grab it, give it to her, let her move on and then say hello to Nick, exchange a few words, and that would be the end of it. But Lord knows why, instead, I lean forward, bending down a little, and almost hiss into the face that has well and truly lost its trusting edge and is starting to look mildly distressed. There's background music, as there usually is in such places, but it is too loud, obtrusive.

"Take my autograph," I try to whisper loudly, separating every word, but it comes out wrong. Like I'm threatening her, and this time she recoils, her face registering a small degree of alarm.

"You do know who I am, right?" I say. "You recognized me, didn't you? I don't mind, really I don't. I'm used to it, I should be." I grin widely, looking more crazy than ever, no doubt. "It happens all the time."

I can feel my features tighten into what I hope is a pleasant smile, but I probably look deranged, eyes wide. I extend my hand to her again. *Give me something, anything*, I tell her urgently with my eyes, seeing Nick almost here. *Any old piece of paper will do, but don't leave me hanging like this just as Nick the Prick joins us.*

I rifle through the contents of my own purse and pull out my wallet. My fingers tremble as I retrieve a business card of some sort, my dentist I think, and I shove it into her palm. I close her fingers around the card tightly and with one hand I hold them there, while with the other I scribble something.

"There," I say, loudly.

"I'm calling the police! I don't want your autograph. Is that what this is?" she shouts. "Why would I want your autograph, you crazy woman?"

"Because I'm famous! Because I won the Poulton Prize!" I yell into her frightened face just as the background music stops and lets my words bounce against the tiles, and I hear Nick in my ear, with one hand on my upper arm, saying, "Are you all right, Emma?"

I stand up straight and turn to him in time to see the amused expression on his face as the older woman says, "I don't want your autograph, you crazy woman. I just wanted you to get the milk pitcher up there for me, on the top shelf."

And to complete my humiliation, Nick, the hero of old ladies everywhere, reaches up to the shelf, picks up a perfectly ordinary white milk pitcher, and hands it to her.

"There you are."

Natalie Barelli

The old woman takes it, shaking her head in disbelief, and moves on, muttering to herself, and turning back, looking over her shoulder to make sure I'm not going to follow her, I suspect.

Nick repeats his question, eyes wide as he does, a picture of sincerity, eyebrows raised in concern. "Everything all right, Emma?"

No, everything is not all right. I have been humiliated, and from the lifting corner of his mouth and the *pat-pat* of his hand on my upper arm, Nick knows it very well.

My face now crimson, I leave my plastic basket right there on the floor, and without even looking at Nick, I walk out of the store with my head down, as ashamed as if I'd been caught stealing.

23

Strange as it may sound, I've only had sex with three people in my life, in total, until today. As of today, it's four. Does four make me a serial lover?

The first time was with a fellow student in college, whose name, coincidentally, was also Sam.

I liked him; he was sweet. I remember we laughed a lot together. He was a year younger than me, but then I wasn't particularly mature for my nineteen years. Most of my peers were no longer virgins, I suspect, or maybe they pretended not to be. At our age, it seemed important to exude an air of sexual experience. I'd been guilty myself of inventing a boyfriend earlier that year, after coming back from summer vacation. Max, I'd named him.

My mother and I never left the city during the summer; we couldn't afford it, and she had to work. So, during vacation, I spent most days on my own, watching TV, making sure the house was clean for her and that the laundry was done. I also made delicious meals in the evening. Nothing fancy, nothing extravagant, just taking the extra time to make something from fresh ingredients, experimenting with flavors. So I didn't mind that we didn't go away. I liked looking after her. I loved my mother.

You could be a cook, Emma. A professional. You're very good at it.

I never corrected her, pointed out that surely she must have meant a *chef*, because I knew her generation had different ideas of how much women could achieve. They were intelligent women who worked hard all their lives, but there were only so many opportunities open to our gender, and it didn't help anyone to complain about it. Something like that, anyway.

There was a young man who worked at the butcher shop down the street, who always winked and smiled at me when I shopped there, making me blush. His name was Max, so I built a fantasy around an imaginary young man who was staying with his aunt for the summer in the same building we lived in, and we'd cross paths on the staircase. I named him Max. One day Max offered me a cigarette, and after that we'd meet downstairs and smoke, and then one day he kissed me and we'd hold hands, and I can't quite remember how the fantasy went, but anyway, he was my imaginary boyfriend for a few weeks, who tragically had to go home after the summer. Back to his mother, away from his aunt and our building.

But Sam, the other Sam, was real. One day he invited me to a party at his friend's house. So I went, not really anticipating anything happening between us, but it did; on a bed covered with coats and jackets that we threw on the floor. He was so eager, and the entire exercise took maybe five minutes, and I remember thinking that if that was sex, then I must be frigid.

We didn't talk anymore after that; not like we used to. We were awkward. The bond had been broken, and neither of us had any desire to revisit an experience that had been embarrassing for both of us. A couple of my friends knew that we'd slept together, no doubt a couple of his friends also, but for my part I gave the excuse that Max was back, and it wasn't appropriate for me to go with two boys. And I preferred Max. I probably did. I'd made him up, after all.

The following year I met Stefan, a young man also at college with me; where else would I meet anyone? Stefan's grandmother emigrated to America during the Hungarian revolution when she was a young girl, no more than a child. Her parents bundled her onto a train, after which she traveled by boat, all the way here to join a family; part of a Hungarian community that was helping their young compatriots escape. She was, still is, the bravest person I have ever met.

Stefan and I dated for an entire year, and when his family announced they were moving to the other side of the country, we cried and hugged, and made promises that we were too young to keep.

And then I met Jim; the less said about that the better.

Sam the ghostwriter has his own story too. He used to be married, but not anymore. They were childhood sweethearts. Sometimes I think Jim and I were too, all those years ago, but not really.

As it turns out, Sam's ex-wife left him to go traveling and decided to stay away. They never had children, so that was lucky, but he would love to, he said. He has time, of course. It's different for men. I want children too, but Jim doesn't really want them yet; he says he's not ready.

"Does Jim want children?" Sam asks.

That jolts me back to the present.

"I didn't tell you. Jim and I aren't together anymore." Which is one way of putting it.

"Oh. I'm sorry."

"Don't be. It's better that way."

"I hope I didn't . . . you know, with that whole business of—"

"It's fine." I put my hand on his arm. "You didn't."

Sam nods, and we lie in silence for a little while.

Is there an opposite of post-coitus, I wonder? Pre-coitus? It was raining, pre-coitus. It probably still is. It feels like forever, but it was only hours ago.

❖ ❖ ❖

"I didn't think I'd ever see you again, Emma Fern."

"I know. Neither did I."

I pushed past him. He was holding the door open, but not so wide as to welcome me in.

"What do you want?"

"What are your standard contract terms? Show me a standard contract, like the one I signed."

"Why? You tore it up, remember? There is no contract anymore."

"Show me anyway."

"You're really worried about this, aren't you?" he says. "Is that what you think of me? That I'm going to trick you? How?"

But he gave it to me in the end; his standard contract. He actually threw it at me. He didn't understand what I was doing, but I didn't care.

I sat down and I went over it again, in minute detail.

"I've called you. I've left a few messages," he said.

"I didn't feel like talking."

"I wanted to apologize. You were right. I should never have gone along with Jim's idea. It was deeply unprofessional of me."

"That's right."

"But I believed him, Emma. You have to know that. I really did think I was going to help you beat writer's block! That's all I wanted to do."

"You told me all that, Sam. I heard you the first time. Sit down," I said.

"Why?"

"I want to hire you."

"Is this a joke?"

"Nope. I want to finish my novel. Will you work with me?"

He sighed. "Do you think we can work together?"

"I can, because I know what I want. The question is, can you?"

He stood up and went to his desk, opened a drawer, and pulled out a handful of pages. He gave them to me, silently, and when I began to read, at first I was confused. I thought that something was wrong with me, because I couldn't make sense of the words on the page. It was as if the letters were jumbled up, or it was a foreign language, and I was about to say something when it clicked: he wrote the first paragraph backward, so that you need a mirror to read it, although once you realize that, you can figure it out pretty quickly.

I turned to him and smiled.

"Too gimmicky?" he asked, biting his lip.

"No, I think I like it," I said gently, and returned to read the rest, which was not written backward.

I couldn't stop reading. The words flew through the air and my heart beat faster in recognition that this was really very good. It was so compelling that I was sorry when it stopped.

"Is there more?"

"Not yet."

"I love it." I watched a smile slowly spread across his face. It was a lovely smile: innocent, happy.

"You wrote all this?"

"I was inspired."

"Even after I told you to stop?"

He smiled, sheepish.

"Where's the rest?" I asked.

He was about to object, but I winked and he laughed.

I read what he wrote, and he told me that he'd never had an experience like this before, of collaborating with someone like this. Normally, he said, he would go away and write the book, but with us it was a team effort. He said it was because I'm so talented. He still believed that I had writer's block, but he said my imagination was unique, and my story was magnificent. That's the word he used: magnificent. And that it was a privilege to work with someone like me. And it was the strangest thing because it was real this time. It really was my story and my imagination.

"You're just my scribe," I told him, and he laughed. He liked that.

Then he touched my cheek.

But now I am lying on the couch in Sam's office, naked next to him, intertwined in a tangle of limbs.

I think I knew this would happen. I had an image of it once, just a flash. Maybe that's what desire looks like.

"I should go," I murmur into his neck.

"Sure." He holds me tighter. I laugh.

"Really, I have so much to do it's not funny."

"Don't go yet."

"I have to."

I lift myself up on my elbow, look into his handsome face. His eyes are still closed, but he's smiling. I kiss him gently on the lips.

I stand up from the couch, and get dressed, aware of him watching me, his arms behind his head.

"Did you copy it on the stick for me?"

"It's on the desk." He points. I spot it, pick it up, and slip it into my purse, just as my cell phone rings. I'm going to leave it, because I think it's that blocked number again. The one that never leaves a message. They called twice this morning, and I don't want to talk to an unknown person.

Except it's not.

It's Terry.

◆ ◆ ◆

Carol did as we planned and emailed Terry. She made it look like a message from Jim, to set up a meeting at the Forum and do *everything in my power to make it right*. That was the night before we took him out sailing.

But Jim never showed up for the meeting. The meeting that was to take place yesterday.

"It's not just that he didn't call," Terry tells me, "which would be annoying in itself, but I can't reach him at all. His cell phone seems to be permanently off, and he hasn't replied to any of my emails. I haven't heard a word since, have you?"

"Since he left? No."

I watch Sam stand up and gather his clothes. He disappears into the small bathroom.

"No phone calls? Emails?" Terry asks.

"I've had no contact whatsoever." Terry called me without prompting. I don't need to add more layers to my story.

"Do you know where he went?"

"What do you mean?"

"After he moved out."

"Nope, I have no idea."

I can hear him sigh. Terry wants something more from me, and I need to give it to him. "You sound worried."

I want him to be as worried as possible. Tomorrow Carol will report Jim missing to the police, and I want Terry to think that Jim may have harmed himself.

"Don't you think that's strange?" he asks.

"I don't know. We didn't separate on the best of terms—"

"I realize that."

"But I agree, it's not like him to disappear completely like that. I don't know what to say. Do you think his phone's out of battery?"

"Maybe. It's just odd, that's all."

"I can give you his parents' phone number if you want."

"Don't worry, I have it."

"You do?"

"He listed his mother as next of kin. It's on file."

And what am I, I wonder—chopped liver?

"Okay." I sigh. "I'll try to call him as well. And I'll email him."

"Good. He may reply to you, even if he doesn't reply to me."

"Did anything else come up yet?" I ask. "From the audit."

I hear him snort a little. "Let's say new information has come to light."

"Yes?"

"It's no longer about the money, Emma. As I said, some of it disappeared, but it wasn't that much, compared to what it might have been, anyway. Jim had full access to the accounts and unlimited power when it came to disposing of it. A big mistake, certainly, and against the rules, but we fell into some bad management habits, all in the name of getting things done fast, you understand? It's possible we're dealing with a record-keeping issue, rather than a theft."

Clearly, Jim has helped himself to the till. But he's not a thief, in the traditional sense. He would have taken what he needed to get away, and no more. Just goes to show, even crazy people have morals. In terms of planting a seed that Jim has done a disappearing act, it's a little thin.

"I understand. But you knew that already, right? That the amount was negligible."

"Just, sort of. I can raise it myself, replace it. But that's no longer the issue anyway. I wish it was."

I feel a prickle in the back of my neck. We're getting somewhere, I can taste it. I imagine Terry sitting back in his chair and running a hand over his forehead. It makes my heart ache a little. Terry never deserved this.

"I have reason to believe that Jim has faked his research. The cornerstone that this place is built upon may well be made of sand."

I can't help letting out a laugh. It sounds like a bark, but he made it sound so poetic, I have to wonder whether this is a line he's been practicing.

"It's not a joke, Emma."

"I know. I'm sorry. Tell me, what makes you say that? What did you find?"

Sam is back. He smiles at me as he sits at the desk. I make a gesture to say, *Do you want me to leave?* but he shakes his head.

"We went back to the original data to replicate the calculations—the graphs, the trends, all the work that the forecasts were built upon—and they don't match up," Terry says.

"What do you mean, they don't match up?" And I ask the question even though I already know the answer, because I'm suddenly aware that while I've been sitting on that information for a long time now, it never occurred to me before today that this is not just about Jim, or me. There are dozens of people who work there. Many of them who have put their faith in the system that Jim developed. There was real hope, among those walls, and outside of them, that the Forum had found the key to a balanced society, and was working with the right people to implement it. To make the world a better place, is what Jim had said. Way back when.

Should I have said something? Probably. I used that information to keep my marriage together, with no thought spared for the people whose lives and reputations rested on that fake research. And while I sit here, reflecting privately on what my actions have meant for these people who are about to lose their jobs and reputations, I am also thinking about what this would do to me, if it came out that I knew. Would I be held partly responsible? Did I do something illegal? Probably, now that I think about it.

Do I need a lawyer?

"I don't know how else to say it, Emma. They just don't match up."

"So you think the original research is fake."

I can hear him sigh. "I'm starting to be fairly sure that's the case, yes."

"But why?"

"Good question. Why would he do it? I don't know. I'll leave that to the psychologists."

"No, I mean, what makes you believe it's fake?"

"Because we've completed recreating the original modeling, and the results are different. Very different."

"I see."

I ponder this for a moment. I remember the late nights; the frantic work Jim did hiding in his office—that's what it was all about. He was trying to replicate the modeling and make it work, as if by some miracle it would all come out fabulously well the second time around.

I should be preparing myself for the inevitable question that will come soon: Did I know? Because at some point, Terry will want to know what I know—or what I knew, more importantly. Am I going to be blamed for Jim's crimes? Like hell I am!

"So I need to find him," Terry says. "I need to give him a chance to explain himself, you see? There may be"—he pauses—"other parts of the research we're not aware of. Reasons why we can't make it add up. We should be able to duplicate it, obviously. Replication of experiments is the bedrock of science."

Cornerstone. Bedrock. Terry should have been a geologist. Or an architect.

"I just want to give him a chance, Emma, that's all. I know things have been . . . awful between you. The breakup of a marriage is always painful. I haven't experienced it myself, but I can imagine."

Huh, probably not in this case.

"But I just want to know if you have any contact with him. If you can help me help him. Can you?"

It's always something of a revelation talking with Terry. Anyone else would have already jumped to the rock-solid, bedrock-like, cornerstoned conclusion that Jim has skipped town and damn the consequences. But Terry, Lord love him, really does want to give Jim a chance to clear his name. There must be a part of him that genuinely believes that Jim was—is—a genius, and the numbers are real. The motivation behind the Forum is real. The tools to make the world a better place are real. Terry wants to believe this more than anything.

"Terry, I think you should consider yourself here, and the other people who work with you."

He doesn't say anything.

"I'm sure Jim meant it when he said he would come to see you, but it's also highly possible that he got scared. If what you're saying is true, about the fake research, what would the consequences be for Jim?"

He sighs. "Seriously? I don't know. Prison, probably."

"Don't you think it's a strange coincidence that Jim leaves me—leaves both our marriage and the marital home—and then resigns? We have no forwarding address, no means of contacting him. I don't think it takes a data scientist to figure out Jim knows exactly what's happening here. I think you need to be proactive, and call the police. Otherwise you'll be the one facing the consequences."

I can hear his sighs as clearly as if I were standing next to him.

"Just do it, Terry."

"Okay, thanks Emma. I'll keep you posted."

Now if Jim's body would kindly wash up somewhere, that would be even better.

"Are you listening, Emma?" Sam asks, not unkindly.

I shake my head. "Sorry, with one ear only. I got distracted by that call."

"That's all right. I know you have to go, but will I see you tomorrow?"

He grins, and I can't help doing the same.

"Sure."

24

Nick's book launch is a trendy affair that takes place in a groovy restaurant in Soho. I bet Nick insisted; it wouldn't surprise me. He fits right in, with his black turtleneck in the middle of summer. At least there's a bar. From that perspective, this is better than having a launch in a bookstore. I may be watching my alcohol consumption, but there are limits.

There are many people here I know, like Gusek, the first person to interview me after I published *Long Grass Running*. He winks at me and makes me laugh. I see many reviewers and writers that I've met. The place is like a who's who of the publishing world, and I wish all this was for me, but soon I too will have a book. It will be a great book, and I will have my own book launch and Nick the Prick is already not invited. I don't care what Frankie says.

It's a bit awkward being here by myself, but Frankie has spotted me and is waving for me to come over. I push my way through the crowd.

"Em, come, let's take a picture," he says.

There's a photographer here, as there would be.

"Hello, Emma, it's great to see you again," Nick smirks, shaking my hand. I want to rush to the bathroom and wash it, but then again I'd hate for him to think it was appropriate to kiss me. He repulses me.

"You're feeling better?" he asks, eyebrows arched as per usual. "I couldn't find you yesterday after you rushed off."

"Yes, I had to. I know that old hag." I shake my head. "She's my stalker."

"Is she?" he blurts, mouth forming a perfect "O."

"Nick, if you hadn't come when you did, I would have had to call security. She follows me everywhere, begs for my autograph, then berates me if I don't give it to her." I raise my index finger and make a circle near my temple.

"Oh no! Emma! That's terrible! Have you told the police?"

"God no, did you see her? She's an old lady, I can't do that. She's obviously got mental issues. She liked you, though, I thought."

He blinks.

"Just keep an eye out. I hope she doesn't start to stalk you. She always makes a scene."

"Come, come, you two." Frankie gathers us on either side of him, his arms around both our shoulders. He's like a proud parent. The photographer takes pictures. Nick tries his best not to look terrified, clearly pondering the prospect of being stalked by a crazy old lady, which is nice. Still, I can't wait to wriggle my way out of here.

Frankie and Nick take their place on the low stage, where two stools have been set up, with a small round side table and microphones. It's very trendy, like I said.

"We're absolutely thrilled to be here today, everyone," Frankie says, "and I'm proud to introduce Nicholas Hackett, who of course none of you have ever heard of."

The crowd titters. I zone out, otherwise I'll puke.

I retreat to the bar.

"Emma? Is that you?"

I turn. She looks vaguely familiar, and I plaster a smile on my face while I try to place her, but she beats me to it.

"Natasha," she says, extending a hand. "We met at Craig Barnes's party, oh, it must be two years ago at least, so don't feel bad if you can't remember."

I shake her hand. I do remember her now, and I'd liked her. She was a friend of Beatrice's, although there was a strange energy between them. As if they'd been close once, but no longer.

"Hi, Natasha, how are you?"

"Oh, you know, alive," she laughs, and then her hand flies to her mouth. "Oh God, how clumsy of me," she says, and for a second I don't know what she's talking about.

Nicholas is speaking now. "I just want to say, I'm so lucky to be working with Badosa Press. They're the best publishers in the world, as far as I'm concerned!"

The crowd laughs and I can't believe they're taken in. *He's not humble, for God's sake, he's playing you. He's a fake, a fraud, and a phony, and you're all falling for it.* I'm disgusted. I raise an eyebrow at Natasha, who smiles at me. I think we understand each other.

"Would you like a drink?" I ask her, noticing that she doesn't have a glass, let alone a full one, and I don't understand what the point of coming to one of these things would be were it not for the free drinks.

"Yes, I'd love one. Whatever you're having."

I turn to the bartender and ask for two glasses of white wine.

I hand one to Natasha. "There. Cheers."

"Cheers."

We both take a sip and exchange pleasantries, and then she says, "I've been delighted to follow your success, Emma. I think when we first met you'd been shortlisted for the Poulton Prize. Are you working on anything new?"

Funny, I used to hate that question. Now I love it.

"Yes, I am. Working on another novel, as it happens."

"Wonderful, I hope it goes well."

"Thank you. And you?"

"The usual. I show with my gallery, it follows its course, I can't complain."

I must be getting a little tipsy, because otherwise I'd never ask what comes out of my mouth next.

"I do remember when we first met, Beatrice introduced me. But the two of you, I don't know, there was something off. She seemed a bit uncomfortable. Did you have a falling out? Not that it's any of my business."

"No, that's fine. Yes, we did somewhat, although I never quite understood why. She had this crazy idea. She wanted me to say that I wrote her book or something. I don't know."

She flaps a hand in the air and my heart stops. It just stops. Completely. Then it restarts, and it's going at five hundred beats per minute. I feel myself going red, I feel my heart climbing up my throat. I put my hand to it, in a manner I hope is natural.

"I know," she says, mistaking my gesture for consternation, and again she flaps a hand in the air. "It was stupid. I didn't know what she wanted me to do, or why she was asking me, but I said no, obviously. 'What would I want with your book, Beatrice? I'm a painter. What would I do something like that for?'"

I turn to the bar and gulp the rest of my drink before handing it to the barman and asking for a refill.

I turn to face her again. "So what happened then?" I ask, through the thumping of my heart.

"Nothing." She shrugs. "But she was never the same after that. It was as if she couldn't forgive me for turning her down. You probably never experienced that side of her, but she could be very selfish, Beatrice."

"Really?" I ask, bemused.

"Yes, surprising I know, since she was also so generous and wonderful and all those things that made Beatrice who she was, but trust me, if she didn't get her way, you were persona non grata."

"Huh!"

"Anyway, that's all in the past." She flaps her hand again.

I want to ask her if she knew the book Beatrice wanted her to say she wrote, but she couldn't have. Otherwise, she would have known, well, everything about me, essentially.

"I don't know if she ever found someone to do that for her," she says, echoing my own thoughts. "Whatever *that* was, because to be honest, I still don't understand it."

"No, neither do I." I take another long sip. I look around for someone I know, anyone. I want to catch someone's eye and pretend I've been called away. I do catch someone's eye. Someone I had not expected to see here.

Sam is talking to someone, but he's seen me. He smiles at me and makes a gesture to indicate he'll come over.

"I'm not surprised she never asked you," Natasha says.

"No?" I turn back toward her, taking another sip.

"You're a writer, you see. She wanted someone who wasn't a writer, someone with no aspirations of their own, at least in that department." She shakes her head. "I don't mind saying, Emma, I think Beatrice had a tendency to use people."

"Really?"

"I shouldn't speak ill of the dead, I'll stop now." She puts a hand on my forearm and smiles, and I do too; what else can I do, since I'm speechless?

"Except maybe Hannah, her agent!" she continues, eyes wide, like she just remembered a juicy bit of gossip. "What about that? I fell off my chair when I found out she killed Beatrice. I mean, of all people! God! I never met her—did you?"

"Me?"

"Emma, I forgot to say! Congratulations!" Nick has materialized by my side, he's touching my elbow, and it's all I can do not to throw my arms around him.

"What for, Nick? Oh, this is Natasha, by the way."

"Oh, hello, I'm a great admirer of your work," he tells her.

"You know Natasha's artwork?" I blurt out, incredulous.

178

He turns to me. "Doesn't everyone?"

"Thank you," Natasha says, "that's kind of you. And congratulations on your book launch."

He takes an exaggerated bow, a grand gesture, complete with one arm at the front and one arm at the back, and I want to knee him in the face. How's *that* for theatrics, Nick? But I'm so grateful he's interrupted our previous conversation that I leave him alone.

"Congratulations on the *New Yorker* article, Emma." He doesn't exactly grin, it's sort of a self-satisfied smile; his lips turned in slightly, the corners raised high.

"Thank you, Nick. I didn't realize it was out already."

"Oh, it's not. Frankie told me about it and I have a friend who works there. He emailed it to me. Oh, you don't mind, do you? Was it all right for me to read it early? It's hitting the stands this week. I should have waited until then. I hope you don't mind?"

Is this guy completely crazy? Or is it just that he'll go to any lengths to make everything all about himself?

Someone touches Natasha on the back of her shoulder and she exclaims with delight at whoever it is.

"What's this about?" Sam's voice asks behind me. He puts a hand on the small of my back. I turn around in such way that his hand falls away. I smile back, a question in my eyes. He leans in and whispers in my ear, "Fancy meeting you here."

"Oh, Emma has an interview in the *New Yorker*. It's coming out Monday," Nick says, helpfully.

"Congratulations," Sam says, with genuine enthusiasm.

See, that's how it's done, Nick. That's what sincerity looks like.

"Thank you. It's for the series they're running on Poulton winners." I say that last bit looking straight at Nick, who still has that stupid smile on his face.

"And of course it's all right," I tell him, while planning how I can kill Frankie in the most painful way imaginable. "Why wouldn't it be all right? We're all, you know, together, working with the best publisher in the world, after all."

He raises his eyes and puts a hand on his chest to illustrate his great relief. I can't tell if he's making fun of me, or if he really believes it looks, I don't know, adorable?

"Well, I can't wait for you to read it. It's wonderful! It's very you, Emma. They really captured the essence of you! You'll be so pleased."

"Thanks Nick!" I say, turning to Sam so as to give him my full attention.

"What are you doing here?" I ask.

"I'm here for a book launch. What are you doing here?"

I laugh. Of course, why wouldn't he be here? We work in the same industry. I just feel more than a little uncomfortable showing the world how well we know each other.

"Can I get you another glass of wine? What are you drinking?" he asks, touching my cheek. I flick my head away.

"Please don't," I say softly.

He lets his hand fall back down. "Sorry," he says, just as I catch from the corner of my eye the smirk on Nick's lips, looking right at us.

25

When I wake up on Monday morning, the first thought that comes into my mind is how perfect it is, that the *New Yorker* article should come out so soon after that embarrassing debacle at Williams-Sonoma. I couldn't have planned it better myself. I don't know if Nick believed my little stalker story, but he looked like he did, so let's hope. I chuckle to myself at the thought of him running away from every little old lady he comes across. God! I wish he'd take his snobbery and his pseudo-intellectualism and his black turtlenecks and jump in the Hudson River.

It's wonderful! It's very you, Emma. They really captured the essence of you! Oh, was it all right I read it before you did?

He must have been *so* jealous to bring it up like that; having to show how happy he was for me.

Well, Nick the Prick will have to wallow in his jealousy for a while longer yet, crushed by the realization that I'm not just a better writer—after all, there's only one of us who's won the Poulton, and, as far as I know, it's not him—but also the more famous. Let him think about that for a while, then he can jump in the Hudson.

I dress quickly and go downstairs to the newsstand and purchase a copy. I'm a little disappointed to see I'm not on the cover, even though I told myself it was unlikely.

"There's an article about me in there," I tell the man who takes my change.

"Really? You're famous?"

"I am. Emma Fern." I tap the magazine. "Take a look when you have time."

"Will do!" he says, brightly.

Back at the kitchen table I flip through the pages until I find it.

> In our Poulton Prize winner series: Emma Fern, or
> don't judge a book by its cover.
> By Al Gonski

I am tingling with anticipation. Take that, Nick the Prick.

> I need to reread *Long Grass Running*.

Good idea, that's great, tell your readers, Al. I could use the extra sales, that's for sure.

> *Long Grass Running* was a surprise win, being
> only the second time that a novel by a first-time
> author received the gong. I can still taste the feel-
> ing of discovery I experienced when I first read it. A
> revelation. A story so sweet and so delicately told,
> playing with time as if—

And I skip through that part since I already know the story.

> But meeting Emma Fern has taught me that some-
> times, there is no correlation between writing a
> great novel and one's ability to express oneself.
> Listening to Ms. Fern talk about her upcoming

> novel is as confusing as reading the subway map.
> And yes, that's the intended analogy: it's impos-
> sible not to get lost.

I have to read that last part again, because I think I've got it wrong. Then I read the rest, and frankly, I never want to think of it again or remember a single word of it.

I'm so angry. It's not actively ruthless or cruel, but it makes me sound like I'm "on the spectrum," as they say. I can write a magnificent novel—and at least he acknowledges that, repeatedly—but you'd never know it, talking to me. He doesn't say it in so many words, but he implies it.

There's a sentence about me having a "shrine to myself" in my office. They even have a picture of my corkboard, for Christ's sake! That has to be the most obnoxious line in the entire piece. I know what a shrine looks like. My mother had one, to the Virgin Mary. Nothing fancy, but on the dresser in her bedroom, she had a small statue of Mary, with a rosary that hung loosely around it, and a couple of candles. She never lit them when I was around, but sometimes when I came home from school and she was there, I could smell the wax. I found out that later that it was a shrine. My corkboard, with a few odds and ends from Lord knows how long ago, tidbits that were too small to make it into my scrapbook, is not a shrine. I don't pray in front of it, for God's sake. Unless *please God give me inspiration* when I sit at my desk counts.

But the worst part, the very worst part of the article, is the bit about me supposedly being reluctant to discuss the influence that Beatrice had on the novel itself. That hurts the most. I told him what influence she had. I discussed it at length. I remember that very well. And anyway, she was a crime fiction writer, so what did he think her "influence" would have been? That I should have killed those characters in the first chapter and then spent the rest of the novel figuring out who'd done it?

Does he think that would have earned me a Poulton Prize? That's what happens to me when I read garbage like this. I forget Beatrice wrote it in the first place. And anyway, I wrote a book about that. What else does he want from me? I thought the interview was supposed to be about me, call me crazy.

That's the problem with *New Yorker* writers. They wish they could write a novel and then win the Poulton. Except that I'm the Poulton Prize–winning author, and you're on the byline, Al.

I should have had coffee before I picked up this piece of garbage, but I make myself a cup now, thinking about what Nick said the other night. *It's very you, Emma. They really captured the essence of you!* What an awful man he is, with his arched eyebrows and fake solicitude. What did I ever do to him, anyway?

My phone buzzes. Before I look at it, I know it's Frankie.

Frankie doesn't even mention the article over the phone when I pick up. He calls to ask me out to lunch, and because I told him I had some chapters to show him.

"I thought you wanted me to deal with—what was his name? Waleed? Exclusively. He's in charge of my novel now, you said."

"But I'm asking you to lunch, and that trumps it," he says.

"Lunch it is. I'll bring the chapters, but they're on a USB stick. Shall I email them first?"

"Just bring them to the office. I want to read them with you there. So we can deconstruct," he says, which makes me laugh.

I know the article will come up, and I also know he doesn't want to put me on the spot. He's more interested in the future. But I don't have such qualms.

"I'm going to put in a complaint, Frankie," I say. "It's really too appalling. Who does this Al Gonski think he is? Do they have a complaint process at the *New Yorker*? Because I'm not letting this pass. I bet you anything the little twerp hates women. Some men are like that, you know?"

"Slow down, Emma. Stop. You're overthinking it. It wasn't that bad."

"Yes it was."

"No, it was fine! It made you sound, I don't know, interesting."

"Interesting? Really? Thanks for nothing, Frankie."

"Stop it. You know what I mean. You can't be pigeonholed. You're too remarkable for that."

"Thank you."

"You're welcome. And I mean it. You worry too much about what people think. He made you sound really interesting, you know. You're reading too much into it."

I sigh. "I believe you're just saying that, but I'll let it pass."

"Come to lunch. I want to read what you've got."

"Apparently what I've got is a subway map."

"Shut up, Emma, and get over here."

"There you are. Don't say I never give you anything."

Frankie looks up, surprised to see me standing there. He was so engrossed in whatever he was doing, he didn't hear me come into his office until I dropped the USB stick ceremoniously on his desk from a great height.

"Tell me this is what I think it is," he says.

"This is what you think it is."

He stands up. "Can I look?"

"That's what it's there for."

I love Frankie. He's already displaying such enthusiasm about it. After the article in the *New Yorker*, he could have been distrustful, to put it mildly, about my ability to deliver. What did that awful man say about my story? *It's like reading the New York subway map, no matter how hard you try, you're still lost.* Or words to that effect.

But Frankie has made it clear that he trusts me. And why shouldn't he? I rescued his publishing firm with *Long Grass Running*. He would be bankrupt without me.

"I know it's going to be good," he says, "and don't worry about that article, okay? It's not you, it's him."

"That I can agree with."

He puts the USB stick in the slot and opens the document, and I can see his confusion at first, because of that very clever opening of Sam's, the backward effect, but I don't give instructions, and I can see from the sequence of expressions on his face that Frankie figures it out pretty quickly, just like I did. When he looks up, he has a funny expression on his face, his head turned slightly sideways.

I take the seat in front of the desk.

Okay, maybe it wasn't a really clever opening paragraph. Maybe I was already in lust when I read it. Maybe it's a stupid idea. I'm very nervous now. Frankie is the first to read it. Did I put too much store in Sam? Is he even for real? Maybe he made it all up—the website, everything. It's very convenient, when you think about it, being a ghostwriter.

Oh yes, I've had at least eleven titles on the New York Times *bestseller list. Which ones? Sorry, that would be telling. Just take my word for it.*

Now I can't believe I've been so stupid. Surely I could have asked for some references at least. There must be something out there for him to prove what he says is true. But no, not me, I'm too busy believing anything anyone says. It's what always gets me in trouble. It's what Beatrice did to me, back then, when she tricked me into—

"It's wonderful." Frankie beams.

I actually put a hand on my heart and it's beating so fast. I love him. I love Frankie again with all my heart and he loves me, I can tell, again, with all his heart, and for this moment, all is right with the world, as we beam at each other. I stand and lean over the desk and take his face in my hands and I squeeze it as I kiss him.

"Okay, okay, thank you, that's good, you can stop now," he says through pursed lips.

I laugh and clap my hands in excitement. "You really love it?"

He stands abruptly. "Yes! I love it, Em! You did it!" And I'm so happy that we jump, and hoot, and whoop, and it's so much fun, and his secretary comes in and says, "Are you okay in there?" but we don't stop jumping, and he hugs me and I hug him, and life is simply perfect.

"How much is there?"

I take a while to get my breath back, after these exertions. "Fifteen chapters."

"Where's the rest?"

"It's coming."

He gives me that sly look again.

"It is! I swear it! I'm frantically working on it, Frankie, but I wanted to show you what we've—what I've got. I knew you'd love it."

"You swear you're working on it?"

"Do you love it?"

"I love it. Do you swear?"

"I swear. Cross my heart and hope to die!"

"Don't say that, just promise me."

"I promise."

"I love it, Em. It's amazing."

"Isn't it? Oh, I'm so pleased, Frankie, for all of us. I mean that."

"I know. I can't tell you what it means to me, Em. I was worried, I can tell you."

"What, that I was a one-hit wonder?"

"Don't say that. I would never think that about you. You're the most talented person I know."

"Thank you, and I'm sorry, but it wasn't easy. You understand, don't you? With Beatrice dying and all that."

"Of course I do. I need to see the rest, though, before I love you too much. When do you think?"

"What about Waleed?"

"After I read the first draft, then you can deal with Waleed."

"Okay. Well, since it's going very well, I'd say a few weeks."

"I'll take that as a few months then. But really, I'm so pleased, Em. I can't wait to get started on this."

"Me too."

"Welcome back, Emma Fern," he says as he hugs me again, then he releases me and says, grabbing his jacket from the back of his chair, "Let's celebrate. I'm taking you to lunch."

"Yum! Where to?"

"The Tavern," he says, helping me put on my coat.

"Wow, that's special!"

"Nothing but the best for you, my dear."

I lightly punch his shoulder. My phone rings, and without thinking I pull it out from my pocket and take the call.

"Hi, Mrs. Fern? This is Charlie from Avis Car Rentals. How are you today?"

I make a face at Frankie, shaking my head.

"I'm fine, thanks, but I'm busy and trying to get out the door, so if you're selling anything—"

"Oh sure, sorry to disturb you, it's just that you left a cell phone in the car you rented on Wednesday. I've put it safely in the office ready to be picked up, when do you think—"

"Excuse me?"

"Your cell phone. You left it in the glove compartment."

But I can't hear him very well, probably because of the sudden rush of blood in my ears. It makes his voice sound as if it's traveling through cotton wool. Thick. Distant.

I say nothing. I'm afraid that if I speak it will become real, this impossible scenario. I'm going to be sick. I need to be very still and not breathe, and then maybe he will go away, the man from Avis. He will realize he has made a mistake. He will apologize and say goodbye and go away.

"Are you still there, Mrs. Fern?"

I try to swallow. "How did you get this number?"

"Hmm, that's the number we have on file. It's the number you gave us when you filled out the rental contract. That's why I didn't call you sooner. I thought you'd come and get it. We assumed that was the cell phone we had on file for you, so there was no point in calling you, but seeing as you didn't come to retrieve it, I thought I'd give your number a try. Is there a problem? I can call you back on a different number if you like."

"I think there's been some mistake."

Please, God. Please let there be some mistake.

"I'm sorry?"

"I didn't rent a car."

"This is Mrs. Fern, right? Mrs. Emma Fern?"

"Yes."

"I have the paperwork right here, Mrs. Fern. You rented a white Buick Verano last Wednesday. Returned it the next day."

26

My hand is shaking. This is not good. I'm completely confused, and I'm frightened. I had to make my excuses. *I'm not well*, I said. Lame excuse, but what else could I do? There was no way I could go through lunch pretending nothing was wrong. Frankie was disappointed, but, as always, he was understanding.

"Call me later, okay?" he said, putting me in a cab. "Get some rest."

I have to lie down when I get home, because I think I'm going insane. People tell me I have done things, but I have no recollection of them. I did not rent a car last Wednesday. And yet it seems I did.

I remember how clean the car was. I even commented on it. I thought to myself, *Carol must be very fastidious, she clearly takes very good care of her things.*

I try to remember any stickers on the windshield. Don't rental cars display something on the windshield? But I didn't pay attention. I had my head down. I kept my sunglasses on the entire time. I just wanted to be let off where we agreed and go from there.

I said I'd call him back, Charlie from Avis, that I had to hang up, I couldn't stay on the phone, but he said, "No need, just come by the office whenever you like, same office you rented the car from. Midtown."

Four blocks from where I live.

Of course I'm not going there. Why should I? I didn't rent the car. They might think I did, but I'm not the one who fronted up and filled in the paperwork, and anyway, don't they need a driver's license? It's the law, surely, to check the ID of the person renting the car, otherwise anyone can rock up and pretend to be someone else—

I spring from my bed and almost run to my purse, sitting on top of the counter, in the kitchen. I empty its contents and grab my wallet. I open it, my hands shaking.

It's not there. It's always in the same place, in the pocket on the left side. I would have it behind the little clear plastic pocket, but it never quite fitted there, so I've always put it in the pocket behind that. Except it's not there now. I go through every pocket, thoroughly. I pull out all my credit cards, the bits of receipts I've been accumulating since God knows when, the business cards I've collected for one reason or another. I flick through everything again but I already know I won't find it. It's always in the same place, and I haven't needed to pull it out for any reason. Someone else did, I'm sure of it. And that person used it to rent a car in my name.

I can't breathe. I can't think. I have to pull myself together and make sense of this.

I didn't rent the car. I couldn't forget something like that, for God's sake. So it could only be Carol. Who else? She must have taken my wallet when we met, and taken my license. When? Did I leave my bag unattended? I can't remember. We only met twice. I replay each scene in my mind, but I can't remember. Then I remember, she wanted to get some soda or something, but didn't have any cash and she took my wallet.

Really? She engineered that situation to take my driver's license from my wallet? Why would she do that? I wish I could call her. But of course I can't. She doesn't have the disposable phone anymore, because

I left it in the glove compartment and forgot to tell her. She must think I still have it. I wonder why she doesn't call me for it? Or has she not noticed?

What's Carol trying to achieve? By hiring the car in my name? She was supposed to bring her car, for Christ's sake. I go through it in my mind again, the plan. It went like this: Carol takes Jim on a boat trip, ostensibly to discuss their escape, away from prying eyes, because he's a paranoid psycho. Or was.

I dressed like him, so that it would look like Jim and Carol, the happy lovers, came back from their little trip and then she dropped him off, at his request, and he was never seen again. His body will wash up eventually, and then all will be clear: Jim went back to the sea and drowned himself. A tragedy, but not unexpected if you have all the facts. Me, I have nothing to do with any of this. When the police come calling, and they will, I'll make clear that I haven't seen nor heard from him in weeks.

She must have reported him missing by now. The police will be in touch any minute. How is that going to look? If she rented the car in my name? And why would Carol rent a car anyway? She's got a perfectly good car. She told me she used it to go to D.C. and back that day we met for the last time. So what's the point in renting another one? And now, by doing something so stupid as to use my driver's license to rent the car, she's put both of us in danger of being discovered. It wasn't part of the plan, for God's sake.

Both of us?

Wait. Wait, wait, wait, wait.

No.

My head hurts. It's throbbing.

No, it can't be. That's not possible.

I drop my head in my hands and close my eyes, trying to stop the wave of nausea from rising. I go back over every minute detail. Jim and

Carol, the happy lovers, did not come back together to the marina, laughing and kissing for all to see. No, Carol made sure that "Jim" came back on his own, except that "Jim" was wearing a hat that he didn't have when he first got there, and a blue windbreaker that I'd put money on that he'd never laid his eyes upon.

I didn't look like Jim at all. I was just some guy leaning against a barrier by himself. Which means only Carol came back.

On her own.

Carol, who told me exactly what she would be wearing, in detail, down to the logo on her cap, so that we could match our outfits completely. So that when I went to take the cooler to the boat, it wasn't Emma, it was Carol. Then everyone saw Carol and Jim together, going to the boat. So if anyone had seen Carol take the cooler earlier—and that was unlikely considering the time of day and the lack of people around—but for argument's sake, if anyone had seen her, and then later Carol and Jim going to the boat, they would have simply assumed that Carol came back after dropping off the cooler.

Carol, who looked like my twin.

Carol, who looked so much like me, anyone would have thought it *was* me. My chest hurts now. It's hard to breathe.

Carol was never there.

Only Emma was there, Emma who rented the car. Emma, who, I'd wager my meager life savings on, also rented the boat. And Jim?

Jim did not come back at all. The only time "Carol and Jim" were together after the boat trip was in the parking lot, and in the car. And if anyone saw us, it won't mean anything. We no longer looked like the same people who went in.

So the story goes like this: Emma and Jim went on a boat trip, and Emma came back alone.

I've been set up.

◆ ◆ ◆

How could I have been so stupid? I slam my palms against my forehead, over and over, until it hurts. How could I possibly have fallen for this?

Carol came looking for me. *You have to help me. Please help me*, she said in her little-girl voice, and I, Emma, the stupidest person on the planet, said, *You need my help? You've got it*. Sure, the fact that Jim was holding that stupid text from Beatrice over my head didn't help.

I don't regret the killing part. He had to die. He really was crazy, and he was going to tell everyone that I'd killed Beatrice and I didn't write my first book. He was warming up to that, I could tell.

God. I feel sick. I'm shaking. I need to do something but I don't know what to do, so I just sit and shake.

Can I steal this car rental contract from Avis? Could I go there and distract them and take the paperwork?

No. I'm not going to Avis in Midtown. I can't be seen there. I have to report my driver's license as stolen. I'll say that I have some idea who stole it, this strange woman I met who *needed my help,* and I never saw her again, but now my driver's license is missing. *Et voilà*!

I wish I understood why she'd do this to me. We killed him. He's not going to hurt her anymore. Why screw up the plan? I've got a headache. I need to go back to bed.

What about the phone? What does it mean for me that Avis has it in their possession?

She didn't know I put her disposable phone in the glove compartment. There was nothing personal in there. So why would she look? Does she even realize it's missing? If she does, she's not necessarily going to assume it's in the car. She would have checked everything else about that car. Maybe she hasn't noticed yet. It's just a throwaway phone.

But I know.

I know she rented the car in my name.

I think I should get that phone, because it's her phone. That phone was a genuine ploy, to avoid calls showing up on hers. Christ, I thought she was so smart, that it was a wise idea. Well, she is smart; I'll give her that.

But she bought it. I wonder if you have to provide some form of ID when you get one of those phones? That would be very incriminating. Whose ID did she provide anyway? Mine?

Oh God.

I have to get that phone back.

27

I need to think straight. I need to stay focused. *Breathe. Just breathe. Now think.*

If the police get involved, it won't be long before they realize that since that boat trip, Jim hasn't used his credit cards or his cell phone; that he has disappeared, and jeez, I wonder what his estranged wife has been up to lately?

I need to call Terry. Oh God.

My fingers tremble as I find the number. Why is everything so hard?

"Emma! Any news?" Terry says, almost shouts, as soon as he picks up the call.

"No, nothing." I try to keep my tone just this side of calm. "That's why I'm calling you. I thought you might have heard from Jim?" I put this to him as a question.

"Not a word," he sighs. "I'm really worried, Emma."

"I know, me too. Have you spoken to his mother yet?"

"No. I've been putting it off. Sorry. I don't mind admitting it."

God, don't apologize. I almost say it out loud. This is such good news. If Terry calls Moira, she'll be beside herself. *My son is my sun,* is what she used to say to me. I used to think that was really sweet. Groan.

But if Terry tells her he's concerned, she'll be at the police station filling out a missing person's report before Terry ends the call. And I can't have that. I'm pretty sure Carol hasn't reported Jim missing yet, because she thinks I have her burner phone, and she wants to get it back first. With my name on the rental car, I can't have anyone reporting Jim missing right now. Not until I figure out what to do.

I wonder if Jim told Moira he left me? I think she would have called me if he had. We sure weren't the best of friends, but she was always kind to me.

"What about the police? Did you speak to them?" I ask. I close my eyes in silent prayer.

"I was thinking of calling them," Terry says. "I thought I'd wait. I know, Emma, you said I should, but—"

"No, wait. I remembered something. That's why I'm calling."

"What's that?"

"When Jim left, he said he was going away for a while." I feel under such pressure that I can't think of anything else to say.

"You're kidding."

"No, I'm not."

"You only just remembered? What else did he say?"

Terry is annoyed with me now. I think he's the only person who is genuinely worried, seriously worried, about his friend.

"Look, it was hard, okay? Some terrible things were said, and not by me. When Jim left, he was upset, and so was I. I didn't really register too much of that night; it's all a bit of a blur." I sound peevish, but what can I do? I'm so desperate right now, I feel like I need to stop the world. Christ.

"Sorry," Terry says, "I shouldn't have snapped at you."

"No, I understand."

"Did he say where he was going?"

I sigh. I want to sound as if I'm thinking back to our imaginary conversation.

"No, I don't think so, but under the circumstances—I mean, we're both worried about him—I've been going back over our last words, and he did say something like, 'Don't come looking for me. I won't be around.'"

Even to my ears this sounds completely idiotic. Not to mention false, off-key. But I'm banking on the fact that Terry is a friend and that he trusts me, so even if his instincts tell him that my conveniently recovered memories are a little lame, he won't pay attention.

"Don't you think that sounds . . . ominous? Isn't that some kind of cry for help?"

"Oh Lord, no! It wasn't like that! No it was more like, 'I'm going away for a while, somewhere nice'"—*should I have said that?*—"'and I don't want you to look for me.' I think that's what he meant, you know? Like he needed some time to think. In fact, I'm pretty sure that's what he said. Yes, that's what he said—that he needed some time to think and was going away for a few weeks."

"Jesus, Emma, couldn't you have remembered that before? I've been going crazy here, even without the audit, which is beyond serious, believe me, but nothing is so serious as someone's well-being. I've been extremely concerned about Jim's mental health."

Mental health. That's one way of putting it. Does being a dangerous psychopath fall under the umbrella of mental health? Probably.

"I'm really sorry. I don't know what to say. But it's good news, isn't it?" Lord, I'm so bad at this.

"Emma, there's something else. Carol called me."

I take a sharp breath, but I don't dare speak.

"Are you there?" Terry asks.

"Yes." I breathe out, my chest feels tight. "When did Carol call? What did she say?"

"Thursday night. Look, Emma, it's not my place, okay? And I'm really sorry, but it sounds like she was expecting Jim to turn up there. I don't know."

"What did she say?"

"They've been seeing each other. He's staying with her. I'm just telling you what she said. But she's worried."

Oh my God. My mind is reeling. Why would Carol call Terry the day after? It makes no sense. She was supposed to wait two days, and then call the police.

"Did she say anything else?"

His short silence tells me that she did. Then he says, "I wouldn't worry about it. She's not exactly impartial, if Jim and her are, you know . . ."

"What did she say, Terry?"

He sighs. "She said Jim was concerned about your state of mind."

"Oh? That's it?"

"That he was worried you might do something."

"Do something? Like what, hurt myself?"

"No, hurt him."

I can't breathe. Everything is happening too fast and I can't make any sense of it.

"Fuck her!" I snap, and I can hear Terry's intake of breath. "I mean, why would she say such a thing? It's a lie, Terry."

"I know it is."

"What gives her the right to be so concerned?" I continue, outraged. "It's no business of hers, is it? She has no business meddling in our lives."

"I know, you've got a point."

"I do. I mean, who does that? Makes a big fuss just because he doesn't show up at her place? For Christ's sake! Isn't that a little strange?"

"Maybe."

"Maybe?"

"Yes, all right, it is a little strange."

"Obviously she wants him back. Now that we've separated. She's spreading lies. About me, and about Jim."

"I don't know what to say."

"I'll tell you what to say, Terry." I must sound shrill, I'm so angry. "Listen to me. Jim told me he needed time out. Give it a few more days. It's a stressful time for him, and he's your friend!" I almost shout that last bit, aware that I made the complete opposite argument the last time we spoke. But my God! Carol calling Terry? That wasn't in the plan. *Oh, I'm so worried.* Yeah, you should be. You killed him.

Breathe, Emma. Breathe.

"Give it a few more days," I say in the most reasonable tone I can muster. "He deserves the chance to redeem himself. We have to afford him that dignity, Terry. It's the least we can do."

I feel like such a bitch. I'm repeating his words back to him, words of kindness from a true friend, and here I am appropriating them for myself.

"Yeah, okay, Emma, but I'm worried. If I don't hear from him by—"

"Friday, Terry. Promise me. End of the week. Okay? Give him that much, for Christ's sake. And don't worry his parents unnecessarily, please." God, I sound so ridiculous. I can tell how hard this is for him.

"Yeah, okay. Friday," he says. "But you keep in touch, all right? The moment you hear from him—"

"You'll be the first to know. I promise. And, Terry, don't speak to Carol again. It's none of her business." I was going to add *she's poison* but think better of it.

"Yeah, all right."

Christ! That was a close call.

◆ ◆ ◆

It's not Charlie at the Avis counter, it's Mike. Mike is very helpful, very sorry they didn't call sooner, but as Charlie explained, they assumed this was the contact number they had on file, and they expected me to inquire earlier. I assure him that's fine and I understand. I mumble something about it being a spare phone and I don't even remember why I brought it along. He nods, then goes to a back room, to their lost and found property holder. He returns with the phone wrapped in a plastic bag, a yellow Post-it note stapled to the top. I can make out what I guess to be the registration number and my name.

I thought briefly of putting my other wig on, my Jackie Collins black wig, but what's the point? What if someone remembered me from that day? "That's funny, you don't look anything like the Mrs. Fern who rented the car from us." Wouldn't that be awkward? I may as well look like Carol, who looked like me.

"Can I see some ID, please? Driver's license will do."

"Ah, as it happens, I recently lost my driver's license."

"Really? Sorry to hear that, I hate when that happens."

"Tell me about it."

"Do you have anything else? I can't just hand you the phone, Mrs. Fern. No offense, but we have—"

"That's fine, I understand, I appreciate that."

I go through my wallet, looking for something that I can use instead.

"What about the credit card you used to pay for the rental?" he says.

"The credit card?"

No, please God, I had assumed she paid with cash. I quickly run through the contents of my wallet. I can't believe it! She stole my credit card!

He checks the contract: "Visa, ends in 0144."

I find it! The only credit card I carry. How is that possible? I pull it out to show him.

He takes it and looks at it closely, matching the details with whatever he has on the screen.

"That's all good. Here."

He hands the card back to me, and picks up the package with the cell phone in it.

"So I used this credit card"—I'm holding it up—"to pay?" I'm shaking, so I quickly lower my hand again.

"Yep, that's the one we have."

"That's odd."

He shrugs. "It went through fine. We wouldn't have accepted it if it had been rejected for lack of funds."

"No, what I mean is, I don't usually carry it with me. I just happen to have it. I forgot I used it, I guess."

"Oh, that's because you paid over the phone, remember?"

Over the phone?

"Ah yes, of course. Thank you. I'm having one of those days." I smile.

"Well, no harm done. I hope you find your driver's license, Mrs. Fern. And maybe you shouldn't be driving anymore."

"Why?"

He taps his temple. "If you're having trouble remembering, you know." He shakes his head. Wonderful. Now he thinks I'm suffering from dementia.

I take the phone from him. There's a part of me that hopes Carol will realize it's missing and call Avis. Let her sweat a little, when they tell her, "But Mrs. Fern, you already picked it up, don't you remember?" Tap, tap, on the temple.

◆　◆　◆

I don't even know why we own a filing cabinet. Who has a filing cabinet these days? Isn't everything in the Cloud? Jim always made himself out to be so technology-minded, up-to-the-minute knowledgeable, and yet you couldn't pry his fingers from that vintage piece of office furniture. It has followed us for most of our marriage, always locked, always in a corner of his space.

But when he left me, he didn't take it, of course. He could hardly lug it out in the elevator. But he didn't bother to lock it. I noticed when I checked it that there are big gaps in there now. Lord knows what used to fill those gaps, but one thing I know is that my credit card statements were mailed to me every month, and he reviewed them, paid the balance in full—*I respect that banks are out to make money, Emma, but that doesn't mean we have to throw it at them*—and I never saw them again. I assumed they found their resting place in the filing cabinet, never to see the light of day again until tax time.

It makes me so angry that he left it behind, along with the other items he didn't want, all the things that didn't matter anymore: his books; most of his clothes; his antique desk lamp, a gift from someone or other; a musical cigarette box that used to belong to his grandfather; me.

I'm rattled that my credit card was used to rent the car—*over the phone, Mrs. Fern, don't you remember?* I make a beeline for those statements the moment I get home. I'd already seen that the two bottom drawers where Jim kept his paperwork, whatever that might have been, have been emptied, but the two top drawers still had files in them, and I didn't look too closely. Until now, when I pull open the top one so hard that the entire unit almost falls over and I catch it against my chest.

There are no bank or credit card statements, not even mine. No financial information at all. He took it all with him. My credit card number was in those papers, I know it. Jim kept records of everything. That's how Carol did it, I'm sure of it. I can smell it. She found my credit card details among Jim's papers, and then used it to rent the car.

I decide to call my bank, to check the last few transactions. I should cancel the card, but then I change my mind. I don't want to raise any flags, not yet anyway, not until I know for sure what I'm dealing with.

28

I know in the back of my mind that it's the wrong thing to do, that I could do it over the phone, stay under the radar, but I do it anyway. I want to check again, to go through the motions, see if I can gather some more clues, anything. I need to know how exposed I am.

After I've been to the DMV and filled in the paperwork to get a replacement license, I go back to the same marina, the same office, ostensibly to ask whether they retrieved a ring from the boat. There's a bit of activity here this morning, and when my turn comes, I speak to a nice man, pen poised over an open ledger, ready to take my booking.

"Hi, my friend rented a sailboat, a catamaran, last Wednesday, for an overnight trip. She lost a ring, and I wondered whether it had been found?"

"A ring? Can't say that rings any bells," he quips. It takes me a moment to get the joke. I smile. "Let me take a look out back. What kind of ring was it?"

"It's a thin silver band with some sparkles."

"A diamond ring, is it?"

"Fake diamonds, lots of them, all the way around. It's not valuable, only sentimental."

He turns away from me and opens a drawer at the back of the room.

"Nope, no ring. Which boat was it?"

I describe it to him. He goes back to the ledger.

"What name?"

"McCready. Carol McCready."

He flicks a couple of pages back, runs a weathered finger down the page, then across the line.

"McCready?"

"That's right."

"Nope, there's no McCready that's taken out a boat last Wednesday. Sure that's your friend's name?"

"Could you check under the name Fern?"

He takes another look, his finger repeating its journey down the page. "Ah, looks like we have a winner," he says. "Yep, Emma Fern. That your friend? How many names does she have?"

I expected it. I knew she would have done the same thing here, reserved the boat under my name. And yet, when I hear it from him, it still makes my legs buckle a little. My head is spinning, and I find myself gripping the counter.

"Different friend," I say. "Can I take a look at the boat? In case it fell in there, somewhere?"

"I think we'd have seen it when we cleaned it, a shiny ring like that, but let me see what I can do."

He goes over to the computer farther down the counter and presses a few keys, one at a time, looking back and forth between the screen and the keyboard.

"Ah nope, can't help you there, the boat's out today."

"All right, thanks anyway."

I turn to leave and he says, behind me, "That's a shame about the ring. I'll keep an eye out for it. They seemed like a nice couple, Mr. and Mrs. Fern."

I turn back to face him. I'm clenching my jaw, my body, my fists, to stop myself from shaking.

"They came together?"

"Yes, when they rented the boat, your friend and her husband. When she dropped the key off, she said they'd been through a rough patch. She said they really wanted to get back on track. 'On an even keel,' I told her," and he chuckles again. I gather there's a boat-related joke in there somewhere.

I come back to the counter, and I ask, "Did she pay over the phone?"

"Why do you want to know that?"

"Sorry, it's my friend. She's confused about losing her things. She lost her wallet too after she came back, not here I mean, but later that day; maybe she lost the ring then, at the same time. It would be good to know what the last thing was that she bought on the card."

He really shouldn't be working in a customer service capacity, this man, because clearly he will swallow whatever lies any stranger tells him, no matter how preposterous. Sure enough, in the next instant, he's back at the computer, typing one finger at a time.

"Yeah, that's what I thought. Just as I remembered." He taps the screen with his finger.

Hook, line, and sinker.

"What is it?"

"It was paid for over the phone, yes."

"Thank you." Just as I thought.

"With Mr. Fern's credit card. So you can tell your friend, her last purchase, it wasn't here."

I stand very still, I don't breathe. Then, just as he asks, "Was there anything else?" I turn around silently and tell myself to put one foot in front of the other and get to the door.

"I hope it works out for your friend and her husband. She looked happy when she came back. She said the trip was a success. It's good to take time out to talk over things, I always say."

I've opened the door, I'm almost outside. "She's got some sense of humor, your friend," he says behind me. "I asked her if Mr. Fern had a good time and she laughed and said, 'Oh, he did, until he got what was coming to him.'"

I feel a sharp pain in the pit of my stomach. I think it's called fear.

I leave the office, keeping my head down, and walk toward the pier anyway. I want to go back to where the boat was moored. I wasn't really expecting the rental to be under Carol's name at this point, I knew it would be under mine, but it still shocked me when I heard my name. But paying for it with Jim's card? That's a stroke of genius on her part. I won't have to wait very long before I hear from the police. They'll know exactly where I've been, since it's also the last transaction on Jim's credit card, and, as far as the rental office is concerned, I was with him.

I walk back up, past the spot where I leaned on the wooden barrier waiting for Carol. It's even more crowded than it was that day, and yet it's an easy line of sight along the pier. If you walked back this way, you couldn't miss me. It's not far, and there isn't another way to go from the boat back to the office. So Carol must have come this way, and I didn't see her. Granted, I had my head down most of the time, but still, I believe I would have spotted her on the way back. Unless she changed her outfit, wore a completely different hat, different set of sunglasses. I wouldn't have been checking for a different outfit.

It floors me, the deliberate treachery that Carol has engaged in. It reeks of resentment and contempt. She must really hate me, to do this to me. Get me to do her dirty work, and then make sure I take the fall.

I make my way back to the LIRR and wait for the train. I feel like I'm outside myself, watching from above. I'm so frightened. The police are going to come for me and they're going to put me in jail for murder. They'll put me away for a very long time.

It occurs to me that this is what Carol is waiting for, before she goes to the cops. She's waiting for Jim's body to turn up, to be washed ashore. It's bound to be easier to frame me for his murder if there's a body.

All I can hope for is that the sharks were hungry that day.

◆　◆　◆

I remind myself that I am one step ahead of Carol: she set me up to take the fall for Jim's death, and as far as she's concerned, all she has to do is report Jim missing and my downfall will soon follow.

I don't think Carol knows how much I know at this point, but she must believe I have her phone.

Her phone. We exchanged texts on that phone. We discussed meeting times and places. When they haul me off to jail for the meticulous planning and carrying out of my husband's murder, does she think I'm going to keep my mouth shut? How is she going to explain those texts?

I stored that phone, still wrapped in plastic, in a drawer in my bedroom. It's still there when I go to retrieve it. Why wouldn't it be? I unwrap it, consider for a moment whether I should wear gloves before I handle it, so as to keep Carol's prints on it intact, but frankly it's too hard to operate a touchscreen phone with gloves on. What difference does it make anyway? I've already held it.

It's still on, but the battery is low. I'll need to check if my charger will fit this one, otherwise it should be easy enough to purchase another.

I press the home button and I'm greeted with a grid of numbers. It's password-protected. I angle the screen toward the window, trying to see whether there's an obvious pattern of greasy fingerprints, but no such luck. I stare at it for a while, trying to remember if Carol ever mentioned anything I could use, like, *Hey, guess what! It's my birthday today, and I always use the first four digits of my birthday as a passcode! Isn't that a coincidence?*

I try "1 2 3 4," but it doesn't work. I try "1 1 1 1." I even try my own passcode, and when I get the alert that says I only have three more attempts, I stop. I just stare at it.

She texted me on this. She used it to plan our little assignation. I have to see what's on it, because it's all I've got.

When it rings, shrill and loud, I drop it to the floor as if it were on fire.

"Sam?"

"Hey, Emma Fern, I've been thinking about you. I was wondering when I'd hear from you again."

"Yes, sorry, I've been busy." I pause. "I was just calling to . . . umm . . ."

"Everything okay?"

It's reassuring to hear his voice. It grounds me. When Carol's phone rang, I figured it must be her, so I didn't answer it. And now I feel uneasy, alone in this apartment. I need to get out. I wonder what Sam would think if I asked to stay with him.

"Are you free tonight? I was wondering if we could do something together," I ask.

"I'm having dinner with two of my closest friends. Come with me. Would you come along and meet them?"

"I'd love to join you and your friends for dinner."

"That's great, I'll let them know, and shall I pick you up at seven?"

"Yes, please. Thanks, Sam."

As I get ready for my evening out, it occurs to me what a big step it is, to take your lover to meet your closest friends. I guess Sam and I are moving forward, and it's a nice feeling.

"Our first date," he says, smiling, when I meet him downstairs. I point out to him that means we had sex not on the first date, but before our first date, and he laughs, blushing slightly.

"Tell me about your friends," I say, when we're in the taxi.

He puts his hand on my knee. "Well, Lisa and I went to college together, and—"

"Wait." I sit up abruptly. "Do they know anything about me? What we're doing together?"

"No, of course not. I told them your name, but that's about it."

I lean back. "Okay, sorry, keep going."

"Lisa has her own marketing business. Don't ask me what she does exactly, because I don't know. Something to do with social media campaigns. Akil is a lawyer. They've been married for—oh, I don't know exactly—almost twenty years."

"Wow. Any kids?"

"One. Noel, who's sixteen. No, wait, seventeen."

Sam leans closer and tilts my head toward him, with one finger, then he kisses me. A long, sweet, gentle kiss. I put my head on his shoulder, trying not to think how strange this is. But I'm happy. When all this is over, I want to be with someone kind and loving, just like Sam. I want to fill my life with people, new friends, and reconnect with old ones. I can't wait to meet Lisa and Akil.

◆ ◆ ◆

Lisa is lovely and warm when she greets me. She hugs me, which I love.

"What a charming home," I tell her, walking over to the big square windows. Their loft is on the corner of the building, so they have windows along two walls of the main room.

"Not much of a view I'm afraid, but it's nice and light during the day."

Akil however, just shakes my hand and it feels a little cold. Perfunctory, even. Especially after he hugs Sam, and the two of them engage in a ritual of backslapping and cheek-pinching. I hide my discomfort by scanning the large photo arrangement on the wall. They make me smile. They're charming. There are a handful of wedding photos where the happy couple and two friends are jumping in the air on a beach somewhere. I realize suddenly that one of the goofy and happy friends is a very young Sam. I turn to look at him, smiling. He's chatting animatedly, and I feel a warmth come over me. I want to get to know him better, and his friends too.

Going back to the photos, I realize with a start that among the many photos of Noel and his parents at various ages, there are many others with Sam, his arm around a petite woman with a dimpled smile. Happy snaps in a variety of settings. In one they're at some kind of ski resort, the four of them together, grinning in the snow, arms on each other's shoulders. In another they're on a boat, champagne glasses held high. I don't want to look at a boat, let alone at Sam's ex-wife in a bikini.

I turn away and Akil catches my eye, but his face remains blank. He hands me a glass of white wine and indicates an armchair for me to sit on. Sam takes the other one and Akil and Lisa sit together on the couch.

"Is that my phone?" I hear it ringing in my bag, which I've set down next to the couch. I start to get up.

"There you go," Lisa says, bending down to pick it up and handing it to me.

I pull the phone out, ready to turn it off.

"Everything okay?" Sam asks. I realize they're all looking at me.

"Yes, why? It's just a phone call." It's a private number again. I've had a number of missed calls like this over the last few days, displaying "private number" instead of the usual caller ID, and it doesn't take a genius to figure out that it's Carol, trying to get in touch with me. I put it on silent.

"So, how did you two meet?" Akil asks.

I turn to Sam.

"At a book launch," he says, and I breathe silently with relief, grateful for his quick thinking.

"That's nice," Lisa says. "Whose book was it?"

"Nicholas Hackett," Sam replies, as I take a sip. "He's a friend of Emma's."

I snort, spraying wine all over my hand. "Sorry, he's not a friend exactly, just someone I know through my publisher." Lisa hands me a small napkin so that I can wipe my hand.

"Oh, you told me about that book launch," Akil says. "That was just the other day, wasn't it?" he adds, looking at me.

I don't know what to say. I just smile at him, feeling a crimson blush rising in my cheeks.

"Yep," Sam says, "and we couldn't be happier." Which makes everybody laugh and lightens the moment.

The dinner is delicious, and I start to relax. I chat to Lisa about her work and then I hear Akil say to Sam, "We got a long email from Barbara the other day. Did Lisa tell you?" and Sam mumbles that yes, Lisa did, and I realize with a start that Barbara must be Sam's ex-wife.

"She's coming back next month. I can't wait to see her; to hear all about her travels," Akil continues.

Lisa shoots me an apologetic glance, and puts her hand on her husband's arm.

"We've got tickets to *Hamilton*," she says brightly, to everyone. "The musical. I have no idea what it's like, but we got free tickets. Have you seen it, Emma?"

"No, I haven't."

"We'll let you know if it's any good. Maybe you and Sam would like to see it too." She stands up and starts to clear the table.

"I'll give you a hand," I say, pushing back my chair.

"No, please, Emma. You're our guest. Sit, sit. I'll get the cheese plate."

We watch her go into the small galley kitchen and Akil gets up, grabs a bottle of red wine from a rack nearby, and opens it.

"I was thinking maybe Barbara would like to come with us, Lisa," he says to his wife, who has returned with the cheese. "It would be great to see her. She'll be back by then."

I put my glass down on the table, my jaw tight. "Is there a problem?" I ask Akil. Sam gives me a pleading look.

"No. Why? Something wrong?" Akil replies, popping a piece of cheese into his mouth.

"I don't understand why you asked me to come tonight. I don't think—"

"We didn't ask you, Emma, I'm sorry," Akil says. "Sam did. Not me."

I turn to Sam, who rubs a hand over his face, but remains silent.

"Akil, stop," Lisa says, finally.

"Why?" He turns to me again. "I'm sorry, Emma, it's nothing personal."

I smirk. "Really?"

He shakes his head. "You don't throw away sixteen years of marriage just like that." He clicks his fingers, looking at Sam. "You two have only just met. I don't want to—"

"Never mind," I say, standing up. I turn to Lisa, who looks crestfallen. "Thank you, Lisa. The dinner was delicious."

Sam gets up too, thank God, because for a moment I thought I'd be leaving by myself, leaving the three of them behind to pick over the remains of my total humiliation.

When we're outside in the balmy air, I don't even look at him. "You shouldn't have brought me."

"I'm sorry."

"You just sat there pretending none of this was happening. You made me feel like a complete idiot, Sam."

"I was waiting for it to blow over. He would have let it go, Emma, I swear."

A few days ago I was gushing over him like a schoolgirl, but not now. Now I regret our intimacy. I should have waited until after the novel is finished. I don't want to let anything get in the way of that novel.

Sam hails a taxi and says, "Come on, I'll take you home."

He opens the door, and before stepping inside, I turn to him and say, "No, I'll go home on my own. I'll you call tomorrow." And I close the door.

◆ ◆ ◆

The apartment is dark and silent when I get back. I go straight to my bedroom and turn on a lamp. I throw my coat over a chair, not bothering to hang it up, and I sit on the bed and cry. My cell phone rings in my purse, but I know it's Sam. He has called three times already, but I let it go to voicemail each time. I don't want to talk to him yet.

I'm so tired, and so confused. Not once did Sam speak up to stop his friend from embarrassing me. I feel ridiculous. Did I overreact by leaving so abruptly? I don't know. But right now, I can't bear to see Sam again, and as I drop my head in my hands, feeling so stupid that I engaged in an emotional relationship with this man, all I can think of is: *How am I going to find another ghostwriter now?*

My phone rings again, so I get it out of my purse and turn it off. I catch sight of the other phone, Carol's phone, blinking on the chair. I go and pick it up. It's almost out of battery, so I plug it into my own charger. I'm about to turn it off too, but then, I don't know why, almost without thinking I try one last password: Jim's. I know his password just as he knows mine: "0 1 1 2." The first four Fibonacci numbers, or so he says.

Bingo!

29

I love my morning runs. It must be the endorphins. Isn't that what they say? You get addicted to it. Well, I have to do something this morning to clear my head after a sleepless night.

The heat is unexpectedly oppressive, reflecting off the buildings, and for a moment I wonder whether it's too hot to run, but I do it anyway, because if I don't, I'll kill myself for having been so utterly, completely, and comprehensively stupid. At least the good news is that if three makes a serial killer, then I'm not one. I didn't kill three people. In fact, I haven't killed anyone in years. That's got to be good, and I hang on to that thought.

Get her driver's license. It's in the pocket on the left side.
How?
I don't know, maybe borrow her purse to get yourself a drink or something. Pretend you have no cash on you.
I'm nervous Jim. I don't know if I can pull it off.
You will. When are you seeing her?
In ten minutes.
Okay. Call me after.
I love you.
I love you too.

Sweat is running into my eyes as I run, and I slow down, wiping it off. I felt ill when I read those texts on Carol's phone. There are others too, but less specific. They're not from Jim's own cell number, so I suppose they both got themselves burner phones. I can't believe she let me take it from her, the day before the trip. They must be desperate to get that back, and no doubt the mood between them must be a little, shall we say, tense? He's probably berating her for being *so stupid*.

They set me up. The two of them. It's all there, in text messages. I don't know how Jim made it back to shore that day, but I can guess. The same way I did. I remember Carol didn't want to leave right away, after we pushed him over the edge. I also remember feeling the boat lurch. It felt strange. But I don't know how to sail, so how do I know what's normal? But of course, he'd just got back on the boat, and that was when we reset the sails.

I just can't believe I fell for it. Jim must be right about me. I'm an idiot.

An idiot with a plan, though.

It took all night to formulate, but I've got it. I know what to do. And it's not something so ordinary as going to the police and telling them about Jim's little stratagem to get himself a brand-new life—and get away with fraud.

I realize now why he stopped harassing me about his research documents. He didn't care anymore. He doesn't. As far as he was concerned, he would be dead, and I'd be charged with his murder.

That is, if someone reports his disappearance to the cops. As long as I have Carol's phone in my possession, she won't do it. I need to make sure Terry won't do it either, but I can do that.

So on that front, it's under control. Or at least that's what I tell myself when my cell phone rings.

"Emma, it's Moira. Is Jim with you?"

It's hot and noisy out here in the street. I lean against the wall and try to get my breath back.

"Hi, Moira, how are you? How's Florida?"

"Oh, Emma, I'm so upset. I don't understand. I've been trying to reach Jim for days. Is he there? He didn't call me for my birthday, you know that? He always calls me on my birthday. Always. Jim would never miss my birthday. I said to Larry that something wasn't right. But Larry said he must be busy and he'll call soon. But he hasn't, Emma! Not a word!"

Her voice is sounding progressively more shrill and I feel a tinge of sympathy as I say, "Calm down, Moira, please." But I can't get another word in, through the "how can I calm down? My son is missing, Emma. What's going on? Is he with you?"

"Moira, stop, listen." I find a scrunched-up Kleenex in my pocket and pull it out to wipe the sweat on my forehead.

She pauses; I can hear her breathing, fast, short, and shallow.

"Where are you?" she asks.

"I'm on my way home."

"He's not there, is he?" she asks, her voice small and almost pleading.

"No. Jim has gone away. But I'm sure he's fine, really. There's nothing to worry about."

"Where did he go? Have you spoken to him?"

"Has he told you about us?" I ask, even though I already know the answer.

"Told me what?"

Of course he hasn't. He wanted to wait until he'd gone away, wherever that was. Tunisia or whatever.

I like Moira, very much. She's always been nice to me. I think she recognizes a little of herself in me: we are both women who married up. Other than that, we don't have very much in common, so most of our conversations center around her children: Jim and his two sisters.

Mostly Jim, because everyone in that family is in awe of him. He can't do any wrong. He could say anything, and it would be treated as pearls of wisdom. If I told her right now that Jim was convinced he was being spied on via his webcam, she'd tell me of an article she'd read recently about the perils of webcams. Or that it happened to a friend of hers. And she'd believe it too. We used to see them regularly for family meals, before they moved south, and it always struck me that his sisters would do a lot to help their mother and father. They'd bring food to store in the freezer so that Moira and Larry would always have a few prepared meals on hand. Or they'd bring Moira a gardening magazine, knowing how much she enjoyed it. On those occasions when we all went to their house, they would help with the meal, and shoo Moira out of the kitchen so that she could "put her feet up." Jim did nothing of the sort, except maybe bring a bottle of wine, but he certainly never got his hands dirty with such mundane activities as clearing the table or stacking the dishwasher. But then again, I used to make up for it.

I brace myself. "We've separated, Moira, I'm sorry." It comes out on an exhalation.

"What do you mean 'separated'?"

"Jim has moved out, he's left."

"Left what?"

"Me, Moira."

"You're getting a divorce?" She shouts that last part, and I have to move my phone away from my ear.

My heart breaks a little. She used to brag that no one in her family had ever divorced. Not her children, not her sister or brother or her parents or Larry's parents, all the way up and down the family tree.

"I don't know, Moira. I hope not."

"But what's happened?"

"Maybe we should talk about it another time."

"But where is he? Why isn't he returning my calls?" She lets out a little sob.

"He's not missing, Moira, okay? Give it a few days. He's a little upset."

"When did he move out?"

"A few days ago." Which is sort of true.

"Oh, is that all?"

"Yes, so you see why we should wait? He told me he was moving into a hotel somewhere, to get his thoughts in order."

Even to my ears that sounds completely unconvincing, but I'm hoping that Moira will let anything persuade her that her son is safe.

"Do you know which hotel?"

This conversation is starting to grate on me. I don't know how many ways I can tell her that I don't know where he is and have no means of reaching him, but I force myself to stay gentle.

"No, he said he would let me know soon, but not yet. He wanted to have some time to himself."

She lets out another small sob.

"I can't reach him, Emma. I tried calling, but I only get his voicemail. I've left messages but I don't understand why his phone isn't working. What if he was in an accident? Have you thought of that?"

"He just needs some time, Moira. He'll call you. I'm sure of it. You'll see."

We go through a few more rounds of this: *Why won't he pick up the phone? Have you tried to reach him? What does his work say?* She hasn't called the Forum yet; she called me first. She doesn't know that Jim has resigned, and I don't tell her. But I do say that he's taken leave from work as well.

"You call me the minute you hear from him, all right, Emma? Promise me."

I know it's not going to be that simple. I can see her in my mind's eye, one hand over her mouth and her eyes darting sideways as she begins to imagine the worst. It won't be long before Moira calls the hospitals, and soon after that she'll ring the police.

Which means that I don't have a lot of time, and I can't stay in my apartment, because that's the first place they'll come looking for me, once they piece it together.

◆ ◆ ◆

I walk briskly back to my apartment, my head down. My thoughts are racing in my mind and I force myself to slow them down. I can't panic now, or I'll make mistakes.

I'm almost back at my building, only another block, when she does it again.

"Emma!"

I jump, almost trip. I turn to the voice, even though I already know who it is, the same as last time, waiting for me in the shadows, whispering as I come past.

"Jesus! Fuck! Carol! You almost gave me a heart attack! Are you trying to kill me too?"

She recoils at that, and I stifle a smile.

"Sorry, I didn't mean to scare you."

"Yes, well, you did. Give me a minute."

I bend down, hands on my knees to get my breath back. It's my composure I'm concerned about. She gave me a shock, leaping out like that. I take a deep breath.

"Do you think this is a good idea? Us being seen together, like this?" I ask.

"Let's just walk," she replies. She seems a little sharp in her movements, a little nervous maybe. She steps up beside me. "No one will recognize me anyway."

"Aren't you hot in that?" She's wearing a hoodie and yet another baseball cap, a different logo this time that means nothing to me, but it is an even larger cap, as usual set low over her eyes, and large sunglasses.

She ignores my last question, takes off the sunglasses. "Do you still have that burner phone?"

Well, that didn't take long.

"Yeah, I meant to give it back to you, obviously, then when I got home it was still in my pocket."

Her eyelids flutter in relief. So she was really worried. I can't say I'm sorry about it. I hope she lost sleep over that burner phone. Now that I see her eyes I'm pretty sure she did lose plenty of sleep.

"Great. I wasn't sure. I don't know. I got really confused. Can I get it from you?"

"I don't carry it in my pocket, if that's what you're asking."

"No, I didn't mean—I mean, I can wait for you here. You can go and get it."

"I don't have it."

"I know, but if you could go up to your apartment and I'll—"

I stop and look at her squarely.

"I don't have it upstairs. I'm in the process of moving out, right now. All my things are in storage. Burner phone included."

Her head does a quick shake, then she does it again, like an electrical impulse she can't control. "But I have to get it back!" she says, urgency in her voice.

"I know." I speak very calmly, unlike her. "Trust me, I don't want your burner phone either. In fact, I was going to throw it out—"

"You didn't!"

"No, I figured you'd call for it, so I waited. It's in my storage unit."

"So when can I get it?" she blurts, then smiles, as if to correct the impression that she's more agitated than she lets on.

"I can get rid of it if you like," I propose.

"No! No, don't. I'll do it. Can you go and get it now?"

I put my hand on her shoulder.

"Stop worrying. I'll get you the phone as soon as I can."

She nods and we resume walking.

"You shouldn't be here anyway, even with your stupid disguise," I add.

"Yes, well, if you answered your own phone occasionally, I wouldn't have to do this."

"You called me? I didn't know it was you."

"I used a different phone."

"Really? You should have texted. How was I supposed to know who it was?"

"Are you crazy? We're not supposed to have any contact, Emma! You think exchanging texts is helpful?"

"Okay, fine, I get it. Call me tomorrow night, okay? I'll get the phone and I'll let you know where we can meet. But I need something from you, Carol."

"Oh yes? What?"

"Jim stole something from me. My old phone. He showed it to me the day he left and he took it with him. It must be among his things. I need it back."

She stares at me, eyes a little wide.

"What kind of phone?"

"It's an iPhone. In one of those hard, protective cases, with an animal print pattern. Have you seen it?"

"Not that I recall. Are you sure he had it?"

"Positive."

"Is it really that important, Emma? What if I can't find it?"

"You'll find it," I smile. "I have complete faith in you."

Her shoulders drop. She just wants her phone, clearly, and she doesn't want to have to do chores for it.

"Tomorrow night?"

"I won't get to the storage unit before tomorrow, so yes, tomorrow night. We'll arrange a time to meet then."

"Okay," she says, reluctantly. "I'll call you tomorrow night."

Then she gives me a quick kiss on the cheek and walks away. I put my hand where her lips touched my skin. That was so strange. I can't work out if she did that for the benefit of onlookers; two friends running into each other.

I watch her disappear around the corner. I didn't ask myself, or her, the first time she surprised me like this, where she came from. But now I wonder. There are no recesses or nooks or dark alleys, and yet she seemed to materialize out of the shadows. Did she observe me from the Starbucks across the road? Sitting by the glass window, afraid to look away in case I appeared and she missed me? Did she sprint across the road behind me?

◆ ◆ ◆

"I forgot about this place," I say, looking around La Masseria. "I haven't been here in God knows how long."

"Well, as you can see, it's still the same," Frankie says, scanning the menu. "What will you have?"

"I don't know." I glance at the table next to us. "Soup, I think."

"*La zuppa del giorno!*" Frankie says to the waiter with a flourish that makes me smile.

He puts the menu down, and we're alone again. "Everything okay?"

"Sure, why?"

"You're a little distracted, maybe."

"Well, since you ask," and I tell Frankie a version of my separation. I'm getting some practice now, it flows easily. I also tell him about my financial situation, which I blame squarely on my economist husband.

He shakes his head. "I'm so sorry, Em. Tough break."

I make the usual noises about how life goes on, and *que sera sera*, and it's all for the best, and it was on the cards, and when I've exhausted the platitudes, I come out with it.

"That's partly why I wanted to see you. I was thinking about your beach house."

"Yes? What about it?"

"I need a place to stay, and—"

"Oh, Emma!" He grabs my hand. "You're not homeless, are you? Did Jim ask you to move out? Why didn't you tell me before?"

I burst out laughing. "Lord no, it's nothing like that. Jim is the one who's left the apartment. I just want to have some time away." I was about to say *by myself*, which makes no sense since I'm already there. "Time away from our home and the memories, just until I work out what to do next. So I was wondering, could I stay there for a while? If you're not using it, obviously."

"Of course, anytime, Emma. Come on, you paid for it," he says sweetly, and we chuckle together. That's one of Frankie's lovely quirks, he always credits me with his "rising from the ashes moment," as he calls it.

"You can stay at the beach house as long as you like. We don't use it at the moment, and even if we did, there's plenty of room."

"Huh, stop right there." I put a hand up, still my favorite gesture. "We?"

"Yes, well, this is probably not the time, under the circumstances— oh, forget it, I'll tell you another time."

To my surprise, Frankie blushes.

"No, tell me now."

"It'll keep."

"Is it good news?"

"Yes."

"Then you must tell me. Good news I can take." I smile. He does too.

"I met someone." He looks down at his plate, surprisingly shy. "You see why it can wait? It doesn't seem appropriate after what you just told me."

"Why? It's great news! Out with the old, in with the new, I say. Tell me all about him."

"You're sure?"

"Positive."

He laughs. "Well, his name is—"

And for a second I find myself praying he doesn't say *Nick*, but no, thank God, it's Brad.

"You're kidding. You got yourself a *Brad*?"

"I know, right?" he grins.

I push my plate away, so there's room for my elbows on the table as I rest my chin on my hands.

"Everything," I say. "And I mean everything. Go."

He blushes. It moves me.

"What do you want to know?"

I take his hand in mine, across the table. "Where did you meet him? Let's start with that."

"At the gym."

"Oh, nice! So he's in good shape, then."

"That's one way of putting it."

And for the next hour, Frankie tells me all about Brad, sweet, beautiful Brad, a financial adviser.

"Watch out for those," I quip. "I was married to an economist. Look where that got me." Which raises a laugh from both of us. "How long ago did you meet?"

"Two months."

"Two months? And you're telling me now?"

"Emma, I've barely seen you! Don't look at me like that. I've been dying to tell you, believe me."

"Okay, I forgive you. Any pics?" I point to his cell phone on the table.

"None you'd like to see," he says wryly.

"I'm not so sure about that."

"None I'd like to show you then. You'll meet him in the flesh; don't worry about that. Hey, when did you want to go to the beach house?"

"Are you changing the subject?"

"Yes, I am."

"Can I go there this week?"

"Sure."

"Can I go there tomorrow?"

"Of course you can."

We discuss the logistics of getting me the key.

"The door to the garage doesn't work properly." There's a trick, apparently. You have to press the button once and then press it again.

"Should I be writing this down?"

I'm about to reach for my purse when I feel a presence beside me, like a shift in the air. Then I hear his voice.

"Hello, Emma Fern."

I look up to see Sam's face, smiling, but there's an edge to his features. I can't quite put my finger on it.

"Well, well, what are you doing here?" I say.

"Same as you I suspect," he says, smiling. "This is quite a place, isn't it?" He turns to Frankie and holds out his hand. "Sam Huntington," he says, friendly, natural.

"Frankie Badosa," Frankie says, half standing.

"Ah, the publisher." There's something in Sam's tone that annoys me. Why would he say that anyway?

"The one and only," I hasten to add.

"Have we met before?" Frankie asks, and my stomach lurches. That would not be good, if it turned out Frankie knows Sam, and his chosen profession.

"Sam was at Nick's launch the other night. Maybe you met him there?" I say quickly.

"Oh, sorry if I met you and I'm being vague, it was one of those nights," Frankie says, charmingly.

"Of course, congratulations, it was a great evening." Frankie nods in acknowledgment. Then Sam turns to me: "I've left messages over the last two days. Everything all right? You left so quickly after the other night."

Okay, right. This is getting a little out of control.

"I've been busy, but I'll call you soon." I'm being dismissive, but this situation is making me nervous. I want Sam to leave.

"Yes, please do, it would be good to catch up." He winks at me, and I smile, wondering whether he's playing some kind of game. Why does Sam seem to pop up wherever I go? Is it really as coincidental as he claims?

I watch him leave us to join a man sitting at a corner table.

"Who was that?" Frankie asks.

I shake my head. "Nobody. A ghost."

30

"I'm going away for a while," I say, nonchalantly.

Sam is sitting a little away from me on the couch in his office. I think he wants to come closer; I can feel it. He reached out to put his hand on my knee, but I pretended not to see and moved a little farther at the same time.

"Oh? Where?"

I study my nails. "I just need some time to myself, time to think."

"Okay," he says slowly. "Should I be worried?"

"What do you mean?"

"I'm out of practice, so I may be wrong, but I get this awful feeling you're letting me down gently."

I turn to look at him. There's a small frown of disappointment creeping up between his eyes.

"Letting you down about what?"

"About our relationship."

"Do we have a relationship?"

"Don't we?"

A frolic on the couch and now we have a relationship?

"Did you really happen to run into me? At the restaurant earlier?" I ask.

He rolls his eyes. "For Christ's sake! I was having lunch. What else would I be doing there?"

I shake my head. "It's just a bit of a coincidence, don't you think? Especially after Nick's book launch." I pick at the lint on my cuff.

"What are you saying? That I'm following you? That I'm some kind of . . . creep?"

"No. Of course I don't think that."

"I went there for lunch. Just as you did. That's what people do in restaurants. We just happened to be there at the same time." He sighs. "I probably shouldn't say this, but after I saw you, I thought it was some kind of sign."

"What kind of sign?"

He shrugs. "That we have a connection."

I burst out laughing. He looks at me sharply, but then a smile spreads across his face.

"Stupid, I know," he says.

"No, it's sweet. Really."

"You haven't answered my question."

"We have a professional relationship, Sam. Let's leave it like that for now, please. Then after we finish the work—the novel—we can see where we want to go. In our personal lives."

He looks down, and this time I'm the one reaching out to him. I lay my hand on top of his.

"I can't believe you just said that," he says.

"Excuse me?" Slowly, I pull my hand away.

"Is it because of the other night? With Lisa and Akil?"

I look into his worried face. "Partly. I think we're going too fast and your friends are not ready." I smile, because it's funny, really. But he doesn't. "Tell me, Sam, when did you and Barbara divorce? How long ago?"

"What does that have to do with anything?"

"Just tell me."

He doesn't look at me now. "We're not divorced yet. But I'm going to get an attorney and get things in motion. Soon, real soon."

"I see. When did you separate, then? You are separated, aren't you?"

"Yes, of course we're separated! What do you think I am?"

He stands up abruptly. Now he's angry.

"We separated late last year. And anyway, who are you to talk? How long have you been single, Mrs. Fern?"

He stops pacing. He's looking at me, triumphant; an unattractive smirk on his lips.

Oh God! I've gotten myself into a difficult situation. I was in some kind of hyper-emotional state. But this is the man who is writing my book, and I just can't afford to throw it all away and start again.

"Sit down," I say, patting the couch next to me.

He doesn't move. He crosses his arms and says, "Are you going back to him?"

My head jerks in surprise. "I'm sorry?"

He leans forward. "Are you going back to your husband? Is that why you're telling me you're going away?"

I don't know whether to laugh or cry. I shake my head, disbelief and disappointment washing through me.

"Don't do this. Please."

"Don't do what?" he asks.

"Act like a jerk. Sit down."

He relents then. He drops his arms to his sides and it's as if his whole body deflates. He sits down heavily on the couch next to me, our thighs touching. I take his hand in mine.

"I got a sense, the other night with Lisa and Akil, that your relationship with Barbara was still fresh. That it was too early for you to bring someone new into your personal life like that. Your close friends are not ready. Why did you, Sam?"

"Why did I bring you?"

"Yes. Why are we even doing this?"

"Hey, you're Emma Fern. It's not every day I get to date someone like you." He turns to me and gives me a crooked smile.

My heart sinks then.

"I'm not going away for long; maybe a week," I say. "I need to think about my future."

As soon as I say it, I know what is coming.

"Am I a part of that future?"

"We'll see." And seeing his features morph into sadness I add, "I hope so." I smile, caress his hand. "There are things I need to take care of, but I'll call when I get back. We can talk about it then."

"When you get back? Why? Can't we talk before then?" He's almost whining. I stop my jaw from clenching.

I smile. "I won't be away long, I promise. Will you keep working without me for a while?"

"If I must," he says, but he's smiling as he pulls me against his chest. We sit like this a little longer, silent, intimate, and it should be nice and comforting, but yet all I can think is, *I've made a mistake.*

When I leave, he kisses me, hard on my lips, his teeth knocking against mine. I let the kiss turn passionate, and when we part he puts his cheek against my own and whispers, "I love you."

He hasn't noticed that I didn't say where I was going.

◆ ◆ ◆

The beach house is in Port Jefferson, a little bay on the North Shore of Long Island. I've been here once before, when Frankie first bought it and he threw a party: a Great Gatsby–themed party that went on and on until the small hours, and we all fell asleep on couches and spare beds, and nursed a hangover for days after.

I set my bags down near the door and put the key on a small table nearby. I stand and look around.

It's larger than I remember. The front door opens directly into the living room, a happy room with white walls and large colorful rugs set haphazardly over a honey-colored wooden floor.

There are two large pale couches at right angles to each other; the type that are deep and soft, and covered in cushions, and it's all I can do not to drop myself on one of them. Everything is either white, pale wood, or colorful pastels. It's the ultimate beach house of my dreams.

On the opposite wall are large French doors that frame the harbor. I open them and step outside onto the deck. There's a round glass table with a patio umbrella and four chairs. Through the trees I look at the boats that float gently around the marina.

I did wonder how it would make me feel to be here; whether I'd be comfortable with the memory it's bound to evoke. And the answer is, absolutely fine. Different marina, different viewpoint. I love it here.

I'm in heaven. I can go forth with my plan from here, then take some time out and make decisions about the future. I feel an incredible feeling of lightness come over me.

I should take the food I bought and store it in the kitchen. I remember this kitchen. Kitchens are my favorite rooms in a house and this one speaks to me. It has the same pale wooden floors, and a marble-top island in the center with white wooden cupboards below it, which match the other cabinets and the high stools. It's not very big, but it has the most wonderful feel. I fill the bowl with the fruit I bought, and store the perishables in the refrigerator. Then I pour myself a glass of white wine, which is not quite as chilled as I'd like, but fine for now, and I return to the deck and watch the light in the sky change colors.

My cell phone rings. Right on cue.

Poor Carol. She really wants that phone badly. She does her best to appear relaxed—nonchalant even—but there's a breathlessness to her voice when I assure her that yes, I have the phone with me.

"You do?"

"Of course, what did you think?" I reply. "I'm a woman of my word." Unlike some people.

"Okay, good. So where can we meet?"

"Did you find my cell phone?" I ask. "Do you have it?"

"Yes, I found it."

"That's music to my ears." I'm so happy, I could almost whistle a merry tune.

"So where should I meet you?"

"Right. Well, I've moved out of the apartment. I'm staying on Long Island, maybe not too far from you."

"Where on Long Island?"

I notice she doesn't tell me where she's staying herself, but frankly who cares? I don't need to know. Not anymore.

"Port Jefferson."

"Okay, it's not next door, but it's fine. There's a place on East Broadway I know. Can you meet me there?"

I pretend to agree, but then I hesitate. I say, "Do you mind coming here instead? I still have so much to unpack. I'd rather stay and keep going."

"You're on your own?"

"I certainly am. The place is tucked away. No one has to see you come or go. It's very discreet. It's almost dark, anyway."

"Okay, that's probably better. Where are you?"

I reel off the address. My mouth feels dry, partly from excitement, partly from nerves. Everything is going according to plan.

"I haven't been in touch with the police yet," Carol says. "I didn't want to have that loose end with the phone. But I'll go and see them right away after I pick it up."

Of course you will, I bet you can't wait. But there's an edge to her voice, a slight rise in pitch. I wonder if Jim is with her, whispering to her. She needs to get that phone back before the police interview me. It would be awkward if I decided to give it to them.

"They called me yesterday," I lie. "I guess Terry must have talked to them."

It serves no purpose for me to say that. The police haven't been in touch yet, thank God. But if it makes her sweat a little, then why not?

I can hear a sharp intake of breath. "Oh really?" she says. "They haven't been in touch with me."

"Well no, Carol, why would they? Jim is—was—married to me, I'm still his next of kin." I'm glad she can't see me because it's too hard not to grin.

"Oh, yes, of course," she says.

Carol is the one who called Terry and made sure he was sufficiently concerned. But she hadn't realized her phone was missing at that point. She must be kicking herself now. No doubt she has her story ready, and she'd like to share it with the police before I do.

"But you haven't seen them yet?" she asks.

"No, not yet. They asked me if I knew where Jim was. I did as we discussed. I stuck to the script. They want me to come over to the precinct tomorrow morning. They said I can file a missing person report if no one has heard from him."

"What if they come tonight?"

"Here? No. They won't come tonight. I told you, I'm expected at eight thirty a.m. tomorrow at the station. They don't know where I am anyway. I haven't told them about this place."

"Okay, good. I'll come over now."

She says it will take her twenty minutes to get here, and I tell her that it's fine by me. But then, when I end the call, it comes over me like a wave. The doubt. Am I really going to pull this off?

The first thing I need to do is check the gun. I didn't ask Frankie if he still kept it in the house, because I didn't know how to bring it up. Frankie is a card-carrying member of the NRA, and that's a topic we have learned, over time, to rarely bring up between us. That's what makes us the best of friends, I've realized. You can have strong, divergent opinions on things, but it takes nothing away from how much you love each other.

And today, I love Frankie even more for being a gun owner, because I need one, and I wouldn't know the first thing about sourcing a gun. I don't exactly know how to fire one either. I have never handled a gun in my life, but as for everything I needed to learn, I went to the School of Google and I looked it up. I'm pretty sure it will be fine.

I know where the gun is. Frankie told me a while back—I don't remember the occasion. I walk to the master bedroom and open the closet. I bend down and pull out a couple of small boxes, and for a moment I think I've made a mistake. But then I find it. In a black plastic carrying case, right at the back.

I am relieved to see that it's still there, in its hiding place.

It's a small gun, a Glock, and I pry it out of the foam lining and take a closer look, making sure it's loaded. I'll have to carry it in my pocket. It's not ideal, but I don't know yet when I'll need it. I just know that I will.

I go through the house and pull all the drapes shut. I make sure everything else I need is in place. I sit down, and then I get up again and walk over to each window, checking that each one is locked, even though I just did them all five minutes ago. I keep feeling for the gun in my pocket, and every now and then I pull it out and carefully tug at the cartridge to check that it's in place. I'm doing that for umpteenth time and almost drop it when the doorbell rings.

31

"This is nice," Carol says when I open the door, stepping in and looking around.

"Yes, I like it." I walk in front of her, leading her to the living room. "What's your place like? You have a view?"

She shrugs. She doesn't want me to know where she's staying, other than what she told me already. Bellmore, from memory. I want to tell her that I couldn't care less, I'm just making conversation, but I don't. We have work to do.

She takes her hand out of her jacket pocket and holds it out, palm up. "Can I have the phone?"

"Sure, come and sit down."

I've poured us each a glass of chilled champagne, a small tribute to that other night a few weeks ago when Jim similarly invited me to partake. Also, personally, I think it's always difficult to refuse a glass of champagne.

The glasses are waiting for us obediently on the large coffee table, next to the bottle of Bollinger in its silver ice bucket. I indicate the couch for her to sit down.

"I don't have the time to stay," she says. "If I could get the phone from you, then I'll be on my way."

Is Jim waiting for her out there? If he is, it's fine with me. The sooner we get this over with, the better.

"Come on, you'll be fine, Carol. Just a toast. Please. To a happy, Jim-free life ahead."

Reluctantly, she sits down and reaches across to take the glass I hand her. I don't sit yet.

"Cheers," I say, "to the future."

"Cheers." She takes a sip.

"I'll get your phone for you," I say, and start to walk away, but then I stop, as if I just thought of something, and I turn back to her and hold out my hand. She pulls my phone out of her jacket pocket and I close my fingers around it.

"Thank you," I say, without giving a hint that, to me, this phone is as precious as if it were a gold bar. As soon as I can, I will delete every last trace of me from that phone, starting with every text Beatrice and I exchanged. Then I'll destroy it. Maybe I'll try putting it in the microwave. That can't be good for it.

"Can I have mine?"

"I'll get it. Relax, Carol."

"I really need to go."

"I know. I'll get it for you now." I make a show of knocking back my drink, as if somehow it was important to do that first, then I watch her do the same, but she doesn't drink all of it. It's all I can do to stop myself from pushing her glass up to help things along.

"May we both find happiness—separately, of course—after a rather rough patch." I pretend to drink the last of my champagne, even though my glass is now empty, and she does the same, which is brilliant, frankly, as I'm running out of happy toasts.

I leave the room, and when I turn to look at her from the door, I catch sight of her tilting her glass to get the last of it.

I chuckle to myself. She really *is* in a hurry.

Bad luck, that.

◆ ◆ ◆

Because of the seclusion of the house, I told her it was perfectly safe for her to park outside. I've never seen her car. I don't even know what she drives. So I have to go outside, hiding in the shadows, and I slowly make my way to the Honda parked a few yards down the street that seems like a good bet. I crouch down, and when I am sure there are no other cars coming, I walk, crab-like, over to the Honda, my heart thumping in my chest so loudly I fear it can be heard in the silence. It takes a full minute for me to talk myself into peering into it, as discreetly as possible, to make sure Jim isn't in it. I almost fall backward with relief once I see that the car is indeed empty. That it is the right one is confirmed when I press the electric key that I retrieved from her bag and it flashes its lights at me.

I drive it inside the garage, which isn't big enough for two cars, but I've already moved mine out of sight.

Back in the bedroom I decide to unpack the suitcase that is sitting open on top of the bed. I may as well use the time efficiently while I wait. That's one thing that Jim didn't leave me much of when he moved out that night: suitcases. He took most of them with him, not that we had that many anyway, and the only set he left behind were the ones we purchased in Rome together. I can't remember if it was on our honeymoon trip, or a different vacation, but we'd only taken one suitcase for the both of us and, unfortunately, one of the wheels had come off. The hotel manager directed us to a small store around the corner, where he assured us we'd be able to buy a replacement. We were amused to discover it was an ecclesiastical vestments and accessories store that sold various specialist items aimed at the clergy, including luggage. We bought two pieces, one small, one large. Jim joked that they were probably blessed. I guess his cup had runneth over, because he left them behind in our closet.

I don't expect unpacking to take long, because how long does it take to hang a few clothes? Not very long, is the answer. But I keep the door open and my ear tuned.

I'm getting quite experienced at this, I think. It's nice, acquiring new skills in life. Mine is calibrating dosages of barbiturates. Getting it just right for the job. Too much and you can kill someone, although I read somewhere that with barbiturates alone you've got to take a hell of a lot, as they don't make them as strong as they used to. Well, since I don't want to kill Carol—seeing as I have quite enough problems as it is—it's not an issue. But too little, and well, you've got a situation on your hands. If your target becomes aware too soon that you're trying to subdue them, they won't let you have another try. You can't exactly come back with a "top-up." Which means you could have a fight on your hands; a few scratches on your face maybe, a bite mark on your skin. How are you going to explain that?

So, best to get it right the first time, and, as it happens, I know what I'm doing. When I peer around the door of the living room, Carol, God bless her, is fast asleep on the couch, the stem of the glass resting in her loose fingers on the floor. I tilt my head, studying her face. I'd like to say she looks like an angel, but that would be a lie. I never really understood what Jim saw in her, frankly, because put the both of us in a lineup, and I'm by far the more attractive of the two, hands down. Asleep like this, her face sags, her jaw is slack, and I wonder if she snores. It wouldn't surprise me.

I take her pulse, which is a little slow; a little weak, but that's to be expected. I need to work quickly, so I go and retrieve the rope I've hidden at the bottom of the broom closet, and I set it down on the floor, next to her. I've already cut it in various lengths, because I believe in preparation, which should be pretty obvious to anyone by now.

I start by tying her feet. That's easier than the hands, because of her position. I remove her shoes first, just like that article said, the one I found from googling *how to tie up a person*. I wouldn't have necessarily thought of it, but of course if the person manages to remove their shoes, then they'll have a bit more wriggle room. Self-evident. Once you know it.

She's wearing running shoes—the expensive kind—and dark grey pants. This is more her "I'm going to the police after this" outfit. Practical and nondescript. Every other time I've seen her, she's been wearing something sporty. I noticed also, that night on the boat, when we moved Jim, that she's surprisingly strong. I must not forget that.

I tie her legs together, below the knee, just like the instructions said, and I make sure not to pull the rope too tight. I don't want to cut off the blood flow. I only want to immobilize her.

I study her hands and arms next. I would have preferred tying them behind her back, but it's too hard, given her position, so I have to tie her hands together at the front. She's wearing pale-pink nail polish. It's a pretty color. I must ask her what it is.

I stand up and take a good, appraising look at her. I think I did a fine job. I reach for the bottle of champagne and refill my glass. I feel quite parched after all these exertions, but I'm happy with the result. Carol is not going anywhere fast.

I'm about to sit down when I hear a phone ring in her bag and I lunge for it, even though I know nothing is going to wake her up right now. By the time I find it in the multitude of zipped pockets, it's no longer ringing. But there is a missed call alert on the screen.

Jim.

I turn off the phone. All I need to do now is wait.

32

I suspect Carol's going to be passed out for at least another half hour, since I am now an expert in such matters, and I leave her there, asleep, and go to the kitchen. I'm so fortunate that dear Frankie let me stay in this house. It's so pretty here; so lovely and welcoming. Frankie has such good taste. These are the things I tell myself over and over to convince myself that everything is normal. Then maybe I can keep the lurking feeling of dread from engulfing me.

Coffee. That's what I should do. Make coffee. Except Frankie doesn't own an espresso machine, which is rather annoying. I make a mental note to buy one for the house. It can be my thank-you present. It's the least I can do. But meanwhile, I find myself this evening having to do with French press coffee, which is just not the same. People say you shouldn't drink coffee after midday, but I must be immune, because it's never stopped me from sleeping. Anyway, that's academic at this point, since I have no intention of doing so; not for a while yet.

It feels like an eternity, but it's only just over half an hour when I hear her moan in the next room. It makes me clench my jaw, just hearing the sound of her voice. It makes me want to hurt her.

"Ah, Carol. Hello. How did you sleep?" I ask.

I walk into the living room as I say this. She's trying to move her arms and legs as if she hasn't noticed she's tied up. Because she's not quite awake yet, it hasn't registered.

Ah, now it does. I can see her eyes flutter open, and then her head lifts. She has a mark on her cheek from the sewn edge of the cushion. Her eyes dart around the room. She manages to pull herself into a sitting position, her head moving frantically left and right. Maybe she doesn't remember where she is. I hate it when that happens. It's a feeling I know well from the days when I was doing book tours—staying in hotels, never more than one night—so I can sympathize. And I would, if it were anyone else.

And then she spots me. She tries to speak, but it comes out all blurry. She smacks her lips a few times.

"Emma, what the fuck?" she slurs, finally.

"What the fuck what, Carol?"

She blinks a few times, her eyes darting around the room.

"What are you doing?" she asks, quite genuinely, which surprises me. I expected more fear from her than this puzzlement. But no doubt that will change.

"I was going to make a cup of coffee, if you must know. I'd offer you one, but you know . . ."

Her eyes are really open now. The light in the room is dim because I've only got the small lamp on in the corner. Even though I've drawn the drapes across all the windows, I keep getting this feeling that Jim is outside, watching.

"Untie me! Now!" she yells.

I come forward so I'm standing in front of her. It's easier for her that way. She's shaking; the tears are starting to fall on her cheeks.

"Don't be scared Carol. There's nothing to be afraid of. I just want to talk."

"Are you going to kill me?"

"Kill you? No! Lord no! Don't be so paranoid! Jesus! I don't want to kill you. If I did that, I'd have to admit I have a problem; that killing has become a compulsion, rather than a necessity. I'd have to join Killers Anonymous." I chuckle. "Do you think there's such a thing? There should be, you know. It's better to get people the help they need before they do the deed, don't you agree?"

I tilt my head at her, waiting for an answer. She shakes her head, takes big gulps of air, like she's hyperventilating.

"Do you want some water?" I ask, helpfully.

"Untie me, Emma."

She doesn't know whether to plead or yell, so her tone is stuck somewhere in between, which is nowhere.

"No," I reply, turning away and moving toward the kitchen.

"Where are you going?" she blurts.

"I've changed my mind about the coffee."

When I get back, elegant glass in my hand—and I'll say this for Frankie, he doesn't skimp on the glassware—I sit down in the lovely plush armchair to the right of the couch.

"You know, it's a real shame that Jim and I couldn't make a go of it," I say. "We were actually really well suited. But he didn't know that." I lean forward, one arm on my knee. "Do you know he did exactly the same to me once? Okay, I'll come clean. That's where I got the idea from. Although he didn't tie me up." I wave at the ropes. "He drugged me with something. I don't know what. Anyway, it was very similar. Interesting to note we had very similar instincts, Jim and I. We should have talked more, you know? Isn't that what they say? Communication is the key to a happy marriage. That's what the man at the boat rental office said too. What a waste." I sigh, sitting back in my chair. I take a sip. "Oh well, water under the bridge, right?" I smile.

Then I lean forward again, bringing my face close to hers. I glance at her trembling chin, then look straight into her tearful eyes. I don't smile.

244

"He was a horrible man, Carol. A sick, cruel, vindictive man, and he almost killed me."

She nods and bites her lip, tears falling down the side of her nose.

I put the glass down on the coffee table.

"So why did you do it?"

She shakes her head. "I didn't do anything," she says, quietly.

It's all I can do not to hit her across the face. I close my eyes and take a deep breath.

"No, of course not. Poor, sweet little Carol, who was so frightened of the big bad wolf. *Help me! Help me!* Seriously, do you think you'd be here, trussed up, if that's what I believed? You think I haven't figured out your little stratagem? Well I have. I know you set me up. You both set me up. Tell me that's not true, Carol, just try."

I say that last part through gritted teeth. She nods quickly, mumbles something.

"I can't hear you."

"We set you up," she whispers, "but—"

"Stop!" I shout, raising my hand, palm toward her. "Don't say another word."

I was determined to remain cool and rational. It's a decision I made, coming into this. But it is harder than I can manage.

"How could you, Carol? How could you trick me like this? You rent the car in my name?" I'm shouting now, I'm shaking and shouting, and my face is red and I'm spitting in her face as I yell into it. "Then you rent the boat in my name? You came to me! *You* asked *me* to help you! And I did! I trusted you!"

"What are you going to do?" she asks, her voice small and trembling.

I pick up my glass again and take a small sip.

"We're going to wait for Jim."

She shakes her head from side to side, frantically. "He doesn't know I'm here! I didn't tell him I was coming here!"

"Don't lie to me. I will never believe another word you say."

I take a deep breath. I need to stay calm, otherwise I'll kill her right here and now. Not that I'd mind, but I need her to be the bait. *Keep the bait alive.* That's the whole point.

"My mother always said I was too nice. 'You're too nice, Emma,' she'd say, 'you're too trusting. People will take advantage, mark my words.' Funny how you get older and you realize your mother was right, more often than not. Have you noticed?"

She nods, continually. She's stuck on a nodding loop, essentially.

"It's not—"

"Shh." I raise my index finger and we both become still and listen to the sound of a car coming down the road. My heart races as I look toward the door, but the car moves on without stopping.

I wait until my heart slows down. I look at the draped windows, the sliding doors that lead to the deck. We shouldn't be here, in this room. We're too exposed.

"We're going to go into the kitchen."

Her face crumples and the tears well up again.

"Carol, stop! What's the matter with you? Do you really think I'm going to hurt you? What do you take me for? I'm not that person, Carol! Although Lord knows you deserve it."

She wriggles on the couch, trying to stand up.

"No no, don't do that, I'm going to leave a bit more rope between your feet so you can take small steps. Okay? Ready?"

I crouch at her feet, all the time looking at her face. I feel my way through the knot and then I look down and retie her legs, leaving a small length of rope between her ankles.

"Okay, I'll pull you up now." It takes a couple of tries, but I manage to get her up. She's shaking as I guide her slowly to the kitchen and help her sit on a hard-backed chair, one of the tall ones around the kitchen island. Then I tie her to it, looping the rope around her and the chair together.

My skin feels hot and clammy from the exertion. I wish it were over. I hope he comes soon, because I don't know how long I can keep this up.

I sit down on the chair opposite, across the kitchen island.

"So why?" I ask her this in the most genuine manner I can. I want to show her this is a real question, that requires a real answer, even though I already know the answer, obviously. But I want to hear it from her lips.

"I—I—" She's stammering, so I wait, give her a little space. "I was frightened. I'm sorry."

I'm so angry at her lies that it's me who's shaking now. I want to tell her everything that I know—that I read the texts, that I remember how cool she was when we came back to the pier, that she didn't look scared to me—but I don't get that far. There's someone at the door.

33

They pull out their ID; bring it forward as I peer at them through a small gap in the doorway.

"Can we come in?"

"Yes, of course. Wait one minute, please."

My heart is pounding as I slip the gun back in my pocket, just before I open the door wider.

I thought it was him at the door. So did Carol. We both gasped when the doorbell sounded. I watched her eyes open wide and I thought she looked as scared as I did.

"You say one word, and I *will* kill you. Clear?" I said as I pulled the gun from my pocket. I went to the living room and crouched by the window closest to the front door. I pulled the drapes back, less than an inch, and peered out at the porch. There were two of them, and I was fairly certain Jim was not there.

I was pretty fast, going back to the kitchen. I pushed a couple of pills down Carol's throat and wrapped a dishtowel around her mouth. She tried to fight me off, but let's face it, she's got a handicap. It almost made me laugh out loud seeing her try so hard.

"If I hear a peep out of you, I will kill you. Okay? Nod if you understand. Okay, good! Just lean back against the chair—that's it. Because you'll fall asleep again in a minute and that just can't be helped. Okay?"

I closed the double doors between the kitchen and living space. She probably wouldn't be asleep in a minute, but she'll definitely be even more out of it than she already is.

"Sorry, I was in the middle of cooking," I tell them as I lead them inside. They exchange a glance.

"Let's go on the deck," I say, because it's the space furthest away from the kitchen, and even if Carol manages to moan we won't hear her; not with the sliding door closed.

"Can I get you some water?" I ask, once they've introduced themselves as Detective McDonnell and Detective Murphy. I try to hide my anxiety, but my hands are trembling a little.

"No thank you," they both reply, at the same time.

I don't know why they're here, but they haven't come to arrest me. They wouldn't be lounging on the deck if they had. I fight the urge to get a stiff Scotch for myself. Just a shot of Dutch courage.

"So, how can I help you?" I ask when I've finally sat down, chiding myself for not asking earlier. I bet that's the number one lesson in the police handbook. Innocent people will ask you right away what you're doing here; who died? Is everything okay? The guilty ones, they already know. They forget to ask.

McDonnell starts to speak. "We—"

"Is it about my husband?"

They look at each other. McDonnell starts to speak but I put my hand out.

"My mother-in-law called me yesterday. She was terribly worried about him. Did she call you?" I already know she did. I knew Moira wouldn't last long.

"Mrs. Fern, your mother-in-law called the police with her concerns about your husband's whereabouts. Because he's been missing for at least—"

"I don't think he is. Missing, I mean. If that helps."

"Is your husband here, Mrs. Fern?" McDonnell now asks.

"Here?" I ask. "No. My husband is not here."

"Do you know where he is?"

"Not exactly. I mean, no, I don't. I have no idea." I sigh.

"Is that unusual?" McDonnell again.

"That I don't know his whereabouts? No, not anymore. Unfortunately, my husband and I are having . . . marital problems, and he has moved out for a while. To a hotel."

"I see. Which hotel?" McDonnell writes something in a notebook.

"He didn't say."

"When's the last time you spoke to him?"

"When he moved out. Let me see." I make a show of counting the days on my fingers. "Three weeks ago, give or take."

"Why did he move out?"

"As I said, we're having marital problems."

"And you're staying here? Permanently?" Detective Murphy asks, looking around.

The question unsettles me. I'm not sure what business it is of theirs.

"Sorry, can you remind me of your name?" I ask, just to buy a little time.

"Detective Murphy."

"Thank you. Yes, Detective Murphy, he moved out first, and a couple of weeks after that I decided to go away myself for a few days. I found it too distressing, alone in that apartment, if you must know." I glare at him. "How did you know I was here?"

"Your doorman told us."

I could kick myself for having left a forwarding address.

"Did Mr. Fern take his belongings with him?" Murphy asks.

"Yes, most of them anyway. He left an old desk and some books."

"Do you expect him to come back for those?"

"I don't know. I'm moving out of the apartment and putting things in storage."

"So as far as you know, no one has seen or heard from your husband in three weeks, is that right?"

I'm about to contradict him, but I stop myself.

There's a pause in the air and I know there's a question I should be asking, but I can't remember it. My brain is swimming in fog.

"Have you been on vacation?" McDonnell asks.

"Excuse me?"

"You're"—he points to his own face—"sunburned."

My hand flies to my cheek before I have a chance to stop it.

"Am I? I've been running. It's been a hot couple weeks."

He writes that down too.

"How long have you and your husband lived in that apartment?" McDonnell asks.

"My husband doesn't live there anymore."

He nods.

"Eight months."

"And before that, you were in"—he flicks through his notebook—"Queens, is that right?"

"How do you know that?"

"You were interviewed as part of a different police inquiry. We have it on record."

I knew he was going to say that. I am in that place again, looking at those two—same play, different actors. I lean forward and look into his face.

"I wasn't *interviewed*, Detective. It wasn't like that. The victim was my friend and I was helping the police. I was concerned." He doesn't even blink. I lean backward again, my back against the chair. "But yes, that's right, we lived in Queens, then we moved to Manhattan."

He looks at me in an odd way. I can't quite put my finger on the meaning of his expression.

"We understand he resigned from his job," McDonnell says, "three weeks ago."

"That's right. So you spoke to Terry? His colleague?"

He nods.

"Was your separation amicable?" Murphy asks.

"Yes."

McDonnell looks up from his notebook. "You wouldn't say it was acrimonious, then?"

"No, I just said so, didn't I?" He makes another note.

"My husband is not missing, Detectives. He left me, and he's gone away for a while. He'll be back."

"How do you know?"

"Because that's what he told me."

"Did you tell Mrs. Fern that?"

I stare at him, uncomprehending for a moment.

"Oh, Moira? Yes, I did. I told her the exact same thing. He's gone away; he wants to be by himself. I don't know where he went, but he'll be back when he's ready. She shouldn't have called you."

I stand up to show them that the interview is over as far as I'm concerned. They stand up too, to my relief, and Murphy pulls out a card, gives it to me and asks, "Will you have your husband call us, Mrs. Fern? When he gets back?"

"Certainly. He shouldn't be long."

I walk them back through the house to the front door, when Murphy says, "Are you celebrating something?"

"What do you mean?" I ask, struggling to keep my voice steady, knowing full well what he's going to say.

He points to the champagne bucket and the two glasses on the coffee table. I move to the front door and open it.

"A neighbor came by earlier. We had a drink, yes. I'm not underage, Detective." Then I smile, because I am relaxed, joking, with not a care in the world, and I have nothing to hide. It would help if I could stop my mouth from trembling whenever I speak.

He smiles.

They thank me again for my time. I close the door after them, and lean against it in relief, before going back out to the deck to watch them go. I look out to the road.

Where are you, Jim?

I open the kitchen door just a touch without walking in, just to see if she's going to lunge at me with a spoon or something, but no, she's sitting exactly where I left her, her back to me.

I walk over to her. She sees me and starts to jerk a little. She's frightened. I can see it in her eyes.

She's half asleep, but she's fighting to stay awake. I remove the dishtowel from around her mouth.

"You're okay? Yes? Good."

I'm glad I didn't have that Scotch. I fill the kettle and set it to boil.

I hear her hiccupping behind me as I spoon ground coffee into the French press.

"Can I have some water, please?" she asks timidly.

I don't want to give her water. I don't want to give her anything. I want her to suffer.

I sigh, grab a glass from the top cabinet and fill it up. I set it in front of her and she moves her hands forward, but she won't be able to lift it. Not the way I have her tied up to the chair.

"Hold on a second," I tell her.

I walk around her.

"I'm going to untie you from the chair, okay? For now, anyway. You move, I shoot. You understand?"

"I understand," she replies quietly.

I remove the ropes. She stretches her back slightly, then lifts the glass to her lips.

"You have to believe me," she says after a moment.

I turn around, set the cup of coffee I've just poured onto the kitchen countertop, and put both hands flat on either side of it.

"Believe what, Carol?"

"It's—it's not my fault."

I slam one hand hard on the marble surface. "Shut up!"

She flinches, and I slam it again and again until my palm hurts. I'm shouting. "How could you? What did I ever do to you? He's a monster Carol! Why would you do this? To me?" I want to tell her, *I thought you were my friend, I thought you were kind*, but I'm too busy shouting, "Why? You could have gone overseas, you could have reported him missing and gone ahead with your stupid plans, but you involved me!"

And all the time she blinks, blinks, and blinks, and the tears are running down her cheeks, and my coffee has spilled all over the marble counter and my cell rings in the living room. *What now?* I go and pick it up because frankly, at this point, if I don't leave the room, I'm afraid I'm going to kill her.

34

"Hi, it's me."

I know it's him. I saw his name on the screen before I picked it up. I wish he wouldn't say "me," as if we were that kind of couple.

His tone is sad, not in the way of "I'm really sad because I just watched the news and what a horrible world we live in," or whatever; no, it's more of the "I'm sad because you make me feel sad" variety. All I really want to say is: *Sam, we made a mistake. We should never have become intimate. I take full responsibility for that mistake, but I was in a strange place. Can we be friends instead? Can you please go away?*

Except, of course, I can't do that. I can only deal with one crisis at a time.

"Hi, how are you?" I say, softly.

"I'm okay. Thinking about you."

"That's nice."

"Is it?" I can hear the smile in his voice.

"Of course."

"I miss you," he says.

I peer around the kitchen door, just to make sure Carol is okay, that she didn't fall over or Lord knows what. I see from the movement in her shoulders that she's crying, still.

"Can I come over?" Sam asks, jolting me.

"I miss you too," I say, as if he hadn't spoken that last part. Then I laugh. "I really do, but I have company, so maybe not as much as I might."

"Oh, is it male company?" His tone is completely different. Abrupt. Maybe even angry.

"No, no, we're just having a cold drink, girl talk, making plans. She's a good friend. I'll introduce you one day. You'll like her."

"That's nice," he says, and I can hear in his voice that the moment has passed. "So when will I see you again?"

"I told you, in a few days."

"I don't know if I can wait that long, Emma. I could come over? Tonight, maybe?"

"Please don't," I say, sharply.

"Oh, of course. I'm sorry. I don't want to intrude."

Now he's back to being brisk, and if I'm going to have to watch what I say all the time, and how I say it, I'm going to have to finish this book in record time.

"You're not intruding," I reply gently. "I have too much to do. It's stressing me out a little."

"Don't stress too much, Emma. You should be looking after yourself. Meanwhile I'll keep working on your behalf."

"Thank you, scribe."

He chuckles. I notice some of the rope has fallen under the coffee table. I bend down to pick it up.

"Will you call me when you have a little time?" he says. "Let me know when you want to come over so we can go over the new chapters."

"Of course."

I go back into the kitchen, carrying the bit of rope, the phone cradled in my neck. Carol sees me and winces. I put the rope back in the bottom of the broom closet.

"I can't wait to do that. I really look forward to it," I tell Sam. I lift an index finger toward Carol, as if to say, *I'll just be another minute*, and just before I leave the room again, she screams at the top of her lungs, "Help! Call the police! Help!" with all the pent-up fear she has in her.

I pull the phone away and jab it with my finger to end the call.

35

"I cannot believe you just did that."

I stare at Carol in complete and utter disbelief, like she's an alien that has slid out of a webcam and materialized in my kitchen.

"What am I supposed to do now, Carol? Christ!"

She does that blinking thing again. Blink blink blink blink, and I really want to slap those eyelids shut.

"Do you think that was smart?"

My phone rings in my hand. I look at it, then look at her.

"I'll be right back," I tell her.

"Wh—where are you going?" she stutters.

"Shut up."

I rush out the door through to the living room, and answer the phone as I go out to the deck.

"Christ, Emma, are you okay?" Sam says. "What just happened? You're okay? Should I call the police?"

I laugh. "Lord, I gave myself a heart attack! I had the TV on in the living room. I forgot, I didn't realize it was so loud! Sorry, darling"—I throw in the *darling* hoping to ease the tension I can hear in his voice—"I was unpacking things in the kitchen, and I walked into the living room just as some poor victim was screaming. It gave me a hell of a fright! God, I hate those shows, don't you?"

"Oh, Emma! You don't know what you just did to me! I think I just had a heart attack too! Oh, let me recover here. I can't tell you the horrible visions I just had. I thought someone had broken in just now. I swear if you hadn't picked up, I was going to call the cops!"

I laugh again. "Well, if I'm ever kidnapped, I'll be sure to call you first."

"Seriously, my heart is still racing. God!"

"Oh, Sam, I'm sorry. You're okay? You want me to call an ambulance?"

He chuckles. I don't tell him that my heart is also racing, that my hand is pressed on my chest as I try to take a steady breath again.

"I don't even know where you are, Emma."

"I'm not in hiding, if that's what you're suggesting."

"I'm suggesting nothing of the sort. Just that I would feel better if I knew where you were, that's all."

"Look, Sam, I need to go, but I'll call soon. Okay?"

He doesn't reply, and the silence at the other end goes on for longer than I'm comfortable with. I sure don't want Carol to start screaming again.

"You're still there?"

"I am, Emma. I feel a little weirded out by all this."

"All this what?"

"Mystery stuff."

"I know, I'm sorry. It's just that with my marriage ending, I want to have time to think about my future. Whatever dreams it may hold."

"You're not breaking up with me?"

I want to say, *No, because I'm not twelve years old and I don't break up with people.*

"Don't be silly, you're my scribe. I need you. You know that."

"Just for that?"

But I can hear the smile in his voice, and frankly, the insinuation is irritating me. Nevertheless, I know I should play along and end this call. So I giggle. "Stop it. You're making me blush."

"I'd like to see that."

"And you will. I miss you, Sam, very much. I'll be back in town in a few days. I can't wait to see you."

"Me too," he says. "Tell me where you are."

"Don't, please."

"You're running away from me, Emma. I can feel it."

I just can't believe what I'm hearing. "This has nothing to do with you, Sam."

"Doesn't it?"

"It has to the extent that I want time to think. About my future, with you in it, of course."

"I don't believe you." I start to say something else but he interrupts. "I know you're with Jim, Emma. I can tell."

"I doubt it, that you can tell, because I'm not. I need to go, Sam."

"Fine."

"Don't be like that. Please." I close my eyes, listening to his breathing, and for a moment I wonder if he's crying.

"You're right, I'm sorry. I'm being a jerk," he says, and I breathe out in relief.

"We'll talk about it when I see you, soon, okay?"

◆ ◆ ◆

When I get back to the kitchen, after we've exchanged sweet goodbyes, it's with an uneasy feeling in my stomach. I stand across from Carol, my hand on the top of the chair closest to me.

"Does it ever happen to you? You sleep with someone once, and they behave as if you're now joined at the hip? They need to know where you are, who you're with, when they'll see you again—is that normal? I'm not very experienced, but it feels a little premature to me, to be so attached. What do you think?"

"I want to go home," she whines.

"Yeah, well, don't we all."

There's a ping on my phone. I assume Sam is being sweet in his own relentless way, sending me a kiss or something. But it's a text from Frankie. Does no one go to sleep anymore?

> All set for tomorrow? Call me if you need anything. Sorry I can't be there, but you should have all the info. Call me after. F. xoxo

Tomorrow? Tomorrow, tomorrow, tomorrow . . .

Oh God. I forgot. How could I forget? I put the phone down and close my eyes, pushing the heels of my hands against them.

"What is it?" Carol asks nervously.

"I'm losing my mind, is what it is."

I can't believe I forgot about the book festival. It's such an important event for me. Frankie is working hard to get me back on the circuit and I can't pass this up. I sit down. I put my fingers against my temples, close my eyes, and cogitate. For a moment I consider canceling, but I can't. Frankie would be furious with me if I did that. He'd give up on me. He really would. Then he'd dedicate himself to Nick's career instead.

I look at her. "Tell me the truth, Carol. Does Jim know you're here?"

She shakes her head. "No. I told you. He doesn't know."

"But that makes no sense, why wouldn't he?" Am I really wasting my time here? After all this?

She sighs. "Because I didn't tell him you had the burner phone."

"Why not?" I ask, even though I don't believe her, not exactly.

"Because he would have been furious, Emma. What do you think?"

"Are you saying he doesn't know it's missing?"

"No. I mean yes, that's what I'm saying."

"Christ."

But maybe that's not so bad. In fact, that could be good. If it's true.

"I want to explain—"

"Look at me, Carol, tell me the truth. Jim doesn't know that you're here, with me?"

She looks at me, straight on. "I swear it, Emma. He doesn't know. Right now he thinks I've gone to D.C. I swear it. I give you my word."

I snap my head toward her. I want to tell her that her word means nothing to me, but I have more important things to figure out right now. I take a breath. "Okay."

I know there's a way out of this somehow. I can fix this. I can make it work. I just need to think.

"So can I go?" she asks, in her little-girl voice again.

I look back at her. "No."

"I don't understand. What do you want from me?"

"From you? Nothing. But you're going to stay here a while longer anyway."

I groan, putting both hands over my face. I have to think, fast.

I text Frankie back:

All set, thanks Frankie, talk tomorrow. E. Xx

I take the coffee cup and the glass from the table and put them in the dishwasher. Then I go to the living room and retrieve the champagne evidence. I could kick myself for being so stupid as to leave that out in full view. I bring it all back to the kitchen, put the glasses in the dishwasher, empty the rest of the champagne bottle down the drain, and put it next to the garbage.

I go to the living room where her purse is still lying next to the couch, and bring it back to the kitchen. She watches me pull out her phone. I turn it back on and give it to her.

"Unlock it," I say.

She takes it from me, gingerly, as if it was going to blow up in her face, and a big part of me wishes it would. Then she hesitates, as if she can't remember her own passcode.

"Just unlock it, Carol."

She gives in and I watch her tap the numbers. Then she hands the phone back to me.

"It's not my fault," she says. "None of this is my fault."

"So you keep saying."

I leave her there and go to the living room.

I press the home button on her phone and I send a text, to a number I know by heart. I text Jim that I'll be staying over in D.C. tonight, but I'll call him tomorrow. And that he shouldn't worry. I sign off, *Love, Carol*, and I turn off the phone.

I go to the spare bedroom and grab the pillows and the quilt from the bed. I recognize the quilt. It's a brand we sold in the store when I still owned it. I'd forgotten Frankie came in once. He wanted to buy it, but I gave it to him. I'm glad it's here, in this house.

But I need to stop reminiscing and start getting on with the task at hand. I take the pillows and quilt to the master bathroom. It has an old-fashioned door with a keyhole and a key, which fits on either side of it. It's meant for the inside, of course, and normally that's where it is, but not today. The other thing I like about this bathroom is that there's no window as such. It has a narrow opening on the far wall, below the ceiling, with a pane of glass slightly angled to let in some air and light, but even if you could get up there, you'd never fit through. It's only a few inches tall.

I make a sort of bed on the tile floor, on top of the bath mat. I don't even know why I'm trying to make Carol comfortable, after everything.

I should get a halo.

I didn't sleep exactly, because I don't know if I believed her or not. So I had to keep alert, in case he came for her. I listened for Carol too, all night long, but once she was settled in her makeshift bed, she was as quiet as a mouse. I waited in the dark, but I didn't hear a peep out of her. I figured it's because of all the drugs she'd ingested last night. I think she just crashed.

But now the sun is shining, it's going to be a lovely day, and I'll be speaking in front of dozens of people. I pray that I'll be able to keep it together. I'm on a panel at the Brooklyn Book Festival. It's something I haven't done in months, and I need to put my best foot forward.

Before anything else, I check on Carol. I unlock the door, but keep it closed, wait a beat, push it open an inch, and finally put my head in to take a look at her.

At first I think she's still sleeping. She's got her back to me, lying on the top of the quilt, her knees almost up to her chin, but then I hear her sniffle.

"Hey, you awake?"

She raises her head and turns to look at me, her face drawn. If she's really had some sleep, I can't tell from here.

She nods, but doesn't answer me.

"We've got a couple hours before I go. I'm going to take a shower, arrange for a taxi, and then I'll make us some breakfast. Okay?"

She nods silently, and lies down again.

"How long are you keeping me here?" she asks, her back to me.

"A while longer."

I'll get her to call him when I get back, and say that she's here. She'll tell him about the burner phone; that I lured her here and kidnapped her. That she was able to get to her phone, somehow. That he needs to come and get her.

I lock the door again, and take a shower in the other bathroom. After I dress, I go to the kitchen and make us an omelet. I can't hear Carol, so I may as well get this done first. I slice an onion, thinly, beat some eggs, grate a little of the Parmesan cheese, and cut up the ham. When I have everything ready to go, I call to organize a car to pick me up, and then I go and get Carol.

I repeat my little drill: unlock but don't open, open an inch and wait, put my head in slowly, then I walk in.

"You need to get up now, Carol."

She doesn't argue. She's like a robot: pushes herself up, props herself on her knees, and uses the edge of the bathtub to help herself up. I go to her.

"I'm fine," she says, a little harshly. I raise my hands. "Okay."

She manages to shuffle slowly, and once we're out of the bathroom, she lets me take her elbow. In the kitchen I help her to the chair.

"I won't tie you to the chair, since when I leave you'll just have to go back to the bathroom." I heat the skillet with a little olive oil and a dollop of butter. That's a trick Moira taught me, but I don't remember why it's a good thing to mix them. Something about stopping the omelet from burning.

I divide the omelet between two plates and put a fork on each. We're sitting across from each other. I'm fascinated to see that she eats it without hesitation. If that were me, after the champagne trick last night, I wouldn't touch it.

Neither of us speaks, and when we're done, I take her back to the bathroom. I watch her lie down on the makeshift bed, and just as I turn to leave, she speaks, in a tone I haven't yet heard from her.

"He was right about you."

I turn back to look at her. "What's that supposed to mean?"

"You're insane. Just like he said." She hoists herself up to a sitting position, her features taut with hatred. I don't know why it surprises me to see her like this.

"He said the most terrible things about you," she continues. "About how crazy you are. Sometimes I even wondered whether it was really true. But now I know. You're so much worse."

I'm so shocked that I don't know whether to laugh or lunge at her. Then she says, "You'd do anything to keep us apart. How long are you going to keep me here? Really?"

I can't help it. I burst out laughing, rocking my head back. It just shoots out of me and bounces against the tiles.

She flinches at the noise, looks away, and starts to fiddle with the edges of the quilt.

"You think this is about you?" I sneer. "You think I brought you here to keep you apart? And I'm the crazy one?"

She snaps her head up toward me.

"You know it is. You hate the fact that Jim wants me instead of you. I make him happy, and you can't stand it. You're vindictive and cruel and all the things—"

"That's enough!" I shout into her face. It takes an effort to control myself, but finally I manage, and I say, more calmly, "You can have him, Carol. You should have gone away together and not tried to pin it on me."

I raise my index finger and point it into her wincing face.

"That's what this is about."

When I leave, I lock the door. I know I lock it. I can see myself doing it, so I know that I have locked that door, and there is no way that Carol can get out.

36

We have a short rehearsal beforehand. It's not really a rehearsal, just a meet-and-greet with my fellow panelists, to show us where we'll be sitting, that sort of thing. I've missed the buzz of these events, and I'm loving being back on that stage; I am ready to shine. And to top it off, I am to be accompanied by three other women writers—yes, it is the topic of the day—and I'm thrilled that Elizabeth Halloway is also on the panel. She is my new favorite author, although I'm loathe to mention it to her. Beatrice used to be my favorite writer of all time and look where that got her.

Elizabeth Halloway writes nonfiction—biographies. But they're so good, I can't put them down. Her style is so personal and so riveting, it's better than fiction. She wrote a biography of Simone de Beauvoir, and I don't mind saying normally that's not my thing. But it concentrated on her relationships, and frankly, after reading it, I had to wonder how she could have been such a feminist, considering what a wet rag she was in her personal life. Sitting next to Elizabeth Halloway makes me feel like I've joined the big leagues, even though I'm the Poulton Prize winner. That says something.

We start by introducing ourselves, recounting our histories, and I have slotted right back in there with the best of them. I talk about *Long Grass Running*, of course, but also about my new novel, and I can talk for a long time about it. The audience is wonderful and attentive, their faces uplifted toward us. They take notes whenever we say something, which always makes me laugh. What if I say something really stupid, like, *I find the best way to get inspiration is to hold your breath for a minute or two before writing anything.* Would they then do that? I don't know why I think like that. Maybe Jim was right and I am a psychopath.

Questions are flying from the audience, and my throat constricts a little when I hear his voice. I'd know it anywhere. I've heard it often enough lately. I wasn't paying attention. I was filling my glass of water again, and my eyes were not on the audience.

"This is a question for Emma Fern."

I snap my head up and there he is, standing, looking very genuine, as if he had never met me before.

My fellow panelists are all looking at me. I realize I haven't said anything yet.

"Hello," I say.

"Hi, Sam Huntington. My question is this. Your first novel, *Long Grass Running*, which won the Poulton, as we all know—"

There's a murmur of assent in the room, and a few scattered claps.

"—did you write it by yourself?"

I don't believe my ears. Everyone at our table chuckles, but I'm frozen; my face feels taut and my mouth is set. I try to breathe slowly and concentrate on relaxing my muscles.

"I was fortunate to be mentored, if that's your question, by Beatrice Johnson Greene. She helped me greatly."

"I understand. I'll rephrase my question: Did she write any part of the novel?"

"I'm sorry?"

I can feel the shift in the room. It's such a strange and particularly offensive question, they're waiting for me to be outraged. They're probably wondering what's taking me so long. I have to say something, but then Sam adds, "With you, I mean? Did you write the novel together? I'm wondering how you found the experience of being mentored."

I let out the breath I didn't know I was holding.

"She didn't write it with me, no, but she helped me. I wrote a memoir about that."

"I see, thank you." He sits back down.

Is that it? His tone made it sound like I was on trial, as if I was facing the jury and Sam was the prosecutor. What an awful man he is. He's sabotaging my event.

"It's surprising how often some readers question the authenticity of authorship," Elizabeth says next to me, but in the general direction of the audience. "Because it is an interesting question, and people believe it happens much more than it really does."

They love this sort of conversation, of course, because they are for real. They are the real deal; they wrote their books, and it's such fun to talk about people who pretend. People like me. But I suspect Elizabeth is trying to deflect the attention away from me, and I am touched by that.

"It is, indeed," I say, but that's all I manage to say, because I'm shaking, and my mouth is trembling, and I don't want to draw attention to myself. I lift the glass of water to my lips, but a little of it spills onto my notes.

Elizabeth raises an eyebrow, as if to say, *Are you okay?* and I nod quickly.

"It's just that—" Sam is on his feet again and I'm going to die, I just know it, "—it was touched upon in the *New Yorker* article, that possibly you are not sufficiently crediting Beatrice Johnson Greene for her contribution. That's all I mean. I wasn't suggesting you plagiarized the novel! I assume you wouldn't!"

Now the panel is laughing out loud, as is the audience, and I force myself to join in. I'm paralyzed. The edges of the room have blurred slightly, and I focus on the door at the back to steady myself. I feel lightheaded. Maybe I should faint, blame the heat in here; tell them I'm pregnant.

Sam sits back down, smiling crookedly at me. He makes me feel ill. I can't believe I once thought it was a charming smile. One of my fellow panelists starts to tell a story about an author who was caught out stealing a book, and another who pretended to write an auto-biography that turned out to be nothing like the life he lived, and everyone agrees these are really stupid things to do, since invariably people will get caught doing them. Someone will know you made up that existence, or you didn't write the book. I nod throughout, and I pray that no one is looking too closely, because I can't stop the tension from creeping through every fiber of my being, and I'm convinced I must be bright red.

Finally someone else raises their hand, and we're no longer talking about people stealing books. I breathe again slowly, gently, meditatively, and I pray that Sam will not stand again and ask another question. Or say something. But I'm going to sue this man when I'm done here. For slander. And hardship.

When it's over, we all stand, but I leave through the back exit before anyone has a chance to stop me. I almost race out of the place, but I feel someone catching my sleeve and I turn with as much force as I can muster, ready to punch him in the face.

"That went really well, I think, don't you?" Sam asks.

He is standing right in front of me, looking wounded, as if it is me who has done wrong by him.

"Why are you here?"

"I always visit the book festival. This is my business, Emma. You know that." He leans closer. "It's nice to see you."

"You're crazy." I stare at him, then I look around me. There are people everywhere.

"Why did you do that? Back there?" I ask.

"I was trying to get your attention."

In spite of myself I let out a laugh. He puts a hand on my forearm, but I snatch it back.

"Hey, don't be like that. I saw your name in the program and I just came to see you. You can understand that, can't you? How else can I see you if you don't tell me where you are?"

I just want to punch him. "I have to go," I say.

He grabs hold of my elbow. "I miss you."

"Don't, Sam, please. Not here."

"Then where?"

"What do you want from me?"

"I just want to spend some time with you. I miss you. I miss what we did together."

"Cut it out, will you? We talked last night, for Christ's sake. Are you stalking me? Are you a fake? Are you really a ghostwriter?"

"That's funny! You're asking me if I'm pretending to be a ghost-writer? That'd make me a ghost-ghostwriter, wouldn't it? Of course I am. I wasn't going to ask about that, back there. I'm a professional. I'd never tell, you know that. And I don't just mean about us fucking." He laughs, a jolly, loud laugh, and I make my decision right then and there. There will be no second novel. I have to get away from this creep. It's like everyone is out to get me. I just can't get a break. I'm going to tell Frankie. I'm going to tell him that I hired a ghostwriter to help me, but then I changed my mind, and I have to start again. I'll think of another way.

"It's not working with you on the book I miss," Sam says, "it's you."

He's crazy. He talks like we're dating and it's charming and *How about dinner? I know this little romantic restaurant around the corner. You'll love it; my treat*, and all I can think is: *This man is dangerous.* I'm surrounded by dangerous men. And Carol.

"I have to go," I say, as I think to myself, *If you kill three, and you promise to stop there, would that still make you a serial killer? No. Not if you promise. To stop there.*

I'll stop there, I promise.

◆ ◆ ◆

I'm exhausted.

I really feel like I don't have my usual resilience. I could have handled this better, and normally I would, but there's so much going on. I can't wait to get home and get this whole Carol/Jim business out of my life.

On my way to Cadman Plaza to find a taxi, I send a text to Frankie to tell him it went fine, and that I'll call him when I get back. I'm sure that once I've had a Scotch or ten, things won't seem so bad.

There's a line at the taxi stand, but I can't be bothered to walk away and find one quicker. I'll just wait my turn. There is a text alert on my phone, and I see that Frankie has replied.

> Great! And guess what? Change of plans. Surprise! We're on our way, almost there, did I say Brad is a great cook too? Dinner's on us, see you at the beach house. F. Xoxoxo

My stomach doesn't just lurch, it flips, then my heart stops beating, and my vision blurs and I'm going to be very sick. Right here on the sidewalk. I'm very sick now. I have to reread the text, but I can't because the words are fuzzy and the letters are jumping, and I can't make sense of it, but it can't be what I think it is. It just can't. I look around for somewhere to sit down, but I'm in a line waiting for a fucking cab that's going to take hours to even show up because guess what! It's rush hour. It's always rush hour in this city.

I bring the cell phone up closer to my eyes and there's a hand on my shoulder and a voice says, "Do you mind moving?" and I look up at a man whose chin is pointing ahead of me. I realize that the line has moved forward while I stood still. He looks at me as if there is something wrong with me. Have I gone really pale? I must have. I take a step forward. I wish there was something I could hold on to. I look at the screen again, and I hand him the cell phone, my hand trembling, and say, "What does it say, please?"

"What?"

I push the phone up as if I'm going to strike his face with it. "What does it say?"

My hand is shaking so much, he says, "Are you all right? Can I get you something?"

Am I speaking Japanese? Why doesn't he do as I ask? I grab the edge of his blue jacket and his face tightens, so I release it immediately, and I repeat myself. "Please, what does the text say? I have a migraine. My vision is blurry. You know how that happens when you get a migraine? Maybe you don't. Well, I can't read properly. Please?"

He smiles quickly, pushes my hand away from him and says, "Just move along, please. Otherwise I'll get ahead of you." I notice then the people behind him, necks craning, wondering what's holding them up.

I close my eyes. Take another step forward. I try and imagine the words I just read. It went something like: *Brad is a great cook, great, we're on our way.* On our way where? Please God, please. There's been a misunderstanding, and Frankie and Brad are coming to my old apartment because, no, he said the beach house, and—wait! They'll make dinner? Supper? When I asked him if I could stay there, I told him I needed some quiet time by myself. I remember that. *Quiet time*, I said. *By myself*, I said. Then it occurs to me that something is really wrong with me, because I should just call him, but I didn't even think of that until now. I'm still shaking, but I'm relieved also to have come up with a solution. I'll tell him to turn back. *You can't come to the beach house.* I'll lie. I'll say I'm in hospital and he has to come and see me right away.

I manage to find the right screen and I hit call, but it goes to voice-mail, and I don't understand why. I try again and get voicemail again, and I keep pressing buttons because I have to do something. I look up and people are walking right past me now, and I see a cab. The man I just asked to help me is stepping off the curb, and I run, pushing people out of my way, and just as he opens the door, I climb inside and tell him it's an emergency. "I'm really sorry," I say, and I shut the door and he says something I can't quite hear as I tell the driver the address and that if he gets me there in record time, I'll give him an extra hundred dollars. Then I lean back against the vinyl seat and get my breath back.

That's the problem with staying at someone else's house. They have no respect for your privacy. It's a little rude of Frankie to just invite himself like that, without proper warning. I don't just rock up to his house any time I feel like it without calling first. If he had arrived unannounced, it would have been different, because I could have explained at least. I could have told him that ever since Jim left me, this crazy woman, Carol, has been stalking me, waiting in the shadows outside my building, calling me, and begging me to meet with her. I could have told him how she spun this crazy story about being afraid of Jim; that he was going to kill her.

"She's completely unhinged, Frankie. She's incredibly dangerous. She tracked me down. Can you believe it? I managed to overcome her and tie her up until the police get here. Where are the police? They should be here by now. I'll call them again. Just to make sure." That's what I would have said.

It wouldn't be very hard to make Carol look bad. Who would Frankie believe? Me, of course. I would tell him that she tricked me into having a drink with her; that she stole my driver's license and dressed like me—pretended to be me—all to get Jim for herself and, frankly, I don't know why she went to all that trouble. She can have him.

"Are you all right there?" the driver says, and I sit up.

"Yes, why?" I put both hands flatly by my side, steadying myself.

"You're talking to yourself," he says.

◆　◆　◆

It's going to take too long. I am stuck in a never-ending nightmare. The entire trip, I'm on redial. Call back. Voicemail. Call back. Voicemail. What the fuck is Frankie doing? Is he on the phone with the police? Telling them to get there right away because there's a strange woman tied up in his bathroom? My face is pressed against the glass, scanning for the police cars. I'm expecting the full police-chase experience any minute now. They'll have the full light show on, dozens of them at least, with their spinning red and blue lights flashing and a megaphone clearly visible above a car roof.

Mrs. Emma Fern, come out now with your hands above your head!

My phone pings. I'm dying. I'm sweating. I'm afraid to look. I put my hand over my eyes and let just a sliver of space show between my fingers before I read it.

Would you mind picking up some milk on the way? F. Xoxoxo

I drop my hand quickly and read it again. It really is from Frankie, and the timestamp says it was sent just now. Where the fuck is he? He's not at the beach house, that's clear. Did we make some kind of arrangement that I've forgotten about? I reread the previous text; the pain between my eyes is excruciating. I scan through dozens of older ones. Was there something else from Frankie that I missed?

The driver is talking to me.

"What?" I say.

"There's some incident on the Long Island Expressway." He taps on the GPS screen next to him.

"So how long is it going to take?" I ask.

He shrugs. "Maybe an hour. I'm going as fast as I can."

I close my eyes. *Kill me now, somebody, anybody.*

"I still get the hundred bucks, right? I'm going as fast as I can."

"Yes. Just keep going. As fast as you can. Go through red lights, I don't care. I'll pay the fines. I'll pay anything you like. Please just get there as fast as you can."

Frankie said he was on his way. I just need to get there first. I try to call him again. Voicemail. I'm going to throw this phone out of the window any minute now. I look at the screen again, at the last text.

Would you mind picking up some milk on the way? F. Xoxoxo

I don't get it. Can't he get it himself? Maybe he hasn't left yet. Maybe I'm dreaming. My fingers trembling, I hit reply, and write:

No problem, anything else? Em. Xx

I wait, leaning against the window and a moment later Frankie replies.

Just you :) see you soon F. Xoxo

Oh God. I bury my face in my hands. Is it really possible Frankie hasn't opened the bathroom door yet? But that's ridiculous. Carol would be screaming if she heard strangers in the house. Is he tricking me? Pretending everything is fine until I get there so that the cops can arrest me?

I think through my options. I could ask the driver to take me to the airport—get a flight to somewhere, anywhere. Then I could send a text to Frankie, explaining that I'm on a plane and the plane has been hijacked, and we are all going to die, but I'm thinking of him in my last, darkest moment.

I can't get out of the country because I don't have my passport with me. I didn't think I needed it, did I? It never occurred to me that I might be the one going to Tunisia.

Did Carol faint? Is she too frightened to call out? She wasn't before, when I was on the phone with Sam. Why would she be all shy suddenly? Maybe she's dead. Maybe she's asleep again, after all the pills I gave her last night.

I type another text to Frankie:

Would you mind not using your master bathroom? I had a little accident in there and I just want to clean up first. Sorry!

Then I change my mind, delete the text without sending it. Surely it's best if I plead innocence? Surprise? I wasn't here and I have no idea who this is. *Oh wait, is that you, Carol? What on earth are you doing here?*

◆ ◆ ◆

I remember to get the milk. I've had the taxi stop and wait at a convenience store because I thought it would be useful in case I needed to tell my story about my unhinged stalker, Carol.

But, Officer, I have no idea how this person ended up here. If I'd done something like that, I would hardly stop to buy milk, would I?

I ask the driver to let me out a good half a mile before the house. I pay the extra hundred dollars. The last thing I need is a scene. It's very quiet. There's certainly no inkling that something shocking has happened in the neighborhood.

I walk up the hill to the house, scanning ahead all the time, keeping my head down whenever a car drives by. There is nothing but peace and silence. The closer I get to the house, the more I expect to see dozens of police cars waiting for me, TV news vans parked in the street, but there's nothing.

When I get there, the lights are on in just about every room as far as I can tell from here. Frankie and, I presume, Brad, are standing by the window, facing each other. I watch their silhouettes as Frankie puts one arm around Brad's shoulders, and Brad lifts a glass to his lips.

They certainly don't look frantic. They don't look like they just discovered a dead woman in the bathroom. They don't look like anything other than two people having a leisurely conversation near the window.

I stand rooted to the spot for another five minutes, watching them chatting, and when they move away from the window, I walk up the steps to the front door. The outside sensor light comes on as I put my ear against the heavy wood, but I can't hear anything from here.

The house and its occupants are a tableau of blissful peace.

I brace myself and let myself in.

37

"Emma! There you are, dearest!"

Frankie must have heard me, he's standing right at the door. He holds it wide open, grinning from ear to ear, and he pulls me inside by the arm.

"Come, come! Brad! She's here! Come and be met!"

"Hello!" Brad's head pops out of the kitchen doorway. "Sorry I can't shake your hand, I'm elbow deep in cornstarch." He lifts both his arms, his sleeves rolled up to show me, although I can't see any cornstarch, but then again, what the fuck do I know? "Can I get you a drink?"

"We got some champagne," Frankie says. "I thought we should celebrate. We have so much to celebrate, Emma, wouldn't you say? And, Emma dearest, the silver champagne bucket does not live under the sink, for future reference." They both laugh.

My face is frozen, smiling. I nod, a lot, just like Carol did last night. I too am stuck on a nodding loop; my eyes darting to the master bedroom. Frankie must have noticed, because he says, "You don't mind, do you? I put your things in the guest room. It's just for a couple nights. I didn't think you'd mind."

I nod some more, then I move my head sideways. "No, no, I don't mind in the least. Of course not."

I missed my calling as a ventriloquist. That I managed to say that many words through my tight smile is nothing short of a miracle.

Brad is all smiles as he hands me a flute of champagne. "It's so nice to finally meet you, Emma. I've heard so much about you." He smiles at Frankie as he says this last part.

"Thank you, it's great to meet you too. I'll just take off my jacket now, shall I?"

They both laugh heartily. "God! Sorry!" they say, in unison, as Frankie helps me take it off. I don't know what's so amusing.

Frankie hangs the jacket up for me. "It's funny, you know, when we arrived, I thought you were already here."

"You did?" I say over the beating of my heart.

"I thought I heard something." He shakes his head. "I don't know what made me think of that."

"Can I pop in to your bathroom to get my toothbrush?" I ask, and I'm stunned no one can hear my heart thumping in my chest.

"Oh, I already moved your toiletries to the other bathroom. You don't mind, do you?" He puts a hand on my shoulder, looks at me, head slightly cocked. I don't know why, but I mirror him, I cock my head too, smiling, glass in hand, frozen. "You did?"

"But yes, please see if there's anything of yours in there. I'm starving! We've been waiting for you. Oh, did you get the milk?"

As I brandish the brown paper bag, it occurs to me that life is a funny thing, isn't it? One minute you think you're going to die, the world has ended, and life as you know it is over, and the next, you know with complete certainty that you will never be this happy again. Ever.

"Yes, here it is! And no! Of course I don't mind you getting your room back! Don't be silly! God, it's good to be back! I'm just going to put this"—I lift my bag in the air—"in my room, and I'll be right back. Brad, what is that heavenly smell wafting out of the kitchen? I'm starving!"

I arrange my things in the guest bedroom, listening for the two of them. They're in the kitchen, laughing and chatting. I open all the closets, all the time expecting Jim and Carol to pop up like a jack-in-the-box. I check the master bathroom, then I go to the master bedroom. The door to the bathroom is ajar; the key still on the outside, just as I left it.

I go in, half expecting to find Carol slumped over the edge of the bathtub, but no, she's not here. There's no one here. There's no rope either. No evidence whatsoever that she was ever in this room. Back in the master bedroom I check the closets. Then I check for the gun. The gun that I put back in its carrying case, right at the back of the closet. The gun that I thank the Lord is still there.

◆   ◆   ◆

It's like I'm a different person. I'm Emma Fern, but I'm not Emma Fern. There's another parallel universe somewhere, with the other Emma Fern in it, and she's been arrested, for sure. She came back to the beach house and Frankie shook his head at her in disbelief and disappointment, and Carol was taken somewhere in an ambulance, and the policeman put his hand on the top of Emma's head as he put her in the back of the squad car. The TV news crews were there also, lots of them, filming her downfall in all its tragedy, and Nick the Prick was probably there too, snickering from the sidelines, and Emma in handcuffs is going to jail for a very, very long time.

But in *this* universe, the one I'm inhabiting, I'm having a really lovely time with Frankie and Brad. We're drinking too much, me especially, and we're laughing a lot. I'm a little over the top, a little too loud, but it's all in good fun, and when I see her reflection beyond the sliding doors, my heart stops, because I think it's Jim, but it's not. It's Beatrice, and amazingly, I'm pleased to see her. We look at each other, and then I turn my gaze away.

I've never seen Frankie with a partner before, and it makes my heart drip with affection to watch him now, sitting at the dinner table, his eyes flicking up to Brad, who is stirring the sauce, his back to us.

"It's nice to see you, Frankie. It makes me happy." I'm starting to slur, but it's a pleasant feeling, coming as it does with a wave of tranquility. The kind of tranquility that comes from looking in every corner of the house, under the guise of *just making sure it's tidy, Frankie, I'd die if you thought me a messy guest!* and finding nothing amiss. Nothing at all. Carol was never here. I dreamed the whole thing. I'm sure of it.

His hand reaches over to take mine. He's looking at me now. "I'm glad, and I'm glad you're here, Emma, after everything with Jim."

I take an audible breath and he apologizes for bringing it up.

"No, I'm fine, really," I hasten to say. I don't want him to worry about me. This is too nice. I want to be a part of this. We're a little family, the three of us. I love them both so much, even though I only met Brad half an hour ago. I wink at Frankie, a wicked wink that says, *How lucky are you!* and he chuckles in his shy way.

"Tell me about today," he says.

I look away, getting my thoughts together. "It was fine. Some of the questions were a bit hard to answer, but you know how it is."

He nods, solemn almost.

"Elizabeth Halloway is very nice. It was great sharing a panel with her."

"Great! I'm glad it went well then."

And I smile, because what else am I going to say?

"How's Nick?" I ask.

Frankie looks down. "Nick isn't very happy."

Do I detect a note of displeasure?

"Why not?"

"Let's just say that the reception so far is not what we expected." His smile is tight and determined at the same time. "I'll leave it at that."

Can one die of joy? I guess I'm about to find out, because my heart is overflowing. I give him an "oh, I'm sorry" look. It takes all my power not to jump up and down with glee.

"I don't understand, you seemed so, how shall I put it?" I'm about to say *enamored* but I stop myself. "Enthusiastic?"

"Yes, well, I was! I am, I mean."

"You don't sound like it."

Tell me more! I want to beg. *How bad is it? Go on! Tell me!*

"What do you mean?"

"Seriously, Frankie? I've felt like you've been pushing this guy down my throat ever since you met him. That lunch! God! I thought you were in love!"

Brad pops his head out the doorway of the kitchen.

"No no, that's just an expression," I assure him.

Brad gives me a toothy smile and pops his head back inside.

"Hey, I had to do something to get you writing."

I turn back to Frankie. He's grinning.

"What does that mean?"

"Were you jealous?"

"Yes! Are you joking?" I cock my head sideways. "So you don't think he's the brightest star in the universe? The voice of his generation?"

"He's a writer under contract, Emma. I have many of those. Badosa Press and its imprints publish many books." He smiles.

I punch him lightly on the shoulder. "I had no idea."

"Thank you for noticing." And we both laugh.

"But why? The lunch and all that jazz?"

"So you'd write, Emma. I was trying to give you a nudge." He grins. "And you have to admit, it worked."

I smile at him, and in that moment, I make a resolution. I'm going to finish that next book. Without Sam. Just me.

Can life get any better?

It turns out that it can, because as Brad brings us steaming plates of scallops in champagne sauce, with a "That's just for starters, guys," and after we've exclaimed our delight, Frankie says, "Hey, Emma, I have good news. I wanted to tell you tonight."

"What's that?"

"Lunch tomorrow, you're free?"

"I—think so." Lord knows what will happen between now and then. "Yes, I'm free."

"Great. There are some people I want you to meet. We can go together." And he winks at me.

I feel a little flutter in my stomach, because this time I'm fairly sure I know who he's talking about, and it's not Nick the Prick.

"Oh, and I forgot to say, your friend called me earlier, just before you got here, in fact."

"My friend?"

"Sam Huntington."

I close my eyes for a minute. "I don't know who that is," I say, because I'm drunk and I'm not thinking straight, and I haven't been thinking straight for something like six hours.

"You do know!" Frankie exclaims. He looks at me, surprised. "The guy from the restaurant the other day. Sam Huntington. He was at Nick's book launch."

"Oh right, yes. What did he want?"

Frankie lifts a scallop to his mouth.

"He wanted to know where you are."

38

"I love this place. Have you been here before, Emma?"

Liz Carmody's long hair falls across her cheek when she turns to me to say this. I wish I had long hair.

"Just once, and I love it. I love Japanese food."

It's not just the food, it's the decor. It's modern and retro at the same time. So unusual, with its curved ceilings, like the inside of a whale. We sit in a white booth and it's a perfect setting for this sort of meeting. There are tall vases of what I think are cherry blossom. I wonder where they got those at this time of year?

I must be delirious, but right now I'm just happy to be out of the house. I'm here with Frankie and two movie producers. Frankie told me about them in the car, just after he told me I looked awful, and did I really get any sleep? I assured him that I was fine, even though I spent all night listening for Jim. Frankie told me something else about the producers' plans, but at this point I couldn't care less if they were going to make a Disney animation of my book. I have no idea what's going on anymore. I have come to believe that I dreamed the whole thing about Carol in the beach house, even though the rope is still there at the bottom of the broom closet. Frankie noticed it when we cleaned up last night. I was determined to sweep the floor, which required no sweeping, inventing imaginary crumbs, because I wanted to open the closet, but I timed it wrongly, and Frankie got there before me.

"Is that yours?" he asked, a bit puzzled. "It's a lot of rope."

"Mmm?" I said. "Oh that? I found it outside, on the grass, I thought it was yours."

"Really? I'll check with the neighbors, but it's not mine."

"Ah, okay," I said, nonchalantly. If that's the only problem I am going to be faced with, having to explain that bit of rope—happy days. I'm in heaven. I can come up with a million explanations for it. Easy. *Give me a harder one*, I want to say.

"So, Emma," Liz Carmody says, bringing me back to the present. Liz is one half of the husband-and-wife producer team we're meeting here. "Firstly, we want to tell you how much we love *Long Grass Running*. It's a beautiful book. And I'm surprised that the movie rights haven't been snapped up yet."

"Thank you."

"There's been a few offers," Frankie chimes in, "but nothing we felt comfortable with. Emma and I strongly believe that for the project to be a success, we need to work with the right people."

It's hard not to laugh. We'd work with anyone. We've been trying to get this movie off the ground for a year now. But I nod sagely, in agreement.

"We are flattered that you think we are the right people to work with on this project. We certainly hope to be. I've explained our vision to Frankie"—she says this to me—"and we have some exciting ideas to share with you."

"I can't wait to hear them, Liz. I'm very excited."

"So are we. Where should we start, Liz?" says Dwight Carmody. But Liz's cell buzzes and she lifts an index finger up in the air, as if to say, *Hold that thought*, and picks it up.

Everyone has their cell phone on the table, myself included. It's the sort of meeting where you're not expected to turn your phone off, clearly. Frankie turns to me and he starts to say something when my phone buzzes as well. I answer it; it's a reflex.

"Hey, it's me."

I hang up. I put the phone back down on the table, a little more violently than I should have, and it startles Frankie.

"Wrong number," I say by way of explanation.

"Everything okay?" he asks quietly, and I nod.

Liz has finished her own conversation and is talking to Dwight, but the waiter has arrived with our sushi, and there's a bit of a commotion at the table as everyone moves glasses and phones out of the way. My phone buzzes again. I pick it up and am about to turn it off, but then I change my mind. I get up from my chair.

"Excuse me."

I go to the ladies' room, the phone still buzzing in my hand. I answer it outside the door, leaning against the wall.

"What the fuck, Sam?"

"What's wrong with you today?"

"What do you want?"

"To apologize, about yesterday. I'm sorry," he says. "I don't know what's gotten into me to be honest. I'm not usually like that."

"You have been a little creepy, Sam."

"Yes, I know. I'll stop now. No more creepiness, I swear."

I don't know what to say, except that I don't believe him.

"Emma, I think we should finish the book, and I think we should put personal feelings on hold while we're doing that. If anything . . . romantic, is to happen between us—and I hope it will—then it needs to be after we've finished our project. I apologize for not having made that decision sooner."

I put a hand on my chest and take a deep breath. When Frankie told me that Sam was looking for me, I think, for the first time, I felt scared of Sam. Frankie didn't tell him anything, thank God.

"I'm not going to give your whereabouts to every Tom, Dick, and Harry who asks, Emma," Frankie had said. "Seriously, what do you take me for?" I told him I'd call Sam, and tell him myself that I don't know him very well, and he's beginning to be a little clingy, shall we say, but Frankie didn't think it was anything to worry about.

"The price of fame, babe," he said, but I knew he was making light of it on purpose, after what happened over a year ago, when I was stalked by Beatrice's agent, for reasons which no one ever found out about, thank the Lord. Frankie didn't want me to worry, and I suspect that if Sam were to call him again, Frankie wouldn't mention it to me. After he'd told him where to go, so to speak. It upset me, hearing that. What does Sam want from me? This isn't just a crush. What did he say that time? *But you're Emma Fern.* Can I please, just once in my life, get a break?

So now I need to ask the question. "You called Frankie yesterday, asking where I was. Why did you do that?"

There's a pause, then Sam replies, "I'm sorry, but I was worried. I tried to call you when you left the book festival and your phone was constantly busy. I couldn't get through and I got concerned. Sorry."

"Okay, Sam, I'm going to say this once, and once only. We're done. There's no book, no contract, no relationship, no nothing. I'll have my lawyers get in touch to terminate the contract. Do. Not. Contact. Me. Again."

After I've hung up and I'm back at the table, I turn off my cell. Frankie puts his hand on mine and leans across. "Everything okay?"

"Yes, fine, really. I'll tell you later," I whisper back. "So, who's going to play me? Jennifer Lawrence?" I ask brightly.

They all look at me as if I have two heads.

"It was a joke," I assure them. "There's no *me* in the book. Unless I lived a previous life as a farmer." But it still falls flat, even though they titter a little.

We don't discuss numbers because that sort of thing is best handled when the talent isn't there, I'm told. Frankie is my agent, as well as my publisher. He'll take care of everything for me on that side.

I lean in to him and say, "Can I stay longer at the beach house? Maybe for a few weeks even?"

"Of course," he whispers back. "Stay as long as you need. Why?"

"So I can finish my book."

◆ ◆ ◆

I go back to the beach house by myself after lunch. It's the first time I've been alone since Carol disappeared into thin air, so it's the first opportunity I've had to try to figure out how she did it. I checked last night, after everyone went to bed, whether my cell phone was still here, the one Jim took from me and Carol brought back. It was. Just as I left it, hidden inside the box of washing powder, along with her stupid burner phone.

I've offered to make coq au vin for the three of us tonight; something I haven't done in years, but Brad mentioned he loved the dish. The weather has cooled, finally, otherwise I wouldn't serve a meal like that. I wish they were here already. I don't know if I'll be able to stay by myself after the weekend, when they leave. I think I'll have to tell Frankie about Jim; that I'm frightened of him. I don't know how I'll ever sleep again otherwise.

After I've put the groceries away, I move slowly from room to room, listening intently.

"Oh, and another thing, Em, make sure to lock the sliding doors onto the deck. It's not as safe as you might think around here," Frankie had said last night, before we went to bed. Needless to say, I had locked the sliding doors. Somehow, they magically opened themselves.

"No, it wouldn't do to walk in and find me hit over the head with a hammer now, would it?" I replied; I don't know why. One of those times where my mouth was running faster than my champagne-soaked brain. They looked at me, startled. I waved it away. "Sorry, I was thinking of something on the news."

"Around here? Hit with a hammer?" Brad had blurted, more dismayed than I'd expected him to be.

"No no no, ignore what I said. I should go to bed, I think." Then I added, just before getting up from the table, "Is there anything else? That I should know about?"

They looked at each other. Frankie started to shake his head, but then abruptly he said, "Just curious, why didn't you park your car in the garage?"

I remember feeling the color drain from my face, because I'd completely forgotten about the garage, where I'd parked Carol's little Honda. Completely forgotten. Totally. For all I knew, Carol had somehow crawled in there. "I . . ."

"Well since you're not using it, we parked the Lexus there," Frankie said, his tone indicating that he didn't think it important. Good.

"Good, good." I even managed not to blurt out something about parking outside in the street on purpose, so that they could bring the Lexus in. Since I didn't know they were coming, that would have sounded a little weird. Note to self: *Do not sound weird*. I didn't ask anything else about the garage. I figured if there was a dead body in there, or something else, Lord knows what, they would have mentioned it.

Then Frankie added as an afterthought, "But again, Em, without wanting to bring up anything scary, the garage door wasn't closed all the way down. There was a gap, at the bottom of the roller door. Probably not big enough for someone to slip through, but you know, you can't be too careful. Especially since I haven't had it fixed yet—the garage door."

It's the first place I check thoroughly for clues, now I'm back. After I've made sure the doors are still locked—and they all are. Including the sliding doors. The garage is clean, as clean as a garage can be, and why wouldn't it be?

Obviously that's how Jim got in. He must have staked out the place, figured out the door didn't close. Then they probably walked right out through the front door.

That's the part I don't understand. Why she went to such lengths to hide the fact that I'd kept her here—against her will, let's face it. That's called kidnapping, and carries a hefty jail sentence.

I've already started cooking when Frankie calls to say they have to cancel tonight, but they'll be back tomorrow night instead. *Please come,* I want to say, but I don't.

"I'll cook something tomorrow night then, okay? Don't bring any food." I say instead.

"I'm really looking forward to it, Em."

I'll make it tonight anyway, since I've already started, and this is a dish that does nicely the next day, if not better. So I spend an hour in the kitchen, chopping and preparing. The distraction of cooking is calming me. I put the pot on to simmer, and go into the living room to put some music on. I flick through the CDs scattered on top of the cabinet, when the light comes on outside, shining around the edges of the drapes, and I drop the CD I'm holding.

It's only an animal or something. It happens all the time. The sensor is too sensitive. Even the wind can trigger it.

I wait, still as a statue, and listen. Slowly I make my way to the window, peer out at the edge of the curtain, but there's nothing. Just the usual distant sounds.

I wait for my heart to slow down. I return to my task of choosing some music, and settle on Claude Debussy. While the pot simmers, I go through the bathroom again, inch by inch. It's so strange. There's nothing there. No evidence whatsoever that Carol was ever in this room. Not even a hair off her head.

Exhaustion overwhelms me, and I tell myself that it's going to be okay. After all, Jim got his Carol back. He has no need to come here again. He'd be stupid to do so. I need to relax and stop being so paranoid. I draw a bath, in which I add a few drops of scented oil, and I light some candles. The coq au vin needs to simmer for half an hour at least, so I have time to luxuriate in the scented water with a glass of wine. I need to calm down. I lay back in the soft water and close my eyes. I could fall asleep.

Am I dreaming? I open my eyes with a jolt. The music has stopped.

He's here. This is it. Oh God. How could I be so stupid? Why did I think he wouldn't come now? My heart thumps in my chest as I wait, listening, but there's nothing. Just eerie silence. I get out of the bath very quietly and pull on the thick robe that hangs behind the door.

"Frankie?" I whisper.

My feet make a wet noise on the wooden floor as I go through the house. It's darker now, and I turn on a lamp in the living room and go to check the sound system. The CD is still spinning. I stop it, then restart it, but there's no sound.

I lean closer, just to make sure, and fear explodes in my chest, because I can see that the volume control is all the way down.

"Frankie?" I shout now. "Is someone here?"

I look around me, desperate for something to use as a weapon, but there's nothing. I run to the bedroom and slip on the floor. I get up, and flick the light switch, my chest thumping.

"Who's there?" I shout. "Jim?"

I turn and scream at my own reflection in the window.

I run to the bedroom, grab the clothes I threw on the bed, and lock myself in the bathroom. I put on my jeans and my T-shirt, then I listen by the door.

I fucked up. I really fucked up this time. Jim is crazy. I've put myself in real danger. Oh God, what was I thinking? I pull at my hair and I let out a low wail when I realize I don't have my phone. I don't have anything to call anyone, and he's on the other side of the door.

I lean my forehead against the door, and listen. There's no sound in the house. Not a creak. Just the distant lapping of water against the boats. Slowly, I unlock the door, as quietly as I can, and open it a fraction. Nothing. I pull it open, wider this time, fully expecting to see Jim brandishing a weapon of some sort.

I need the gun. *Think, Emma, pull yourself together. You can't go crazy like this.* I force myself to breathe, big, deep gulps of air, and keep my hand on my chest, waiting for my heart to slow down.

I go back out to the living room. Nothing has changed. There's no one here. The disc is still spinning. I make my way to Frankie's bedroom, but then I hear something. In the kitchen. It's getting louder. It's the pot. The lid is jumping on top like a pressure cooker that hasn't been closed correctly. The noise is too loud, and I want it to stop, so I run to the stove and the flame is up high, at the highest possible level.

I scream.

39

I can't breathe. There's a hand over my mouth. I reach up to pull at an arm, to get a hand off my face. I can smell him. Oh God, I can't breathe. I can't—

"Shut the fuck up, Emma!" he hisses in my ear. "If you scream, I'll break your neck. Do you understand me?"

I nod, frantically, and he releases his grip, slowly. I take in big gulps of air, he lets me go, and I fall on hard my knees.

"What the fuck, Emma?"

I don't have the gun. After all this, I don't have the gun.

He grabs hold of my hair. I try to hold on to his hands.

"Did you miss me, sweetheart?" he hisses in my ear.

"Jim, stop! Please!"

"I don't get you. I really don't. Kidnapping Carol? What's the matter with you? I had to come here to get her out, can you believe it? And it wasn't easy, I assure you."

He lets go of my hair and I put my palms on the floor. I just have to breathe.

"Get up."

I take hold of the chair leg next to me and somehow heave myself up. Leaning against the kitchen island, my palms behind me on its marble top, I turn to look at Jim. His face is stretched into a strange mask. He grins. He almost looks happy.

"I knew it," I say, crying. "I knew you'd come. The police are on their way. I called them. And Frankie. Frankie's coming."

"Oh, Emma. Honestly. You expect me to believe that?"

"You should go. Just go."

"Carol is a mess, Emma! Do you realize that? You're sick! Thank Christ I found her. I knew she wasn't in D.C. I couldn't reach her. All night, Emma! I couldn't find her! Then I figured you'd have something to do with it. Because you're sick. All I had to do was ask Dennis where you'd gone. *Et voilà!*" He opens his arms wide, like a magician at the end of a trick.

"You have to leave. Frankie will be here any minute." I gulp.

"You should pray that neither Frankie nor the police are on their way. Trust me." He laughs. "How many people did you kill, Emma dear? Were you going to kill her too? Hey! I have an idea: why don't *I* call the cops?"

"Oh God. Oh my God. You're a monster."

"Jeez, Em. Aren't you happy to see me? Smells good, by the way. What are you making?" He goes to the stove and lifts the lid. The liquid sputters onto the flame. "Ha! I knew it! Coq au vin; my favorite. Were you thinking of me, Em? That's nice."

He pulls up a chair and sits down, takes out a cigarette from his shirt pocket, and lights it from the stove.

"All I want is to be rid of you," he says, exhaling a stream of smoke. "Don't you get it? You have been a thorn in my side for years, Emma! Years!" He's shouting now. "I don't trust you. Even if you had given me my research back, I still wouldn't trust you. I'll never trust you. I need to disappear, and you need to shut the hell up."

"I won't say anything. I swear. I won't tell anyone you were here if you leave."

"I didn't want to kill you," he says, dropping ash on the floor. "I just wanted to discredit you; for you to go to jail for a very long time. For killing me, so that Carol and I can start again. God!" He slams the top of the kitchen island with his fist. "It was perfect! We were about to leave, you know that? We were all set to go, start a new life, away from here—and then you go and kidnap her?" He looks at me, shaking his head, and his tone shifts. "I was really worried about her, you know that? I couldn't bear to imagine what you might be doing to her. Seeing that you're a murderous psychopath and all."

I keep my eyes on him while trying to remember what's behind me, what I can use as a weapon.

"I never left Carol," he says now, almost thoughtful. "We kept seeing each other the entire time I was with you, and thank God for that, because I don't know how I would have coped otherwise." He looks straight at me now, cocking his head a little. "It was her idea, did she tell you? To make it look like I was crazy." He waves his fingers in front of his face, his eyes open wide, and he says, "So you'd believe her when she came to you, all scared, wanting your help." He drops his arms to his sides, looking away, as if caught up in the memory of it. "She's a smart woman, that one."

I can't breathe. For a second or two, I forget all of it: why we're here, everything that happened before. I'm overwhelmed by the feeling of betrayal. It's slicing at my heart as memories tumble over each other, each one a different moment of love or happiness, of trust and hope. Of what I thought my life was. Even the recollection of running into Carol that first time comes into my mind, and how grateful I felt for her kindness to me. I am crushed by such a deep sadness that I drop to the floor, losing the fight I thought I had in me.

"So go," I sob. "I'm not stopping you, Jim. You should go, you and Carol; disappear. Why involve me now?"

"Because," he says slowly, looking down at me, "it's surprisingly difficult to disappear in this day and age. It's much better to die. Or pretend to die. And by setting you up to take the fall, I've killed two birds with one stone!" He raises his arms again in a gesture of triumph almost, then lets them fall back down. "It was brilliant, Emma, and then you went and fucked it up for us. What am I supposed to do with you now?"

It's funny really, the power of words. Hearing him say *by setting you up to take the fall* jolts me back, and when I stand up again, I know I'm not going to let myself be crushed into oblivion by this man. I don't care what it takes.

"If anything happens to me, that package will be sent to the right people," I say surprisingly calmly, brushing imaginary dust off my knees.

"That package will be sent to the right people," he mimics, a sneer on his face. "You've been watching too much TV, Em. You're not that smart. Is it here?"

"Here? No."

"I don't believe you. I bet you keep it close at all times. Your little treasure trove. Give it to me."

He stands and comes toward me, menacing, and now I'm really scared and I run to the other side of the kitchen island.

"Oh, this is fun," he smirks. He makes a false run to the left, then to the right.

"You're crazy."

I'm backing away. I feel the edge of the stove behind me, the hot liquid sputtering on my hand, and he comes around the island toward me. I move sideways, feeling my way along the bench. He lunges forward and I reach behind me for something, anything, and I remember the knife rack but I can't reach it and the flame of the stove is burning at the side of my waist and his hands are around my neck and I'm scratching and clutching at them but he squeezes and I'm going to die and there's a flash of light at the edge of my eye when the lid from the boiling pot jerks and drops at his feet. He yells and lets go, and all I want to do is hold my throat, but instead I reach behind me, and then there's a sound, barely human; a guttural scream that comes from me as I plunge the knife into his neck.

"I did it for you!" I scream. "Everything! I did it all for you!" and I fall to my knees.

Does three make me a serial killer?

40

There's no one gawking at me. It's nothing like in my nightmares. There's a grand jury, and I am sitting at the defense table with my attorney, who is not a woman called Katherine. It's a man called Emmanuel Solomon, and Frankie got him for me. Frankie has taken care of everything. He was the first person I called.

I am calm, resigned to my fate. I've had enough. Let them send me to the chair. I don't care anymore. I'm so desperately tired.

"So, when you discovered the irregularities in the modeling, what did you think?" the prosecutor is asking Terry, who is in the witness stand. Poor Terry. He looks awful. He's nervous. I feel so sorry that I put him through this.

"At first, I thought there must be some mistake."

"But then, after you reviewed the results?"

"I knew that Jim Fern had faked the data."

"Why did he do that, do you think?"

"For the prestige of running the country's foremost economic think tank. For the money. It was a well-paid position. Not at first, but once the contracts came in, he benefited enormously. His salary went up tenfold."

Terry doesn't believe that. He knows as well as I do that Jim didn't do this for the money. Jim had delusions of grandeur, sure, but he didn't care about the money. He thought he was smarter than everyone. He thought he could solve the world's problems. And when he couldn't, he made it up. He can't be the first one.

"How did the defendant approach you?"

"She didn't. I approached her. I asked her to come and see me. I explained the situation to her, and she told me that after Jim, her husband, moved out of the marital home, she found some documents he left behind."

"Can you tell the court what documents you're referring to?"

"The full set of results from the original research. The real data, before he tampered with it."

"And those documents prove that he deliberately misled everyone?"

"Without a doubt. He edited them to support his original theory."

"What happened after she told you about finding them?"

"I said I wanted to see them. We arranged for her to come back and give them to me."

"I see. And why do you think he left them in their apartment? They must have been precious to him."

"He meant to retrieve them later. You'd have to ask him why he didn't take them when he left."

"I can hardly do that. He's dead."

"I know."

"So how do you know this was his intent?"

"I don't know directly, but considering he went to kill Em—Mrs. Fern—and get those documents back . . ."

"Did you ever speak with Mr. Fern after he resigned his position?"

"Yes, I did. Once, the day after he resigned. He came to see me."

"Did he tell you he was intending to divorce Mrs. Fern?"

"Yes, he said she had something of his; that he needed to get it back and it was still in the apartment. He wanted me to help him."

"I see. Did you know what it was?"

"He said something like, 'If it became public, it would ruin me.' I told him I wouldn't help him. It was a matter between him and his wife."

"What did he say?"

"He was livid. Furious. He couldn't understand why I wouldn't help him. Then he said, 'Trust me, Terry. I'll kill her before I let those documents become public.'"

"Did you tell Mrs. Fern about that?"

"No, I did not. I didn't believe him, and I've been losing sleep over that. I've told her how very sorry I am; that I should have said something, so she could have gone to the police about it."

"Thank you, Mr. Mundy. No further questions."

My lawyer stands up. "If I may, Your Honor, one question."

"Go ahead."

"Mr. Mundy, do you, in your conscience, in the truth of what you know, believe that Mr. Fern went to the beach house with the intent of killing my client, Mrs. Fern?"

"Without a doubt. That's what he said. He wanted to kill her."

"Thank you. No further questions."

They've let me go, the Grand Jury. They took no time at all to decide that there was no case for me to answer. Self-defense, they said. Which was true. Just this once, it was true. Although the other times were also self-defense, as far as I'm concerned. But I couldn't explain that. And anyway, I wasn't on trial for the other murders I committed, so what do I care?

I'm free. I'm innocent. That's what they said, and I could never have proven it without Terry.

He lied for me. On the stand. He took the oath, laid his hand on top of the Bible, swore to tell the truth so help him God, and then he lied.

I did give him the documents. I gave him the sealed envelope, and I said that if anything ever happened to me, he was to open them and do with them as he saw fit. He didn't know what was in them. But the way he described it in court, it didn't happen that way. I didn't find the documents he "left behind," obviously. Even to my ears that sounds so far-fetched. But let's face it, I was the aggrieved wife. I was famous, and everyone loved me—those who hadn't forgotten about me, that is. Jim, on the other hand, had been outed as the cheating, thieving, philandering, murdering, lying husband who had tricked his way into getting government agencies to hand over a lot of money. They don't like that, government agencies, as it turns out.

With Terry's testimony, no one looked too closely after that. No one was interested in restoring Jim's good name. Which means that they didn't even go near the whole boat business. What difference would it make, since we didn't kill him? He was not meant to die that night. No one cared whether I rented the car, or the boat, or Lord knows what.

The day they let me go, my lawyer gave a short statement on my behalf to the journalists gathered outside, while I stood silently next to him. When it was over, I looked around and saw her watching me from a few feet away. She waved at me. A small wave, her face inscrutable. But I know what it meant: a kind of warning. As if she were saying, *Remember me? I'm still here.* I stared back at her. *Go burn in hell, Carol,* I thought. Then I looked away.

I ignored Sam sufficiently enough that he stopped contacting me, but I saw him again, just once. He was standing on the subway platform, his arm around the shoulders of a petite brunette with a pretty, dimpled smile. I was relieved they were back together, he and Barbara. He saw me, standing a few feet away, but he didn't acknowledge me, and I just walked away.

But there is one thing I did in all those months to while away the time. I thought of Frankie, the only person who believes in me, and I wanted to make him proud. So I sat down, pulled out my leather-bound notebooks, opened my laptop, and achieved something I didn't know I had in me. I wrote a novel. I threw away everything Sam and I did, including that stupid backward first paragraph, and I started again.

It's the story of a woman who wakes up in a hospital after being hit by a car in an accident she can't recall, and the only memory she retains of her life is that she murdered someone, but she doesn't remember who or why. It's a tale of obsession and guilt, and it spilled out of me as if guided by the hand of God. I dedicated it to Beatrice.

I don't see her anymore. Not since that last time, and I don't even know if I dreamed it, or whether it really happened. But when Jim had his hands around my neck, I saw her, in the light that flashed for a fraction of a second. She was standing at the edge of my field of vision, smiling, and as my world turned to black, I watched her lift a finger, just a quick flip, before the burning lid fell to the floor.

Forgive me, I almost wrote in the dedication.

Traces in the Water, that's what I called it. And it has done very well, my novel, after everything. Killing someone and getting hauled up in front of a Grand Jury is a fine publicity technique, as it happens, even if you don't get indicted. They can't print it fast enough. And everyone thinks the Twitter campaign was a stroke of genius.

◆ ◆ ◆

"There you are." My handsome fiancé grins as he gets up to greet me. I'm filled with a wave of affection as I kiss him on the cheek. He takes my face in his hands and puts his lips to mine. I feel a shiver of pleasure down my spine.

"Have you been waiting long?" I ask.

"Not long," he says, pulling my chair out for me to sit.

"Emma Fern?"

I'm still standing as I turn and look at the elegant woman standing by my side, smiling.

"Yes, hello," I say, extending a hand.

"It's lovely to meet you. I heard you moved to Port Jefferson. I'm so pleased. I just wanted to tell you how much I loved *Traces in the Water*."

"Thank you," and as I gesture to introduce my fiancé, she turns to him and says, "The eminent economist. Of course. My husband and I are very familiar with your work."

Terry shakes her hand, all smiles, and for a moment it's as if I'm not here, and I don't mind one bit. I'm left out of the conversation as they talk policy and economy. I sit down and look out the window, at the waves gently slapping against the boats.

◆ ◆ ◆

I love it here. Most people think I'm crazy, after what happened. But in fact, it was my release, that night. I truly am free now, and I love this place. I love it so much that we bought a little house just down the road from Frankie's.

After *Traces in the Water* was published, I decided to retire from writing. Tend a vegetable garden, maybe. I'm still young enough to have children, and Terry and I want to start a family.

We're working on our house, renovating it together. We look like an ad for a bank loan, with paint in our hair, pastel colors on the walls, and the view of the bay in the distance. I saw myself in the future. Three children around us. In the kitchen, of course. I'm making them breakfast. Terry, my talented, intelligent husband, with his attaché case ready to go to work, kissing me goodbye, and I'm laughing in his hair because the dog has jumped up to get the children's toast with strawberry jam. This is me now, I decided. It was always me. I'd just forgotten.

But then, something incredible happened.

The New York Times
Emma Fern shortlisted for the Poulton Prize, again.
By Pushpa Sharma

Most of our readers are familiar with Emma Fern and her first novel, *Long Grass Running*. Three years ago, Ms. Fern won the prestigious Poulton Prize for this novel, and since then it has sold over four million copies all over the world. Being chosen was already a feat, since she's only the second author to win the prize for a first novel. But now Ms. Fern has gone one better: she's been shortlisted a second time, and should she win, she will be the only author to win twice.

Already on the *New York Times* bestseller list for fiction, *Traces in the Water* is an unusual love story that promises to engage and delight even more readers in months to come.

Ms. Fern's husband, Jim Fern, the disgraced economist who himself has featured a number of times in the pages of this publication, died tragically eighteen months ago. Ms. Fern was subsequently presented in front of a Grand Jury, although not indicted.

Frankie Badosa, the publisher of both Ms. Fern's novels, has announced that the film rights for *Long Grass Running* have been acquired by Carmody Productions, with the main role rumored to be played by Jennifer Lawrence.

ACKNOWLEDGMENTS

My heartfelt thanks to the lovely people at Thomas & Mercer, and especially to their editors, whose patience and sharp eyes helped bring this novel to life.

To my dearest friends and family. You are always supportive and enthusiastic, and it means the world to me.

And a massive thank you to my husband, who always ensures I am fed and watered while I plot my way into killing fictional ones.

ABOUT THE AUTHOR

Natalie Barelli can usually be found reading a book, and that book will more likely than not be a psychological thriller. Writing a novel was always on her bucket list, and eventually, with *Until I Met Her*, it became a reality. *After He Killed Me* is the second and final book in her Emma Fern Series.

When not absorbed in the latest gripping page-turner, Natalie loves cooking, knits very badly, enjoys riding her Vespa around town, and otherwise spends far too much time at the computer. She lives in Australia, with her husband and extended family.